'Fabulous... A delight. Nattrass again and again had me wondering at her skill and marvellous turn of phrase in filtering complex eighteenth-century history in a way that resonates with our own times'
S.G. MacLean, author of *The Seeker*

'Danger and mystery trapped inside a rocking barrel, far from home. Artful and authentic historical fiction at its best'
A.J. West, author of *The Spirit Engineer*

'I absolutely loved this book. Full of intrigue and excitement with a brilliantly realised cast of characters and a totally immersive setting, it's a superb historical thriller'
Philippa East, author of *Little White Lies*

'I loved this rip-roaring tale of murder and intrigue on the high seas. Brilliant'
Trevor Wood, author of *The Man on the Street*

'A compelling and spectacular nautical murder mystery. Superbly written characters in a convincing historic setting'
Guy Morpuss, author of *Five Minds*

'Such a thrilling read. Characters who utterly drew me in and didn't let go until the final page. Spectacular'
J.M. Hewitt, author of *The Eight Year Lie*

'I loved *Blue Water*. Even more welcome than an extra rum ration on Christmas Day, and slips down as easily'
Robert Lloyd, author of *The Bloodless Boy*

BLUE WATER

Also by Leonora Nattrass and available from Viper

BLACK DROP

BLUE WATER

LEONORA NATTRASS

First published in Great Britain in 2022 by
VIPER, part of Serpent's Tail,
an imprint of Profile Books Ltd
29 Cloth Fair
London
ECIA 7JQ
www.serpentstail.com

1 3 5 7 9 10 8 6 4 2

Printed and bound in Great Britain by
Clays Ltd, Elcograf S.p.A.

A CIP catalogue record for this book is available from the British Library.

ISBN 978 1 78816 5945
Export ISBN 978 1 78816 5952
eISBN 978 1 78283 7411

AUTHOR'S NOTE

I N 1793 WAR BROKE out between Britain and Revolutionary
France. In 1794, John Jay, an envoy from the United States,
arrived unannounced in Europe, on a mission to repair the
strained relations between his country and Great Britain, or,
alternatively, to seek an alliance with the French. The British
Government, eager to avoid war on a second front, entered
into negotiations of a new *Treaty of Amity and Commerce* with
their old colony.

The Jay Treaty was signed in November 1794 and dispatched by sea, aboard the *Tankerville* packet ship, for urgent
ratification by the American Congress.

CAST OF CHARACTERS

THE POLITICIANS AND THEIR CIRCLE

Lord Grenville, Foreign Secretary in Downing Street
Laurence Jago, a disgraced Foreign Office clerk in his
secret employ
Mr Gibbs, Laurence's dog
William Philpott, loyalist journalist and staunch defender
of the Jay Treaty
Theodore Jay, son to the American envoy John Jay,
and bearer of the Treaty home to Philadelphia
Peter Williams, slave, valet and secretary to the Jay family
Frederick Jenkinson, War Office official

THE CREW OF THE *TANKERVILLE*

Captain Morris, of Flushing, Falmouth
Mr Peters, his sensible first mate
Mr Trevenen, his handsome second mate
Mr Rogers, his choleric third mate
Mr Kidd, the surgeon
Mr Smith, the gunner
Mr Spiers, the carpenter
Mr Hind, the cook
A superstitious sailmaker
Ben, the cabin boy

THE PASSENGERS

Comtesse Emilie de Salles, a French noblewoman fleeing
Revolutionary France
Maximilien de Salles, her nephew, a former soldier in the
French Royalist army
Obadiah Fletcher, business agent to Eli Whitney and his
cotton gin
Lizzie McKendrick, an Irish actress
Bruin, her bear

THE ENEMY

Captain Benoît, of the French brig *Lovely Lass*

PART ONE

Satan, now in prospect of Eden ... at length confirms himself in evil, journeys on to Paradise, whose outward prospect and situation is described, overleaps the bounds, sits in the shape of a cormorant on the Tree of Life, as highest in the garden, to look about him.

John Milton, *Paradise Lost*, The Argument, Book IV

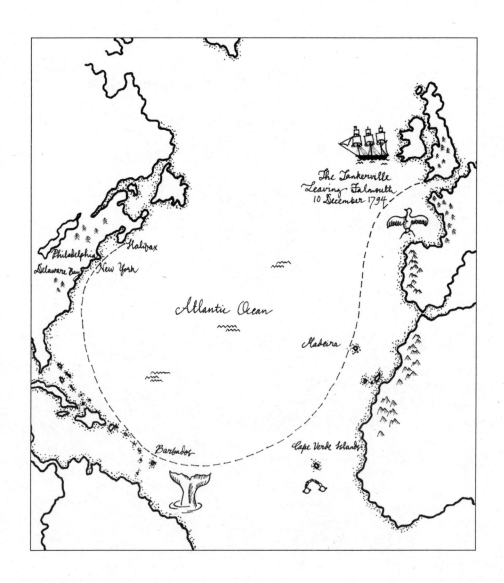

The Tankerville
Leaving Falmouth
10 December 1794

Philadelphia
Delaware Bay
New York
Halifax

Atlantic Ocean

Madeira

Barbados

Cape Verde Islands

Somewhere Off Ushant
16 December 1794

Look closely now. No, closer. Shield your eyes from the
Spray and train your Gaze down to that Spot, there, in
the moving expanse of Water. Do you see it? That dark
Smudge, blinking in and out of the Ridge and Furrow
of the English Channel, is the TANKERVILLE, a Packet
Ship plying her trade for the Post Office between
Falmouth and America, carrying Letters to the West
Indies, Dispatches to the Captains of naval Warships,
and a handful of seasick Passengers to America.

The TANKERVILLE is small and three-masted, with
a blue and gold Trim. Eighty feet long by twenty wide,
she is tolerably tidy, despite the Cow and the Turkeys,
the piles of coiled Rope and spare Sails, and the good
spread of Canvas towering near a hundred feet above
our heads. If she ever escapes this d—d contrary Wind in
the Channel, she will waft us three thousand miles, from
Falmouth to Halifax, Nova Scotia, with stops between
at Madeira, Barbados, Delaware and New York.

But to my reader, good John Barleycorn at his
English Fireside, perhaps these place-names are but
Words with little meaning. And so, John, for your
better enjoyment, I have drawn a Map, as you can see,
with the circuitous path of our Voyage marked upon
it. If I were addressing the Gentry by their more comfortable Hearths, I would call the Shape of our Journey

something akin to a Chafing Dish, but for your easier understanding, I will rather call it a Swedish Turnip or Mangel-Wurzel – a bulbous Shape, to be sure, somewhat baffling to the Eye when a direct passage across the Ocean might seem vastly more convenient. But, John, there is a world of Winds and Tides quite beyond the ken of men like you and I, with which the Captain wrestles, puzzling out our Position and the consequent dispositions of Canvas, from his own admirably unpuzzled Intellects.

From the captain's log

17 December 1794
Latitude 48°, 43' N and 06°, 30'W
Off Ushant

Rose just before dawn, at eight bells in the morning watch, and occupied myself with the ship's provisions and other matters. What a blessing occupation is to a troubled digestion. Winds against us. Heavy sea.

REPORT OF LAURENCE JAGO

My Lord

You will hear as many accounts of this voyage as there are passengers aboard, but, being your eyes and ears on ship, I think it my duty to give my own report, to counter the wilder stories you will no doubt receive in good time. (I am mainly thinking of my supposed employer, Mr Philpott, and the raft of articles he means to post home for *The Weekly Cannon* when we make port.) My reputation as a disgraced clerk, dismissed from your service, has proved as useful as you hoped, for it seems scoundrels will make their feelings and plans known to such a one without much scruple.

Having nothing but time at my disposal, you may find this report overlong, for I have made copies from the captain's log and from Mr Philpott's copious writings, as well as other documents that have come to my hand and might shed light on our journey. But knowing, as we both do, how undeserved was this role you have forced me to play, you shall have your money's worth and be damned.

I

DEATH ARRIVED WITH the cormorant. It came aboard on the seventh day of our voyage, and settled itself at the bowsprit, wings akimbo, to dry its feathers in the brisk wind. It was too far from shore – probably blown out to sea by the tremendous gale we had met at the mouth of the English Channel, which kept us beating about Ushant for three full days, perilously close to the French port of Brest. The poor bird was exhausted, and not at all inclined to take to the wing again, despite all the efforts of the superstitious crew.

'Quite the most extraordinary thing I ever heard in my life,' Philpott remarked loudly, wedged into the open door of my cabin. As usual he wore a farmer's suit of uncommon antiquity – long coat with flapped pockets, leather gaiters and a broad-brimmed hat – and was obliged to bellow his remarks over the roar of waters and the grate of the ship's timbers. 'They seem certain it's unlucky, but there's no agreement whether it heralds a storm, a dreadful accident or is merely the ghost of some miserable sailor doomed to roam the seas till Judgement Day.'

He stepped neatly over the piss pot, which was sliding cheerfully from fore to aft with the swoop and soar of the ship. A count of five one way, and then five the other. I lowered my copy of *Paradise Lost* as he inserted his bulk more comfortably into the two-foot space between my bunk and the cabin wall, blocking out the only light. I could hear the cow mooing dismally from the deck above, and a faint but persistent barking, which told me my dog was annoying the turkeys again. Sometimes I feared the gobbling racket he provoked among the offended birds would tempt the crew to toss him overboard. But the cabin boy had grown attached to him and, when he wasn't teasing the livestock, Mr Gibbs followed the child about the deck all day.

'I talked to the gunner,' Philpott boomed on. 'A Mr Smith. A very sensible man, by God, and a veritable fount of information. You should seek him out, Laurence. He tells me we have left the European moon behind us in Falmouth, and the next we shall see is the American one, when we pass the Tropic of Cancer. God damn me, I have seen both these moons a hundred thousand times, in both continents, and never noticed the difference in all these years.'

Unmoored from his usual pursuits on land, where he was canny enough, Philpott's grasp on facts was growing foggy. I drew a breath to acquaint him loudly with what little I knew of astronomy, but I was distracted by a shadowy figure passing behind him, with a bucket, from the direction of Theodore Jay's cabin. The figure belonged to Peter Williams, Theodore's slave, and I therefore deduced first, that the bucket held vomit – for the American envoy's son had been spewing ever since Falmouth – and second, that Mr Jenkinson of the War Office was once more barricaded in the passengers' water closet, preventing its easy disposal. Poor Peter Williams would be obliged to take the bucket all the hazardous way to the *heads*, the open grating that jutted out to the figurehead at the very prow of the ship. A very public water closet, and a precarious one, regularly washed clean by the waves, and just now swooping and soaring with the motion of the ship.

Philpott's mind was still on the gunner's fictions. 'He says we're bound for more wonders.'

'A second sun, perhaps?' My stomach was troubled, which made me testy, and Philpott frowned at me, his small eyes disappearing in his broad face, as a particularly violent wave made the ship shudder and almost tossed me off my bunk. Not for the first time, I envied the sailors in their hammocks, which might be less genteel but were certainly more practical.

'Not in the least. No, no, he was telling me a fine tale of their last voyage. Blown off course by a *hurricano* such as this, they found themselves suddenly becalmed in the Sargasso.'

'Alarmed in the what?'

'*Becalmed*. In the *Sargasso*. Damn me, have 'ee not heard of it?'

I suspected Mr Philpott's knowledge of the subject was only half an hour older than my own, but I only shook my head, for his face had taken on its hectoring look, and he grew, if anything, louder. 'The *Sargasso*, my boy, is a strange and cursed sea all its own, a weird vortex amid the wild Atlantic, where ships are becalmed, the compass loses its mind, and eels of enormous size and number frolic amid unnatural fields of weed.'

This was going too far, even for the gunner. 'Nonsense. We have an eel at home, in the farm pond, and it has never been known to frolic.'

Philpott turned slightly purple. 'And are you more well-acquainted with the Atlantic Ocean than Mr Smith? 'Tis absolute truth, I assure 'ee. The sea boils with snakes, and any poor soul who goes overboard is snapped up at once.'

'It would be exceeding unlucky to fall in, however, being *becalmed*.'

He ignored or did not hear my disbelief, but we were saved from further arguments by the advent of the formidable Comtesse de Salles into the mess, rapping along the passageway from her dignified seclusion in the captain's saloon, which he had rented her for a considerable sum. Her nephew, Max, had a cabin among us commoners, and she liked to keep her eye on him. Just now the mess was otherwise empty, only Max cleaning his pistols at the table. He was a vigorous man of thirty-five who looked the soldier even in his civilian clothes. He had a medal for valour pinned to his coat, a broken nose, and a scorch mark across his cheek that made me think he had peered into hell and backed out again.

'There is a sheep,' the comtesse announced in enigmatic English, as Philpott leapt to attention and I climbed down from my bunk and followed him out into the mess. When Max didn't look up, the comtesse rapped his knuckles with her cane. 'A sheep! Directly outside my window.'

Her nephew raised his eyes and spoke with his usual studied brevity. 'It's a vessel out of Liverpool, *Tante* Emilie, an Indiaman I believe. We are taking on a passenger.'

'Will you watch 'im come aboard?' She was already dressed for the deck in a voluminous cloak, though her impractical hooped skirts would make any ascent of the ladder a lengthy business.

'It's damned cold and wet.'

The comtesse gave her nephew a glare that would have discomfited a charging lion and resorted to a rapid French that, unknown to her, I perfectly understood. 'Don't be feeble, Maximilien. I have never missed a morning walk these twenty years, rain or shine.'

For so powerful a man, he gave in easily and sloped off for his boat cloak, while Philpott, comprehending the import if not the actual words, grinned and jerked his head for us to follow the old harridan's broad beam up the ladder. I found I was still clutching the copy of Milton and was happy enough to lay it down on the mess table beside Max's pistols. The fall of man and the judgement of God had turned out to be disagreeable topics in the current circumstances of my life.

On deck, the comtesse was an imposing spectacle. The wind whipped her cloak, there was high colour in her wrinkled cheeks, and she was altogether a magnificent contrast to the half-drowned figure crawling up the ship's sloping side from a small boat which had just crossed the hundred yards of lumpy waves between us and the wallowing East Indiaman. The Indiaman looked monstrously big, with an array of real and pretended gun ports along its affluently gleaming sides.

'Sail ho!' a voice shouted down from the masthead above us, and Captain Morris glanced up from his arriving passenger to the lookout at the crow's nest, who cried out with some dark significance, 'Bearing east, north-east, sir. A French frigate.'

The crew of the small boat, hearing this information wafting down to them on the stiff breeze, found it ample reason to turn back towards the Indiaman without delay, and the poor fellow climbing up our side was left hanging perilously over the open sea. A couple of sailors hastened down to help him, and when he finally arrived on deck, dripping and frightened, he turned out to be a small, squat man in a long overcoat.

The captain was somewhat distracted.

'Mr Obadiah Fletcher, is it? Yes, yes, we were expecting you. I would make the introductions, but it seems we must be underway again directly. Welcome aboard, in any event, sir, welcome indeed.'

Fletcher was apparently too dazed by the terror of his arrival and the strange faces of the crew around him to notice much, as the second mate kindly took him by the arm and led him below. Philpott hastened over to the side, hampered by a large wave which, if he had happened to be on fire, would have left him very adequately quenched. The captain climbed nimbly into the rigging, and the comtesse peered out into the grey mist, her vast dignity suddenly diminished. Her nephew Max was fresh from Austria, fighting for the French Royalist army. Why they were bound for America I didn't know, but if any French ship took us, they would doubtless be sent back to Paris for summary execution at the guillotine being, by birth alone, enemies of the new Republic.

I felt the usual torn mixture of kinship and repulsion as I watched Max join her at the rail, his body taut with agitation. I, too, had been ill used by a Government that should have protected me, but I had been called a traitor for sounder reasons. Moreover, the very idea of fleeing French nobility always made me uneasy. I have spoken enough foolishness in my time, to those I ought not, to render even the largest dose of Black Drop laudanum feeble against regret.

The lookout called something new from the masthead, and the captain, who had now reached the cross trees, moved his glass a point or two. The sea heaved under clouds that touched the water, and the ship wallowed in the swell, scarcely moving against the westerly wind. I followed Philpott to the rail. 'I can't see anything.'

He was looking up at the sailors crowded in the rigging, mainly visible as a congregation of bare soles. 'Still too far to see from deck, but they're saying it's there all right.'

The Indiaman was already hull up, attempting a return, back over the hard-won miles towards home. 'Damned fools,' the captain called down to the first mate at the wheel. 'They're caught on a beam reach, and the Frenchman's seen them. They cannot possibly escape. Well, well, it's an ill wind, as they say. Come up a point, Mr Peters, and we'll creep off as best we can and hope they don't see us.'

Philpott had hastened off to the wheel and was now hob-nobbing with the helmsman and eyeing the lookout at the masthead as if he meant to climb up and join him in his perch on the plunging arc of the mast. Before he could fix me with his china-blue eye, and require me to go with him, I made my way over to the other passengers who were standing at the stern. The cabin boy was prancing about his turkey crate as unsteady on the plunging deck as a new-born lamb, with Mr Gibbs bouncing and barking in enthusiastic wolfish atten-dance. I paused to pull the dog's ears, and he gave me a cur-sory lick.

Theodore Jay was emptying his guts over the stern rail. He had apparently just emerged from his bunk, and was dressed only in his shirt and breeches, his hair tousled by the stiff wind. He had lost all his young dignity and seemed abjectly grateful for any kindness when I came up to where he was standing with his black servant. Peter Williams was stiff with ill humour, his face turned away, so I took the slave's duty on myself, handing Theodore my handkerchief with which to wipe his mouth. He hesitated, glanced at his manservant, and put it back in his own pocket, likely judging Peter Williams in no mood to be presented with more of his vomit. I don't think Peter Williams had yet forgiven Theodore for the peril-ous dance the boy had led him these past months through the stews and prostitutes and molly houses of London.

'She's seen us.' The call from the masthead was shriller by a note or two.

'God damn their eyes. Come a point or two closer to the wind, Mr Peters.'

Theodore's skin was transparent, with none of its usual rosy glow, and his red lips were cracked by wind and salt. But I probably looked no better than he did, and quite a different man to the one he had known in London. No wig, no sober dark Whitehall suit. I was bareheaded, dressed in my farm clothes, which were the warmest things I had with me, and my green spectacles were held together at the bridge with a twist of wire. If the Government wanted me *incognito*, I was certainly obliging them. In the darkness of my cabin, My Lord, I had regretted any obligation to please you in any way, and half-thought I should pocket the parcel of money you had sent me and abscond into the American wilderness. But, like Peter Williams, who had elected to return to Philadelphia with Theodore instead of claiming his freedom in London, I found I couldn't bear to turn my back for ever on my family and those others I had once foolishly loved.

The lookout called again with more bad news. 'She's changing tack. Coming about towards us.'

Captain Morris closed his spyglass hastily and clambered down to the deck, where Philpott was standing with the comtesse, her nephew having temporarily disappeared. Philpott took the captain's sleeve. 'They have abandoned the Indiaman?'

'It seems so, and yet that vessel will be brim full of silver.'

'And what does that signify?'

'General orders to intercept the mails if we're lucky. A special interest in our cargo if we ain't.'

2

A COUPLE OF SEAMEN were preparing the mail bags for sinking, while Max de Salles looked ripe to explode with bottled-up nervous energy. He was now in earnest conversation with the fanciful gunner and the third mate and was following them towards us across the heaving deck.

'What do you think I should do with the papers?' Theodore asked rather more loudly than seemed prudent. 'Should I sink them? My father bade me do it if we were taken.'

'Not yet, surely to God.' The French ship was less than a smudge on the horizon and, despite the general gloom, my landlubber mind couldn't imagine it would possibly catch us. I had replied more quietly, for the gunner and third mate were uncomfortably near at hand, but they seemed absorbed in pointing out the cormorant to Max, which had now alighted at the very top of the mainmast. The third mate scowled, and the gunner waved his hands excitedly, until Captain Morris called them back to their duty in a sharp voice and they moodily obeyed. Max remained gazing skywards, scarcely an arm's length from where we were standing.

Theodore was still worrying, still too loud. 'Mr Monroe

wanted to show the provisions to Paris, but Father refused. He was adamant it's only for President Washington's eyes.' Monroe was the American Ambassador to the Revolutionary Government in France and hated the British as much as anyone.

'Mr Jenkinson will know what to do,' I said, quite aware that Max de Salles was near enough to hear all this if he chose. But he was still looking up into the rigging, apparently quite oblivious to us. 'Where in God's name is he?'

'Locked in the water closet again.'

In fact, the War Office official was just now appearing out of the companionway to the mess, and a moment later he was with us. Jenkinson was egg-shaped, with a pudgy hand clamped to a huge, bell-bottomed wig that would have looked out of date a hundred years ago. I had hardly spoken to him since Falmouth, partly out of discretion, not wanting my true purpose aboard ship to be generally known, and partly because the man had scarcely left his cabin. He had handed me a new set of instructions from Your Lordship the day we sailed, but he hadn't taken me into his confidence and barely acknowledged me. I had chosen to take this as proof of my importance, rather than the reverse.

Jenkinson was already addressing Theodore as he came up, with equal disregard for secrecy. 'You must give me leave to hide the Treaty at once, Mr Jay. We cannot afford any mistake in the event the French take us.'

'My father told me to throw it overboard at the first sign of trouble.'

'A measure of last resort, I assure you.' If Mr Jenkinson was an egg, he was at present an extremely harassed one, beckoning impatiently with his stubby pale fingers. 'Oh, very well, very well, I promise you I'll sink it if I must. But we shall hope for better luck than that.'

'Luck!' The third mate was passing. 'There'll be no luck till that fucking bird's off the ship.'

'Like Satan in Paradise,' I remarked, to no one in particular. 'I have just read the very passage in Milton. *Up he flew, and on the Tree of Life, the middle tree and highest there that grew, sat like a cormorant.*' The third mate turned his eyes to me at the exact moment the bird took exception to this slander, flew down from its lofty perch, circled the deck slowly on its shaggy wings, and voided its bowels with scrupulous aim on to the left lens of my spectacles. I removed them and wiped them clean. The mate was still staring at me and I smiled to hide my discomfiture. 'Well, Mr Rogers, is that good or bad luck, according to your sailor lore?'

The mate didn't deign to answer, only shook his head, and turned back to where the gunner was hastening below with Max de Salles. It seemed Max had found some outlet for his restlessness, as had Philpott, who had not climbed the rigging but was now swaying away towards the companion ladder in close consultation with the comtesse.

Peter Williams roused himself from his reverie and followed the third mate with his cool gaze as the man strode off. Jenkinson, who had no time for my nonsense about birds and had not been listening, was addressing Theodore in urgent tones. 'Come, come, Mr Jay. Do as I bid you. I shall find a *very* safe place for the papers, I assure you; one where the French will never think of looking.'

Theodore turned appealingly to Peter Williams, and then to me, but neither of us had the authority to overrule Jenkinson. In fact, as Your Lordship will remember, your secret instructions bade me obey the man in everything, so I only shrugged as Jenkinson rolled away clumsily towards the companion ladder, still clutching on to his antique wig with one hand, while Theodore reluctantly followed. I exchanged looks with Peter Williams, who remained behind, leaning on the lurching stern rail, hands folded. After a moment's hesitation, I went to the ladder in my turn. I needed to know how I should behave in the event of capture, and Jenkinson was the only man I could ask.

Max and the gunner were already coming back up from the mess. Max's face was blazing, while the gunner was holding a pistol, which he handed to the third mate, and they hastened off forwards. 'If we can only wing it, 'twill be enough to put it overboard.' As I put my foot on the ladder, there was the sharp report of a gun, and the poor cormorant fluttered up into the rigging beside the lookout, who turned and flapped his hands, but the bird only settled again and preened its feathers with admirable sangfroid.

Below, the howl of the wind was suddenly muffled, the creak of timbers louder. The hull protested and writhed, water seeping in through the labouring joints. Philpott and the comtesse were examining each other in the gloom as I stepped off the bottom rung. They were as alike as two peas, being both pink-faced and rather stout, but the comtesse had regained some spirit and was wearing an expression that would have curdled milk, while Philpott's face was cheerful as ever, eyes gleaming beneath his broad-brimmed hat. He was, at present, bellowing at an unnecessary volume, apparently labouring under the impression that, having imperfect English, the comtesse must also be witless.

'*Madame*! You are in very great danger. If the ship is taken, you will be captured and returned to France.' He mimed the guillotine with some gusto and the comtesse scowled. I could have intervened, translated one to the other with perfect ease, but Your Lordship's instructions had flatly forbidden me from revealing my fluency in French to anyone aboard. Philpott knew it, of course, but at this moment he was far too agitated to remember I might be useful, as he narrowly escaped decapitation himself from the wildly swinging lantern.

The noblewoman's polite English vocabulary prevented the more pungent retort she obviously had in mind, and she contented herself with a glare. 'I know this *parfaitement, monsieur.*'

'And, so, we must hide 'ee in some way.' Philpott was casting about as he spoke, but any hiding place was hard to imagine in the neat and tidy packet ship, with everything stowed away against the rough sea. Even Jenkinson's confidence he could hide the Treaty seemed misplaced. Hiding a woman was surely impossible.

At this moment, Kidd, the surgeon, appeared from his cabin beyond the bulkhead with a roll of instruments which he began methodically to set out on the mess table, while Mr Philpott explained the comtesse's predicament to him in some circuitous detail. 'Her nephew might pass for an Englishman,' he finished. 'But she cannot, with her strong French brogue. Where can I hide her?'

Comtesse de Salles bridled at the impertinence of their pity as they conferred, heads together. Worse, Kidd was cool, as though her safety was hardly his problem. 'Dress her in men's clothes.'

'Absurd.' But Philpott's eyes lit up at once.

'If we are taken, there'll be shots fired. We'll cover her in blood and lay her on the table as a wounded crewman.'

The gleam I well recognised was blossoming across Philpott's rosy face. 'I'll see what I can find.'

'No,' Comtesse de Salles said sharply, above the general racket of the groaning ship. 'No, and no.'

'But, *madame* ...' Philpott looked chagrined at any

obstruction to such a delightful scheme, while the woman's own conflicting thoughts were equally plain. Pride, warring with fear. For a moment it seemed pride would triumph, but then the ship tacked, she lost her footing, lurched, and smacked her shin on the corner of the fixed bench at the mess table. The pain decided her, though she remained magnificently dignified and spoke as if conferring a great favour.

'Very well, I permit you, *monsieur*. Make it so.'

Philpott gallantly declared his own clothes would drown her, which I highly doubted, and procured others from steerage, which anyone could have seen were far too small. Not gentlemanly, but too good for sailor's clothes, they were perhaps land-going Sunday best for a pious Methodist among the crew. When the comtesse re-emerged from her cabin, squeezed into them as tightly as Mr Jenkinson into his waistcoat, she climbed the ladder back to the deck, shoeless, her fine stockings wicking up wetness. Philpott followed, and when they were safely out of sight I went on to Jenkinson's cabin.

He opened his door just as I raised my hand to knock and, seeing my questioning look, fell back to let me enter. I didn't know what instructions he had received from the Ministry regarding me, but he was always hoarsely civil. 'Well, this is a pickle, ain't it, Mr Jago? We must ensure the papers are well hidden, for whatever the Jay boy says, I'll be damned if I'll sink them and render our whole voyage useless.' He had thrown a boat cloak about his shoulders in preparation for the numbing wind and cold on deck. 'Do you have any suggestions?'

My mind ran over the possibilities and was again defeated by the packet's spartan naval simplicity. The comtesse's cabin was bare and light from the stern windows. The mess dark, but sparsely furnished, with the row of small passenger cabins down one side. Then the forward space of steerage where the crew slept in hammocks above their dunnage neatly stowed away in sea chests. The surgeon's cabin, and the galley. Several small hatchways to spaces under the deck where they kept provisions and ropes. And then a large hatchway down to the dark hold, and the brooding ranks of water, beer and beef casks. Nothing to deceive a searching French seaman who knew his business.

I shook my head. 'No, sir, I'm afraid I don't.'

'Well, I have a couple of ideas might fool 'em. When the deed is done, I'll let you know the upshot.'

'And if we are taken? What shall I do?'

'Nothing, Mr Jago, for as far as the world is concerned you are only a journalist in Mr Philpott's employ. I suppose, if all else fails, I'll sink the Treaty, though it will break my heart to do it and President Washington will be most displeased.' He looked about himself calculatingly, then turned to me again. 'In the event of my death, you must take it from its hiding place and go directly to the Ambassador in my stead.'

It was only then our danger really hit me. But I thought that if only one of us was to survive long enough to deliver the Treaty, it might as well be me. Jenkinson shook his head dismissively, evidently more intent on the immediate problem of hiding the thing, and I left him, finding the surgeon once more alone in the mess, pensively sharpening his saws, his drugs set out on the table. I had never thought the place where we ate our dreadful meals was also a butcher's slab for wounded sailors, but on reflection it didn't surprise me. Nothing is ever as it seems.

'Just a precaution,' he said, as I hovered at his shoulder, eyeing the bottles of rum and laudanum, the two most sovereign remedies against pain and despair. 'She's forty guns to our eight. If she catches us, we're buggered, and no point in fighting.'

Still, I lingered.

'Something you wanted?'

I had taken too much of the Black Drop laudanum in London and had since renounced it at great cost to my health and peace of mind. A Herculean effort that would not bear repetition, and I should certainly never let the stuff pass my lips again.

'A quantity of laudanum if you'll spare it,' I said, without the slightest hesitation or shame. 'I left mine in Falmouth, in error, and have had a pounding headache this past week.' The surgeon could probably hear the tell-tale eagerness in my voice, but what was it to him? His hand reached for the flask and I watched him pour a dram into a small glass phial and push in the cork. It was a coward's refuge and would set me squarely back on the road to damnation. On the other hand, it would give me joy, a scarce commodity this past year. I didn't take it straightaway. I still had some modicum of self-control, and there was pleasure in the anticipation – the weight of its presence in my pocket.

On deck, the ship had thrown itself another point closer to the wind and was now shouldering through the waves with uncomfortable activity. The comtesse was again at the rail, though for a moment I didn't recognise her. Despite the danger of the chase, the crew were taking time from their urgent business to laugh at her gamey legs in the too-tight breeches, her pigeon breast in the too-tight coat. Philpott was also admiring her transformation as I came up, but whether she could carry off the disguise at the point of a boarding Frenchman's cutlass I rather doubted, especially as her bonnet made a mockery of the rest.

'A fifth-rater out of Brest, ma'am,' the third mate was volunteering as I came up beside them, clearly taking pleasure in his gloomy news. 'A fine, large vessel bristling with cannon.'

'*Mon Dieu!*' She seemed to take refuge in bad temper, as another might resort to drink or opium. 'Then we are all dead.'

'Never in the world.' Philpott's button eyes disappeared as he smiled too close into her face. 'I have been talking to the captain, and he is *quite* cheerful, I assure 'ee. 'Tis but a lumpish creature, this enemy ship. Dreadful clumsy, he says, especially with a French crew that don't know their arse from their elbow, and with a turn of speed we'll soon be quite clear.'

'She's closing,' the lookout cried out at this juncture, discouragingly, and Ben the cabin boy leapt into the rigging, in the direction of the unlucky cormorant, now asleep with its head tucked under its wing. Perhaps he meant to shoo it skywards, as though that could possibly avert our danger. Meanwhile, Mr Jenkinson was rolling up beside us, looking haggard, all drooping jowls and large, bruised eye bags, as he removed his enormous wig and bowed to the comtesse, revealing a head as round and smooth as a billiard ball. 'For you, *madame.*' He bent from his invisible waist and proffered his monstrous headpiece. 'To finish your ensemble.'

What an old fool he was, grovelling to nobility amid all this danger. The comtesse apparently thought so, too, and looked about to wave him away, but then she paused, seeming afflicted by another inward struggle. After a moment she took the article he proffered with a bad grace and a frown, probably fearing it harboured a colony of nits. But the tremendous proportions of Mr Jenkinson's peruke seemed, at last, apt for a purpose. In place of her bonnet, it covered her own hair entirely, and with her grim old face she certainly looked the gentleman – albeit one from our grandfathers' time. Mr

Jenkinson watched, nodded, politely tweaked the angle. There was the gleam of a satin ribbon among the luxurious curls. 'I'd be grateful if you'd keep a hand on it, *madame*. 'Tis my only one.'

I raised my eyebrows at him questioningly and made to follow him out of earshot to hear what he had done with Theodore's Treaty, but he raised a deprecating hand, suddenly grey, and trundled away hastily forwards towards the heads. The movement of the ship was certainly dreadful, and his bowels apparently brooked no argument. Looking about me, I saw that Theodore was also missing, probably occupying the passengers' water closet again, leaving the open grating at the forepeak as Jenkinson's only recourse. As I turned my eyes back out to sea, I thought I could now make out the white shape of a sail on the horizon, despite the spray and the darkening winter sky. Behind me, Max stalked away, his whole body emanating furious rage. 'To be taken here! Before we have even begun!' He was right, of course, but one thing I had learned was that fate would screw you if it could, and the only remedy for that hard-won knowledge was safely in my pocket.

From the captain's log

17 December 1794
Later

Took on a passenger from the Ponsborne, then sighted a French frigate in pursuit. Will take customary evasive action through the hours of darkness, with passengers confined below, though they will no doubt protest. Mails ready for sinking.

3

THE THREAT OF CAPTURE might have been real, but it unfolded with dreamlike slowness after that first burst of activity. We sped on through the short winter afternoon, the sky gradually deepening its shade of grey from woodsmoke to pewter, as the invisible sun declined towards the horizon. The frigate was inexorably gaining but, with the wind against both of us, it would be hours before she could make good her capture.

'And there is all the long night to come,' Captain Morris comforted us, as darkness fell. 'With luck, and a little seamanship, we will escape. But we must show no lights, gentlemen – *madame* – no lights at all.'

We went below reluctantly, as if to an early grave, and settled about the mess table under the only lantern permitted. The ship groaned with the pounding waves and unexplained crashes from above deck periodically made me startle like a rabbit. Theodore was back in his bunk. The new passenger, Obadiah Fletcher, had not yet emerged from his own. Mr Jenkinson was also missing, probably in his cabin, trying a recumbent position as a remedy for nausea. Max scarcely acknowledged the rest of us as he helped himself to a glass of claret, holding it firmly against the ship's incessant motion, and gazed into some dark inner world of his own, his fiery face working.

I had no appetite for the dreadful supper in preparation in the galley and wanted nothing but the intimacy of my cabin and an assignation with my old friend the laudanum. But if chance presented itself, I should knock at Jenkinson's cabin door. Just at present, there were far too many eyes on me to make the attempt and I was obliged to stay at the mess table and accept a lukewarm bowl of slop from the cook, which had been stewing all day over the now extinguished galley fire and excelled even Mr Hind's usual standard of dreadfulness. Mr Gibbs had come back to my side, as he always did with the nightfall, and lay at my feet, await-ing the usual good harvest of inedibles, while Philpott patted the comtesse's plump hand before tucking into his own plate with misplaced gusto. 'You'll be back in your skirts by morning, *madame*, the captain *quite* assured me.'

It was then the new passenger finally appeared from his cabin and joined us. Obadiah Fletcher exuded a faintly amphibian gleam as he sat down beneath the lantern and answered Philpott's polite enquiries about his travels. Yes, sir, the town of Liverpool had proved a very disgraceful place indeed. The Indiaman was all show and no comfort. He was damned glad to be going home to Savannah. It wasn't entirely clear if he understood the danger we were in, for he exhib-ited no undue alarm while the peril only seemed to make Philpott more sunny. The two of them might have been in a cosy Piccadilly tavern instead of a ship in danger of sinking in a winter sea.

'But what the devil brought 'ee to Lancashire in a freezing December?' Philpott grasped hold of his supper bowl with one strong hand, shovelling a spoon with the other as the table tipped and bucked.

'The devil himself, Mr Philpott, I do believe.' Fletcher's voice was as glutinous as his exterior, and almost at once I found myself wishing he would clear his throat. 'I have never felt warm these three months. At home – a plantation, sir, of near three thousand acres – I scarcely wear a coat from February to November. But to answer your question more plainly, I have been visiting the cotton mills of Manchester.'

'You raise cotton on your plantation, I suppose?' Philpott slurped at his wine and eyed the American over the rim of his glass.

'Quite so.' Fletcher pushed away his own plate untouched, though whether from nausea or disgust was unclear. It slid perilously close to my lap as he took out a cigar from his waistcoat pocket. 'And have lately gone into partnership with the inventor of a new machine for the cotton trade. I was showing it to the mill owners.' He frowned slightly, as if his demonstrations had not gone particularly well. 'There are some obstacles to resolve, but we will get there in the end.'

The captain came quickly through the deck hatch and hastened to his cabin, where he bent over the charts on his table, the door left open to the mess. With his face lit from below by a single candle, he was framed like a Rembrandt. Running to fat about the middle, a full head of straight black hair brushed to one side of his forehead, and a swarthy complexion from so long in warmer climes. But there was always an unhealthy look about him, and even from here I could see that his hand trembled in a way not exactly encouraging in the circumstances.

'It is a long way to come,' Philpott observed, after a cursory glance of his own at the captain and seeming to see nothing amiss. 'Are the English mills so vital to your business?'

'Vital!' Obadiah Fletcher croaked a laugh and stood up, apparently meaning to light his cigar at the swinging lantern, but Captain Morris looked up from his charts at once and informed him curtly that smoking was only permitted in the galley. Fletcher sat down again with a thud. 'Why, there ain't no cotton trade at all without the Manchester mills, for we have none of our own.'

All this time, Peter Williams had been moving quietly to and fro in the shadows. It was on his third journey between Theodore's cabin and the water closet that he leaned close to the comtesse's ear and spoke deferentially. '*Madame*, might I ask you where you got those clothes?'

'Got 'em out of steerage for her,' Philpott answered before she could, loud and cheerful. 'A fine-looking gentleman, wouldn't you say?'

Peter Williams's eyebrows raised a fraction. 'That's my second-best suit.'

He was a good-looking man, and the comtesse turned pink. As usual, confusion made her cross. 'I shall change directly.'

'Not until we're clear.' Peter Williams's face was unbending. 'Anyways, you can keep the wig. It ain't mine.'

'I'd advise you to speak to your betters more courteously,' Fletcher admonished him. 'Or better still, not speak at all.' With his gleaming skin and sticky croak, the American reminded me of nothing so much as a glossy squat frog as he dropped his wide-set eyes back to his glass, apparently expecting no answer. His mind was already returning to the new machine he'd taken for the inspection of the Lancashire mill owners. 'Yes, yes, it's an American crop in its infancy, Mr Philpott, but my machine will change all that. If the planters take it on, and the factories approve the results, damned if it won't increase production fifty-fold in the space of five years.'

'And what is the machine?'

Fletcher beckoned Peter Williams over, rather as he might a dog. 'There's a small wooden box in my cabin, boy. Run and fetch it.'

Whatever he thought of this instruction, Peter Williams did as he was bid. When he returned, Fletcher took the box from his hand without a word, while the rest of us cleared a space among the jostling dishes. I realised then that we were all eager to distract our minds from what was happening above deck. The ship periodically heeled violently, as the crew presumably sought to fool the French with an unexpected change of course. A fine strategy, if they didn't sink us first.

Inside the neat, hinged lid of Fletcher's mahogany box was a model, wonderfully exact in every detail, he explained, taking it out and placing it on the table. 'It's simple enough. But my partner, Mr Whitney, has made many fine adjustments and improvements to perfect the design.'

'What does it do?' Philpott's curiosity was roused, and even Peter Williams took up a station behind me to watch, as Fletcher cranked a little handle and a small wooden drum, studded with metal teeth, revolved quickly on its spindle.

'Cotton makes a fine yarn, but it's a mass of seeds when it comes off the plant,' Fletcher answered. 'To pick 'em out by hand is a devil of a job. Takes a day to clean a pound of cotton.' Fletcher reached into the box again and took out a white cloud. 'But with this machine, one slave may clean fifty pounds in a day. Fifty times the produce ready for dispatch in a year. Fifty times the crop to be grown.'

'And fifty times the slaves needed to grow it,' another American voice said behind me. Obadiah Fletcher's eyes shot up.

'What's that you say?'

'Fifty times the slaves, I suppose,' I repeated, and Peter Williams poked me gratefully in the shoulder.

'Quite so. And unless the darned abolitionists have their way, a welcome increase to your nation's own trade in Africans.' Fletcher packed away his little machine. 'Yes, we must sell our cotton to you, for that's our market, but I wish there was no need for such commerce, after all that has happened these past twenty years.'

'It is early days enough,' Philpott said easily. 'Scarcely more than ten years since we stopped killing each other. For my own part—'

'Oh, I am quite aware of your views, Mr Philpott.' Fletcher snapped the brass catches of the wooden box home and absently handed it back to Peter Williams, who took it away with strange meekness. 'You've spoken up for John Jay in your paper every week for a year. But he won't find himself or his Treaty welcome in Philadelphia, nor these spineless French aristocrats here, buying their way out of danger with their dirty money.'

At this, Max stirred from his inward turmoil and gave Fletcher a measuring look, but he said nothing, quite as cool under the man's insults as Peter Williams, and I thought I liked the Frenchman almost as much. The comtesse was incapable of such detachment and, from her affronted expression, it seemed she could scarcely credit the man's insolence. Meanwhile, Fletcher was oblivious, apparently believing neither understood him, and still eyeing Philpott. 'But what takes *you* back to America? The Treaty ain't agreed, I hope?'

'Well – well …' Diplomacy was not Philpott's strongest suit.

Fletcher slammed his hand on the table and his froggish face squeezed into a frown. 'That damned grovelling envoy! He'll get a rough ride back home, whenever he comes with his bit of paper. Burn him in effigy, I don't doubt.'

'But as your trade is with England, sir, you ought to welcome a treaty of commerce.'

'Ought to, my ass. Your Government locks up any man who smuggles his know-how with him to America, and thanks to such tyranny there's scarcely a cotton mill in the whole of the States. But it will change, Mr Philpott, whether your Ministry wills it or no. At President Washington's inauguration, he was proud to wear a suit of pure American manufacture.'

'At a fee would fund half a battalion, I heard tell—'

But their argument was interrupted by a curious and resonant *thunk* from Fletcher's cabin, rather like a piano being dropped from a considerable height. A moment later, Peter Williams emerged, his face a mask of indifference, but with a collection of dangling wood and metal parts in his hand. Philpott and Fletcher might disregard our immediate danger but for composure he had no equal. ''Fraid I had a mishap with your little toy, in the dark, sir.'

Fletcher was on his feet directly. 'You whoreson,' he said, staggering with the ship's sudden motion, and craning his broad face sideways to peer up at Peter Williams. 'Did it a-purpose, did you?' He looked round at Captain Morris, who had chosen this moment to come hastening out of his cabin. 'God damn me, Captain, this villain deserves a dozen lashes.'

But Captain Morris had no time for him, as he headed for the hatchway back to deck. 'We don't flog aboard packet ships, sir. The sea's damned rough, and footing hard to keep, especially for you landsmen.'

'The ship certainly heeled like the devil,' Philpott put in untruthfully. 'Just at the very moment we heard the smash.'

Thwarted of sympathy or immediate revenge, Fletcher's squat face sagged and he retreated into the comfort of money. 'Then I'll thank his master, whoever he is, to recompense me

36

the full value of this delicate instrument, the work of so many months.'

As the captain banged out of the hatch again, deaf to Philpott's shouted questions as to the state of the chase, I made my excuses and went to my cabin, tired of the quarrel. Jenkinson was seemingly abed for the night and there was no good excuse for me to rouse him in front of all these witnesses. The siren call of the laudanum, which had hummed at the edge of my hearing all evening, was suddenly a loud and insistent clamour.

4

MY CABIN WAS SCARCELY more than a man's height in length, and scarcely more than an arm span in width, but with the door shut, it was my own domain. I lit my candle in the sconce by the bedhead, took out the phial of laudanum and measured a few drops into the wine I had brought from the mess table. The surgeon's formula proved mild enough, rather like the Godfrey's Cordial I used to take in more peaceable days before I found myself entangled in the fate of nations. But even so, the glorious warmth I remembered suffused me at once, and I lay back gratefully on the hard flock mattress, listening to bare feet slapping urgently overhead, and watching the watery tar drip through a gap in the caulking on to the shoulder of my best coat. I had sailed before, on coasters plying their trade between London and Cornwall – had even once crossed the Channel to visit my mother's family in France – but this was another kind of voyage entirely. When we first saw the *Tankerville* in Falmouth, it had seemed impossible that this creaking wooden tub (however beautifully appointed and skilfully manned) could really propose to venture thousands of miles from shore, its thin planks all that separated us from the depthless fathoms of the Atlantic Ocean.

It had been early December when Philpott came to find me at home in Cornwall and asked me to return with him to Philadelphia as his assistant. He had come home from America the previous June to champion the Treaty in England, and was now returning to Philadelphia to argue for its ratification. He also brought me the first letter from Your Lordship, which hinted I might be reinstated to the Foreign Office if I acted for you *incognito* on this voyage by looking after young Theodore Jay and the important document he carried. Being otherwise stranded at home, without hope or future, I agreed to go. It was my birthday, and my mother wept to see me leave, though to my eyes Philadelphia could hardly seem more remote than London from our roaring Cornish hearth.

Philpott showed me the article he'd begun – an attempt to clear my name and free me from the Ministry's grip – but even he knew it was hopeless.

I have with me, in my Employ, a young Man of thirty named Laurence Jago, who has suffered most cruelly at Lord Grenville's hands. He lately uncovered a Scheme of Lies and manufactured Evidence in the prosecution of the Radical Reformers, most disgraceful to the Government. Worse, on attempting to expose this Malpractice, he found himself dismissed from the Foreign Office on trumped-up Charges of perversion among the Wh—s and Sod—es of London's notorious Stews. Unfounded Charges, which punished him with Disgrace only for seeking Justice. Men's lives mean nothing to the Ministry, and the poor Lad found to his own cost how they wink at Murder in the Alleys as well as on the Scaffold.

But, 'God damn it,' he said dolefully, screwing up the paper in his brawny hand, 'I cannot print any of this, or risk the scaffold myself. A half sheet wasted.'

Theodore and Peter Williams had come down to Falmouth from London by stagecoach, a long and weary journey, but Theodore was no sailor. 'If I die, Laurence,' he said to me, as we sat on a barrel on the quayside and looked up at the packet ship's gleaming new paint, 'tell my mother I always meant well. There has been some disagreeable correspondence between her and my father, and I'd not have her think me a rogue.' I wasn't surprised. If either of us had been the frequenter of prostitutes and the molly walks, it had not been me. He'd spent his six months in London in pious search of redeemable sinners, with Peter Williams in hot pursuit, for it would have been highly embarrassing for the dignified American envoy to have his son discovered in such places.

The tide crept in and out, twice a day, without much fuss across the flat calm harbour while we waited the arrival of the other passengers. Further out, the line of sea on the horizon was broken, which meant an easterly breeze, Captain Morris told us affably, a fair wind that would waft us gently out into the open ocean. 'It can't last,' was all Theodore said, glumly. 'Not in December.'

The egg-like Mr Jenkinson arrived that night after dark, rolling up the gangplank by lantern light with a seaman carrying his large portmanteau, and he nodded to us as he passed down into the mess to find his cabin. 'That's the man from the War Office,' Theodore said, even more glum than before. 'Here to make sure I don't toss the Treaty into the sea on a whim. I'd hoped my father would trust me for once.'

'The man likely has business of his own in Philadelphia,' I answered, but Theodore only shook his head.

It was young Trevenen, the second mate, a handsome youth of five and twenty from Penryn, who told us that French passengers were joining the ship. We were sitting in the snug of the Grapes tavern on the quayside, the candlelight reflecting off our tankards, eating the last good meal I have tasted. Trevenen shook his head. '*She'll* give us some fun.'

'A woman?'

'A comtesse.' He wiped a sleeve across his mouth. 'Comtesse de Salles and her nephew, running from the guillotine, I don't doubt.'

'Poor things.' Philpott, having been hard at the inn's heady brew, was dewy and sentimental. 'It's a dreadful curse to be exiled. Moses, and so forth. And God damn me, I shall miss my wife most dreadfully.'

'Where are they from?' I asked the second mate, trying to ignore the sinking feeling that had beset me at their aristocratic names.

'Somewhere in deepest France.' Trevenen was vague, already exchanging amorous glances with the barmaid. 'Took 'em a fortnight to reach Calais, and then bad weather made 'em wait a week for a crossing. Come down tonight by stagecoach, like Mr Jay and his man.'

We left the second mate to his last carnal pleasures before departure. The ship weighed anchor before dawn, the broad hump of the Lizard Peninsula brooding behind us, a darker shape against a dark sky. The town was mostly asleep, except for a few lights that revealed a flurry of activity on the quayside, as fishing boats also scrambled to catch the tide. We barely set a sail, just enough to catch the whispering air and direct our passage out of the harbour and into the blackness of the Channel, and Philpott's voice roused me from discouraging reflections.

'Well, I'm glad you're with me, my boy. A new start, in a new continent, what do you say? You shall make a finer journalist than a clerk, I make no doubt.'

I wished I could tell him my true purpose, but though Philpott had handed me the letter that began this adventure and knows almost everything about my troubled past, Your Lordship had enjoined me to *absolute discretion*. A needless injunction, in fact, for secrecy has worked itself into my bones over the course of years, and there are a good many things I hope never to confess, except, perhaps, to a priest at the point of death.

I HAD HALF THOUGHT of staying awake and rousing Jenkinson after the others were finally abed. But instead, the laudanum plunged me deep into slumber, Mr Gibbs a heavy weight on my legs, and it was only the mighty boom of a cannon, just past dawn, that woke me. I fell out of my bunk half dazed, pulling on breeches, coat and shoes before spilling through my door into the mess, the dog at my heels. It was still dark in the empty room, only a grey rectangle of light in the hatchway to deck. Very early morning, and despite all his efforts, it seemed Captain Morris had failed to make good our escape from the chasing ship.

I scrambled up the companionway and came out into the raw December morning. The quarterdeck was crowded with crewmen, the whole ship's company there to witness the danger. The captain and helmsman were at the wheel, while a posse of seamen was moving something surreptitiously behind their backs, hidden from the approaching ship, perhaps one of the ship's eight small cannon. I hardly paid it any mind, being more taken up with the apparent certainty of impending death.

Our movement had stalled, and we were gliding slower and slower, while a gigantic vessel sped towards us across a sea that, I realised now, was much flatter. But the Frenchman's speed only seemed to increase as the distance diminished, a monstrous lump of metal and wood hurtling towards us. Would they ram us? Board us? They were showing no colours, and neither were we, but it seemed their cannon had already claimed a victim, for as I looked around for Philpott, I saw he was at the forepeak with a small knot of figures, bending over a fallen body at the heads.

Trevenen, the young second mate was passing, and I stopped him with a hand on his arm. 'We didn't escape, then?'

'Oh, we dodged *that* one,' he answered. 'This is another. Like bloody Charing Cross round here. Too close to Brest, see.'

At what seemed the last possible moment, the new French ship executed a turn, and came up broadside to broadside with us, less than fifty yards away across the rippling water. One fear was rapidly replaced by another. Monstrous, other-worldly, in the empty expanse of ocean, she loomed over us with her two decks, her extravagant gilding, and rank upon rank of open gun ports. I froze as I looked at the cannon mouths, and my scalp crept, as if my own flesh wanted to escape me. I crouched and pulled Mr Gibbs into my arms, though whether for his protection or my own comfort I cannot say.

But when I dragged my eyes from the guns' mouths, I saw only resignation on other faces. *If she catches us, we're buggered, and no point in fighting*, the surgeon had said yesterday, and my heart gradually slowed. Outclassed as we were, there could be no resistance. For his part, Philpott was gazing up at the monster towering over us, his expression positively bright.

Assuming we lived, it would make a tremendous tale for his paper.

It would also be the end of the Treaty's journey to Philadelphia, over before it had even begun. I looked around for Jenkinson, but he was nowhere to be seen, perhaps off cowering somewhere with the precious thing clutched to his bosom. Back on the gigantic ship, there were now faces lining the rails – obscene gestures – raucous, mocking cries. Captain Morris put his spyglass to his eye and swept the enemy from stem to stern, then shouted out an order, and a moment later our flag ran up the mizzen. A blue and gold swallowtail – packet colours – which would tell any intelligent enemy that he had succeeded in capturing the precious mails and, if he was even better informed, the treaty Jenkinson and I had been taxed to guard.

A cheer erupted from the big ship. Laughter echoed across the space between us, and a moment later the red ensign blossomed at its stern. For a moment I failed to understand what it meant, until the men around me cheered too. It was not a French warship at all. We were, instead, in the colossal presence of the Royal Navy.

'Silence, there!' An English voice boomed out across the water, attached to a figure on the poop, dressed in a white shirt and rapidly donning a blue jacket. 'The *Tankerville*, is it? Captain Morris?'

'Yes, sir. And you are the *Brunswick* of the Channel fleet? Captain Fitzgerald, I think?'

'The very same. God damn me, I was on the point of knocking away your spars.'

'And I of opening fire with my great battery of guns.' A laugh of relief all around. There was a rare smile on Captain Morris's sallow face. 'We've spent the night in company with a fine French frigate, sir. Have you seen her?'

The naval captain was still amused. 'No, Captain Morris, I'm afraid you'll have to find her on your own.'

Another ripple of laughter. I stood up, releasing the dog, who scampered forward towards the huddle of figures at the bow.

But Captain Morris was serious again. 'There was an Indiaman with us, sir, off Ushant. She turned back for the Channel, but ...'

Captain Fitzgerald sounded grave now. 'Then, much as I would like to offer you dinner, I'd best go to the rescue.' They had seen the knot of men at the bow and the prostrate figure, and there was some consultation among the officers. 'We ain't killed one of your crew, I hope? 'Twas only meant as a warning shot.'

'No, no, sir. Only an accident in the rigging, I'm afraid. Good day to you.'

'And to you.' Captain Fitzgerald raised his hand as the sails altered on the huge ship, and slowly, slowly, she began a sweep back in the direction she had come.

I looked around again. Jenkinson was still missing, and when my gaze followed Captain Morris, who was hastening forward to the bow, I noticed that the fallen figure was small, spherical and stout. I found myself following, with a growing sense of foreboding.

The third mate met me with an upraised palm. 'Wouldn't look if I was you.' But I went on, to where the captain was bending over the body in consultation with Kidd the surgeon. The only man aboard who had known my true business, and the only one I was sworn to obey, lay spread-eagled on the grating of the forepeak – where he had presumably been relieving his troubled bowels again, for his breeches were folded around his ankles. He was still breathing, but his head was split neatly open and the surgeon was trying in vain to stem the pulse of blood and other matter from the wound. Ben, the cabin boy, squatted at the poor man's side, and I thought with half my mind that he was too young to be witnessing such horror. Above us, a couple of crewmen were examining the frayed ends of rope in the rigging.

And, of course, Philpott was there. 'Very bad luck,' he informed me, with some relish, as I took in the spray of blood and brains pooling around Jenkinson's head. 'They think a spar broke loose under the strain of the chase. A heavy beam that would have fetched him an almighty blow, probably before flying off into the sea, for look, there's naught left but those frayed ropes.'

My first thought was that Jenkinson had been wise indeed to instruct me on my duty, in the event that I, alone, reached Philadelphia. My second was that he would have been wiser still if he'd passed on the whereabouts of the Treaty so I could fulfil those orders. I should have resisted the laudanum last night and crept to his cabin as I had intended.

'Has he spoken?' I asked. 'Has he said anything?'

'Was whispering in young Ben's ear while he still had any brains left in his head.'

This seemed only too literal a description from the evidence trickling across the deck boards. 'What did he say, Ben?'

The boy looked up at me. He was shocked, no doubt about it, white as a sheet and with dark bruises under his eyes. He said something too low to catch, and then shook his head.

'What does he say?'

The captain had been listening with a frown. 'Gibberish, that's all. Something about nakedness.'

'He was ashamed to be seen like this,' Philpott said. 'We should cover him up, poor devil, and let him meet his maker with some dignity.'

As he took off his coat and draped it over Jenkinson's buttocks, I sighed. It was a terrible pity he'd left me no instructions, but he could hardly have been expecting death when it came, for what man would choose to meet his maker with bowels blowing and gushing? Who could predict the random fall of a spar from the rigging?

Ben had stood up to go, and I caught his arm as he passed me. 'Say again, Ben. What did he say to you?'

'*Thou art naked.*'

'Thou …?'

'Art naked, sir.' His eyes looked past me, and I realised Theodore was listening at my shoulder.

'Poor man. His wits were quite deranged,' he said to Peter Williams, who was at his side.

And then a general sigh erupted from all around us. 'He's gone, poor feller,' someone said portentously, as Kidd closed Jenkinson's eyes and took away the cloth he'd been pressing to the bleeding wound. But there seemed to be scant time for reverence. With almost indecent efficiency, the first mate and the gunner turned the body over on to a square of old sailcloth, while someone else threw a bucket of water to wash away the mess. Captain Morris called over the sailmaker to sew up the body, ready for a decent burial.

'Poor Jenkinson,' Theodore said again to Peter Williams. 'Harping on nakedness at the very end. Shocking how carnal thoughts afflict the unredeemed, even at the moment of death. But my father rated his judgement very highly. I shall miss him, though his views on original sin were regrettably vague.'

As I looked around, Max de Salles was watching silently from the edge of the crowd, a frown between his dark brows, while Obadiah Fletcher was, as usual, missing.

On Sailors' Superstitions

I wonder what the D—l you would make of these Packet Sailors, my dear John Barleycorn! The Navy snatches many a Man like yourself away from Hearth and Home, to man its Walls of Oak, but these Packet men are of quite another Stamp. Bred from generations of sailing Folk, I don't doubt, they have made for themselves a rich and preposterous Lore, and woe betide the man that offends against it!

It was only on our second day at Sea that the Third Mate, and another charming, bearded Fellow I was later to know as Mr Smith, the Gunner, took umbrage at my Manners.

'No whistling?' I exclaimed. 'But why the D—l shouldn't I?'

'Just you wait and see,' the Third Mate answered. 'Just you watch the Sails. There'll be a Tempest before nightfall, sure as Eggs.' (As a by-the-by, the Third Mate has the most devilish Face you ever saw, quite as battered as a Steak under the cook's Mallet, and about as cheerful.)

'Nonsense,' I said, for the Sea was as calm as a Millpond all around, from horizon to horizon, and the breeze a mere gentle Zephyr.

'Can't whistle up old Neptune, Mr Philpott, on a Whim. Just you wait and see.'

Yes, it is hard to credit such Superstition in our

enlightened times. I warrant, John Barleycorn, that your Family has long left off tossing children's shoes up the Chimney-place to ward off Witches. But these men are a Breed apart, and scarcely live in the same World as Newton and his Apple.

Still, it would be churlish if I did not admit to a strange Occurrence soon after. The Weather, having been as mild as Milk since we left Falmouth, now took on another aspect altogether. The Wind inexorably rose through the Afternoon, to a wailing Fury by bedtime. And so, dear John, I find myself wondering, against my better Judgement, if they know more of these matters than I! For did not the Cormorant bring on a Death, just as they predicted, and then left at first light, having fulfilled its malign Destiny? At any rate, I am begun on my Encyclopaedia of Nautical Fancies, and shall share my further Discoveries with you, just as often as they arise.

5

THE SAILMAKER'S AUDIENCE was relieved into a paroxysm of ghoulish hilarity after the various terrors of the night and morning. '*Quite* a cauch. Old Humpty got *addled*, ins and outs all backsyfore.'

Mr Gibbs had gone with the cabin boy. The comtesse was at the rail close by, in low French conversation with Max, and I listened unnoticed, just an ignorant foreigner to their minds and hardly worth troubling over. She seemed indifferent to the dreadful scene we had just witnessed. 'I mean to speak to the captain, Maximilien, if you will be so good as to summon him.'

Max looked doubtful, and she raised her voice for emphasis. 'Our coffee is lost somewhere in the hold, and no one seems willing to institute any kind of search, despite my repeated requests. And besides, I have been pondering the captain's meaning yesterday. *A special interest in our cargo*, I heard him say, as though we carry something that puts us all in danger from Paris. We are owed an explanation.'

As ever, there was no disguising the presence of strong emotion on Max's battered face. 'Aunt Emilie, the cargo is me.'

'*You!*' Her surprise was unflattering, and I smiled, my head turned away.

'Even if there weren't all this against us as a family, any officer in the Royalist army would be a great prize in Paris, let alone one of noble birth and decorated as I am. And with François—'

'You dare compare yourself to *him*?'

'It's what Paris thinks that matters. And they see us all in the same light.'

But whatever his worth to the French, and however alarming the intensity of his dark gaze, Max was no match for his aunt. He was summarily dispatched on his errand, only to return promptly with the first mate and bad news. The captain had retired to his cabin after the exertions of the night, and could by no means be disturbed until the funeral. Yes, the mate himself would certainly look into the matter of the coffee – very irking indeed. A little chest, weren't it? Dear me, so easy to mislay.

The cabin boy passed by, singing what sounded like a hymn in reedy tones that whipped away in the wind as the comtesse was skilfully palmed off and thwarted. She looked vexed and then, glancing up at the sailors' bare feet in the rigging, poking out obscenely white and pink from their muffling overcoats, faintly repelled. 'I have a dreadful headache,' she said. 'Wake me for dinner.'

Philpott joined me as the comtesse departed. He looked more than usually solemn. 'Damned hazardous business this sailing, ain't it?'

'And *you* said the only danger would be boredom.' Philpott had bought a prodigious crate of canary wine in Falmouth on the strength of this conviction. I had hardly known what I needed but, with his words in my mind, I had quickly bought my tattered copy of *Paradise Lost* from a small shop in a back-street, while Mr Gibbs loitered outside in sexual congress with a mongrel bitch.

'Boredom and the after-life,' Philpott said now. He was growing portentous. 'Much the same thing, to the injured party I dare say. I never can hanker after an eternity of praising, can you? Still, you'll enjoy the ceremony, Laurence. Burial at sea is a grand sight. There were three such committals, I recall, on the voyage out from Philadelphia last spring.'

'Three!'

'Oh, but much more dignified deaths than Jenkinson's, I assure 'ee. A mother and infant in childbed – most affecting – and an old man worn out by the journey. Deaths quite in the way of nature, not fool accidents like this.' He frowned. 'The third mate swears it all comes down to that accursed bird. Was jabbering at me just a minute ago in the most unaccountable way.' He sighed. 'Aye, aye. We are surrounded by a mob of superstitious fools, Laurence, there's no doubt about it.' But then he smiled, his good humour irrepressible, despite everything. 'And that being so, my encyclopaedia is coming on handsomely.'

Until the hour of the funeral, the passengers had little recourse but to settle back to their usual occupations below decks and recover from the alarms of the morning. Philpott went to his cabin, door wedged ajar, writing up the morning's business with an absorbed face, while I went to my own.

I took the smallest drop of laudanum to blunt the memory of the death I had just witnessed, along with previous deaths it had recalled to my febrile recollection and, as the cow groaned dismally from the deck above, addressed my mind to Your Lordship's secret instructions, which Jenkinson had brought me the day we sailed. They had been in the usual Ministerial code, and I had deciphered them against an old, illustrated edition of Gray's *Elegy,* which Your Lordship had sent me by separate cover. *You will assist Mr Jenkinson in protecting and defending the Treaty against French attack. Mr Jenkinson also has other important duties of which you are unaware. If he requires your assistance in these matters, you are duty bound to obey.* Your Lordship's last line had tantalised me. *A small office in Downing Street (and other inducements) may await you in the event of success.*

I had often speculated what Your Lordship's *other inducements* might be. Would I be permitted to renew my addresses to your under-secretary's stepdaughter, before she hastened into marriage with entirely the wrong man? Such a reward, at least, was worth winning, whatever I felt about you personally, My Lord, and now I began to wonder with equal interest what Jenkinson's *other duties* had been, and if I should try to find out, being the sole surviving representative of the Ministry aboard the ship.

As the cow grumbled again, and the laudanum fizzed in my brain, I reflected how pleasant it would be to stay abed all day in another opium daze. Instead, I climbed down from the bunk and came out into the mess, where, as usual, I was temporarily blinded by the contrast with my cabin's candlelight. The passenger cabins ran in a line along the hull. The furthest belonged to Jenkinson, next to the water closet, whence the shadowy figure of Peter Williams seemed to be coming with a bucket. He passed me with a nod, and as soon as he was gone, I lit a candle at the lantern and went to Jenkinson's cabin door, which groaned on its hinges so alarmingly that I shut it quickly behind me, before setting the candle in the holder.

Jenkinson had been a tidy man, his papers neatly stacked in the drawers beneath the bunk. It was the work of a moment to establish that the Treaty was certainly not among them, and I had hardly expected anything else. Far more likely it was still tucked away in whatever hiding place Jenkinson had finally settled on. It was the work of another moment to put my hand on a letter from Downing Street for, unlike me, Jenkinson had had no need to hide his allegiances. It was likely a set of instructions similar to my own, and I stuffed the letter in my pocket for later perusal before beginning to dismantle the bed, rummaging among the sheets and shaking the flock mattress, listening for the tell-tale crunch of papers stuffed into its innards.

Hearing nothing there, I went on to investigate the piss pot, and the mysterious depths of the latticework cupboard that reached back under the bunk to the gently seeping hull. The ship lay low in the water, so the cabins were submerged in any kind of sea, a thought which had jolted me awake more than once in the depths of the night when the ship's bell tolled the half-hour. Now, as I rummaged around in the hutch under the bunk, feeling blindly for the hidden papers, half-drugged and with an unpleasant stink in my nostrils, it seemed more than usually disagreeable. I backed out of the cupboard on all fours and promptly impaled my knee on a darning needle which had caught itself point upwards between the planks of the floor. It was an instrument of some considerable length and it was a mercy I hadn't stepped on its sharp point when I hurried into the cabin, or I should have been as lame as a worn-out hackney.

After a yelp of pain, which pretty well stung me out of any lingering opium stupidity, I retrieved the needle and restored it to the huswif I had seen in Jenkinson's drawer, then looked about me, contemplating the problem. I was certain Jenkinson had taken the Treaty into this cabin the day before, but it was definitely not here now. I remembered him climbing back up the ladder in his boat cloak. Had he hidden the papers somewhere before trundling off to the heads? Or had he still been undecided? He had, after all, made no attempt to tell me where he'd put them. Had he still had them on him, then? Good God, they were about to consign his body to the water, and the Treaty might still be in his pocket.

'IT WOULD CERTAINLY be a pity for the thing to go to the bottom now,' was all the captain said, sucking on his empty pipe and bending over me with detached interest as I wielded a knife on the waxed stitches of Jenkinson's shroud. As the stitches parted and I peeled back the wrapping, there was a faint whiff of the meat locker. I tried not to look at the gash in Jenkinson's skull. It had been a hellish blow. His face was grey as the waves that scattered past, his bald head grey as a pebble which would belong well enough on the seabed. There was something nightmarish about the heavy stillness of his body as I pushed my hands into his empty pockets, and then patted him down, listening, again in vain, for the rustle of paper. Philpott, who had also been watching, now reached in with less ceremony, yanking off his shoe, revealing plump toes in sober stockings. Philpott felt inside the shoe, tossed it down, and then yanked off the other. 'Nothing here.'

'Well, that's that,' the captain said regretfully. 'I am grateful to you for drawing my attention to the matter, Mr Jago, but you need trouble yourself no further. I will see the document is found – if it is still aboard. I wonder if he sank the damned thing when we expected to be boarded after all?'

I sat back on my haunches and rubbed at the bloodstain on the knee of my breeches where the needle had impaled me, while the captain called the sailmaker over to resew the shroud. Not in Jenkinson's cabin. Not on his body. I stopped the sailmaker's hand as the stitches reached Jenkinson's neck. There was a glint of gold at his collar, and I pulled out a cross from the folds of his shirt. A sharp tug loosened it, and I examined it in my palm. It was set with topaz, almost too feminine an article for the egg-like Jenkinson, but perhaps his wife had sent it with him as a good-luck token. If so, it had signally failed in its purpose.

'Sin to rob a corpse.'

I looked up to meet the sailmaker's disapproving glare.

'I mean to send it back to his family in London,' I answered. 'I'm sure they'd rather have it, and Jenkinson won't miss it, I assure you.'

The sailmaker only hissed and muttered something to himself, apparently concerning my dealings with yesterday's cormorant. Perhaps this was an answer to the question I had asked the third mate – whether bird dung in the eye was considered as unlucky an omen as everything else. Though Jenkinson might have borne the brunt of the bird's ill will, the sailmaker seemed to think I was also tainted by misfortune; and inasmuch as I now found myself left alone without Jenkinson's aid and counsel, I thought he was probably right.

THE CAPTAIN WAS DISTANT and cold as he read the burial service and consigned Jenkinson's body to the deep. Captain Morris was an enigma to me. He had been all affable, tobacco-scented smiles in Falmouth, but since we set sail, he had been by turns vexed, surly and anxious. His hand was trembling now as he passed it across his hair. He was coming to the committal, and the sailors at the plank's end were preparing to tip it. 'In the sure and certain hope of the resurrection to eternal life through our Lord Jesus Christ, we commend to Almighty God, Frederick Jenkinson, and we commit his body to the depths, ashes to ashes, dust to dust.'

The plank tipped, and the weighted bundle slipped into the water and sank quickly. 'The Lord bless him and keep him. The Lord make his face to shine upon him and be gracious unto him. The Lord lift up his countenance upon him and give him peace. *Amen.*' The captain closed his prayer book and bowed his head briefly, before hastening away in the direction of his cabin without another word.

The sea was falling, and I realised now that the wind had been dropping all day, the motion growing easier on my stomach. Philpott stayed at the rail, and I leaned beside him as the others dispersed. The sailors had looked at me strangely, I thought, as the body slipped into the water. Like the sail-maker they had seemed unaccountably hostile, inexplicably grim. I could only think he'd told them I'd taken the cross from Jenkinson's neck. I found it hard to believe they'd not take what they could, for most of them looked halfway to pirates.

'Do you think the crew might have snaffled it?' I asked, my train of thought returning to the more pressing problem at hand.

'Snaffled what?' Philpott was absent-minded, exhibiting all the cheerfulness commonly brought on by a stranger's death.

'The Treaty. Before they sewed him into his shroud the first time.'

Philpott turned his head. '*You* are uncommon exercised by the business. God damn me, Laurence, you've been fussing about it all day.'

'Exercised? Well, I suppose I am, having written out the

confounded thing half a dozen times. More, if you count all the spoiled pages I had to throw away.'

Philpott's face was changing, greeting an unseen figure behind me. It was Max de Salles, who had come up so quietly I wondered how much of this exchange he might have heard, and I remembered another line from my instructions. *As far as the rest of the world is concerned, you have left our service under a cloud, and have now taken up Mr Philpott's offer of a new career. You may, if it please you, exaggerate your chagrin at this turn of events, so that men may think you disaffected.* At the time, this had made me laugh bitterly. But Max seemed not to have heard anything inopportune. He only bowed with excessive formality and requested our presence in his aunt's cabin forthwith.

From the diary of the Comtesse de Salles

I am set adrift. I dream of goat's cheese and figs, peaches warm from the tree, soft brioche and fresh eggs. Instead, I eat something they say is bread, with flabby grey bacon that makes me gag. Everything is gone, there is no solid ground beneath my feet, and the only certainty that if our countrymen take us, we will find a swift path to the guillotine.

I miss the broad fields and woods of the chateau. The churchyard, where my husband lies safely asleep under the chestnut trees. How much simpler to go to bed in the earth beside him. To give my soul up to God, and to seek my dear son in his heavenly Father's arms. The cards give no answer, though I call and call across the darkened abyss.

6

THE COMTESSE HAD the use of the captain's broad saloon, and when her harsh voice bid us enter, I blinked in the bright light from the large stern windows. She was sitting at the table, surrounded by hints to the captain's character. A shelf of books, a rack of pipes and a set of mementos apparently from his travels. A large conch shell, a wooden platter inlaid with mother of pearl, and a glum human skull, painted with mysterious diagrams.

'My mind is troubled,' she announced, bidding us take a seat. The ship heeled a little, the window glass shivered, and a wave dashed past with a boom like a cannon, scattering into a dozen smaller waves in our wake. 'There is much that puzzles me, and I find myself with desire for a newspaper. But then, my nephew points out that there are newspaper men aboard who might advise me.'

'Very happy, ma'am.' Philpott sat down on the worn cushions of the window seat beside Max. The velvet was stained and faded from ingress of water and sunlight, and bore a curious pattern of streaks, like lichen on wood. I settled on the corner of the table, for want of a better seat.

'Please to explain *Monsieur* Fletcher's *effronterie* at dinner last night,' the comtesse went on. 'My nephew promised me we fly to safety in America, but this man was exceeding rude.'

I had, for my own part, been wondering with equal curiosity what had made Max flee the battlefield, when the medal he wore still spoke so loudly of military pride. Something to do with their family, he had said to his aunt that morning, something that made them more than usually abhorrent to the new regime in Paris. Just now he was watching me with a penetrating eye, and I realised he was likely speculating about my own flight from Downing Street. I straightened from the examination of a set of strange playing cards, laid out on the table in the shape of a cross.

Meanwhile, Philpott was looking pleased at the opportunity to sermonise. 'Your nephew is quite right, ma'am, safety awaits you. Philadelphia is a thriving town, and you'll slip in quite unnoticed, I assure 'ee. You will scarcely credit the variety of human life that throngs its streets, from presidents to paupers, all cheek by jowl and huggermugger, as cosy as bugs in rugs.'

The comtesse frowned, as though this was scant consolation to her patrician soul, but Philpott did not notice, nor particularly add to her comfort. 'We English are quite as unpopular as you French aristocrats, *madame*. But you must grin and bear it, for you are obliged to shoulder the sins of your forebears, just as we are.'

Max looked at Philpott with a disbelieving gaze. '*You* don't grin and bear it.' He was abrupt and his scorched face fierce, but Philpott didn't mind it, only laughed.

'No, God damn me, I don't.' He peered out at the ship's wake, a sudden brief flash of sunlight gleaming off the wave tops and glinting on the window glass. 'But someone must argue for the Treaty against the tide, and against the tide is where I'm best.'

The comtesse looked impatient. 'But, *voilà*, 'ere is another thing. What is this *Treaty* everybody speaks of?'

'A vastly important document, ma'am, which seeks to keep America neutral, and make some inroads back to friendship between our nations, after all these sorry years since their revolution. American men of business, like Fletcher, are fools if they don't welcome it, and in these perilous times 'tis equally vital for us. 'Twas France and Spain coming in with the Americans that lost us the colonies, and now France is extending her influence every day. Spain looks likely to succumb, while the radicals in Hibernia court the French as allies. We cannot afford to make America such another. But too many of 'em are persuaded that, as France helped 'em throw off British rule, so, now, the Americans ought to support France.'

The comtesse frowned, perplexed. 'But it was Louis, the French king, who 'elped the Americans in their war against you, *non*? And yet now the Americans wish to 'elp those who—'

'Chopped off his head?' Philpott broke in cheerfully. 'Quite so, ma'am, very sharp indeed. But politics makes fools of us all, and there is a terrible great enthusiasm among the American public for the French Revolution. They cast off dear old King George and have a dreadful thirst for the overthrow of all constituted monarchy. The president for his own part desires no such thing and sent his envoy – young Theodore Jay's father – to England last summer, to hammer out a treaty of neutrality.'

'And where is Theodore Jay's father now?'

'In Paris, placating the French Government, for the Americans don't want to fight them either. America can't afford a war.'

'And where is the Treaty?' Max asked.

Philpott spread his hands. 'We haven't the faintest idea.' And that was, without any dissembling, the entire truth.

The comtesse waved a dismissal and we rose, obedient as ever, turning for the door. Philpott paused to examine the strange skull on the captain's table, his cheerful blue eye meeting its hollow gaze. 'God damn me, this is quite a curiosity. I have heard of this nonsense but never saw it before. Some strange German notion, I believe,' he added, seeing the comtesse's look of enquiry. 'I heard about it somewhere.' The depths of Philpott's knowledge, as well as his ignorance, sometimes astonished me. 'One fellow even thinks good and evil reside in the bumps on your head, not in your immortal soul. Blasphemous notion.'

If I had earlier thought that the stout, pink comtesse and my stout, pink employer were remarkably similar, then the affable Philpott and the captain's gloomy skull now presented a veritable study in contrasts. 'But I'm surprised the crew will tolerate such an occult article aboard,' Philpott said, tapping it affectionately. 'Damn me if it don't look spiteful enough to conjure up every sea monster in the ocean.'

J ENKINSON'S LETTER FROM Downing Street, which I had guessed to be his instructions from London and had taken, limping, from his cabin, still rustled in my pocket. Once alone, I took the paper out and recognised Your Lordship's familiar, dreadful hand. It was in code, of course, the same kind of code I had spent ten years deciphering by the dozen in the garret of the Foreign Office. It was dated, and there was a number in the bottom right-hand corner, which indicated the source as a page in a book. The quickest glance confirmed it was not the same code based on my Gray's *Elegy*, but there had been a modest row of volumes in Jenkinson's cabin, such as any gentleman might possess. With luck, the key to this cypher would be among them.

When I came into the mess, Peter Williams was emerging from the galley with a hot iron, apparently engaged about the business of pressing Theodore's linen on the long table. 'I need a moment in Jenkinson's cabin,' I said quietly in his ear. 'Don't tell anyone. And try not to let anyone else come in.' He looked serenely incurious, just as I knew he would, and only inclined his head a little.

'And if anyone comes down give me a sign, to save me bursting out like a fool.'

'A sign?' He raised an eyebrow.

'A cough. A sneeze. A shriek.'

He laughed at that and went back to his business. I opened Jenkinson's creaking door for the second time that day, shut myself in, and ran my fingers along the spines of the books where they lay in their sober cloth-boarded covers under his bunk. There were a dozen, and the source for the cypher could be any one of them.

The method was simple. The number on the sheet indicated a page number, and the cypher began with the first letter on the page, which stood for A, then B and so on, missing out repeated letters until a full alphabet was formed, to be checked against the document, and translated in reverse into plain English sentences. The whole secrecy relied on the book chosen as the source, regularly changed, and indicated for Whitehall by the date beside the page number at the bottom of the sheet.

Well, there was no choice but to try them all, and hope a comprehensible word emerged eventually, to show me I had picked the right volume. I smoothed out the paper and laid it on the bunk. Now I noticed that the page had been neatly scored and torn, a third of the way from the top, and when I turned it over a line of text was bisected by the rip. The top third of the letter, including the greeting to the addressee at the beginning and Grenville's signature overleaf at the end, was now missing.

Another mystery, but perhaps the reason would become clear when I had decoded the rest. I began to work methodically through the books in Jenkinson's library. It was easy enough to dismiss the wrong ones, even after a couple of letters. XC MTRE, the first declared. DI FADS announced the second. BS WABY was the unhelpful verdict of the third. The sixth of the set yielded MR, and I was about to discard it as similarly meaningless, when the following four letters spelled JAGO.

Mr Jago has been a pious fool, but is an intelligent one nonetheless, and may be relied upon to help you, if it comes to it. As to that other matter, make it your main concern. We know the agent is to come aboard the TANKERVILLE, *and we are certain of their intent. It will be wise for you to apprise your colleague of this matter as soon as is practicable, and to explain that the matter is of vital importance to the Crown. – So vital, in fact, that his assistance in this matter will be sufficient to grant him full immunity from all former slights, and the fulfilment of all promises personally given by—*

And there the paragraph ended, the rest ripped carefully away.

I sat back, hardly knowing how to take it. I was *a pious fool*. Yet, as I was surely also the *colleague* in question, here was a cast-iron promise that if I took on Jenkinson's mission against this unknown agent – not to mention sought out the missing Treaty in whatever hiding place he'd put it – I would be allowed to return to my little office in Whitehall, with which Your Lordship had tempted me in my own instructions. I imagined walking back up Downing Street, among the jostling clerks, through the door of the Foreign Office, across the chequered floor, and up the wide staircase to Your Lordship's room. The under-secretaries awaiting me, the musty smell of old tapestry and snuff. What would I do? Bring a pistol and blow all your heads to kingdom come? Or fall on your necks? I have hated you in my time, My Lord, but, I reluctantly confess, it is as a child might hate a guilty parent – bitter disappointment, sharpened by involuntary love.

I looked back down at your letter. There was nothing else of much interest, save the name and address of the British Ambassador in Philadelphia, to whom I should deliver the Treaty if I ever found it. Whatever paragraph had proved too sensitive to keep – whether at the beginning or end of the letter – was gone, and there was no hint remaining as to its contents.

From Captain Morris to his family
in Falmouth

My wife and girls will be pleased to hear we have outwitted another Frenchman. If they continue so slow improving in sailor's arts, we shall certainly win the war.

Tell Catherine I have not forgot her sprigged muslin and shall be sure to find the very shade of blue in Madeira to match her eyes. Has that young Bennett been visiting? He has not a penny to his name, Hannah, and you must discourage him.

I suppose Flushing is still wet and cold. Here the sea quietens with every hour, and I dare say Madeira will be disagreeably warm. God knows, we are never satisfied. My belly still gripes, but Kidd prescribed me a grain or two of Epsom Salts, and I believe I am a little eased.

We have a pretty sober complement of passengers, and there is little amusement to be had at the dinner table, except from Mr William Philpott who is exactly as you might imagine. His apprentice, Laurence Jago, is a quiet young man who watches and listens but says very little. There is a disagreeable American planter who fancies himself a speculator, and the young Mr Jay who seems to have wool for brains. The two French aristocrats I told you of are as haughty and aloof as you could picture. If I was a common Frenchman I would hang 'em both directly.

Yes, a dull company, even without the poor gentleman from the War Office whose brains were dashed out a few days since by a falling spar. I hardly dare tell you more, knowing how you will fret, but I have been at sea these five and twenty years without seeing anything quite like it. 'Twas a one-in-a-million occurrence, and I dare say poor Mr Jenkinson has saved us all, for the rest of time, from the repetition of so unlikely an event.

7

I STAYED AT THE MESS table after breakfast until every other passenger had loitered off on his own business. I had been considering the problem of the missing papers all night and had even resorted to searching my own cabin, on the off chance that Jenkinson had been cleverer than wise and thought to hide the thing among his accomplice's belongings.

But he had been wiser than clever, and I was now turning my mind to other possibilities. All I could be reasonably sure of was that, unless the crew had rifled his dead pockets the moment our backs were turned, he had not brought the documents back on deck with him.

There was a pile of books lying in the middle of the mess table, the common property of the various passengers aboard, and that seemed a likely place to start, for where better to conceal papers than among other, more innocent ones? I took up the volumes one by one, but no loose pages fluttered out. There was a book of sermons that probably belonged to Theodore since they seemed squarely aimed at errant womankind. I had left my Milton on the table among them, but it wasn't there now.

I opened the lockers and hunted among napkins and carving knives, and the comtesse's sewing basket, which made me think about my knee where Jenkinson's needle had impaled it the day before. It was still sore. Philpott's canary wine had a compartment all to itself, but there was nothing tucked behind the bottles.

Of course there wasn't. These were all hiding places far too obvious, for hadn't Jenkinson said, *I have a couple of ideas might fool 'em?* I looked about for a cranny more obscure, and my eye fell on the pot-bellied stove. It hadn't been lit for a week, the sea being too rough to risk a flame anywhere but the galley. I squatted down and opened the door. Dead coal ash. My fingers were blackened almost at once, and at the risk of my shirtsleeve I pushed my arm up the stove pipe as far as it would reach.

Philpott surprised me in this undignified posture, bursting out from his cabin where he had been writing. 'You look like you're midwife to a cow,' he said cheerfully from behind me. 'What the devil are you up to? Not that damned Treaty again? You are grown quite fanatic.'

I ignored him and climbed the ladder to walk the sloping decks as best I was able in the stiff wind. I even went back to the heads, but there was no possible hiding place there. I explored the muzzle of the carronade the ship carried at its bow in an equally veterinarian manner, and then the other seven guns, while the crew went about their business indifferent to my searches, until, in the end, I admitted myself defeated.

When I came into the mess for dinner, with Mr Gibbs at my heels, Philpott was regaling the other passengers with my inglorious history in a way that made no mention of the *piety* you ascribed to me in your letter to Jenkinson. Having despaired of the truth as too hazardous a story, he was imparting my concocted tale to them in a way that would have pleased you all in Downing Street. For myself, I was nettled. False calumny, even if agreed upon, is still painful. To do him justice, he was not gossiping behind my back, for he made no attempt to moderate his tone or dissemble as I came up behind him, where he was sitting at the table with a glass of canary.

'A very estimable young man,' he was saying cheerfully. 'Whatever his proclivities among the citizens of Sodom and Gomorrah, Laurence is a man of integrity, with a good head for a story. He'll make a fine journalist, now he's shaken the dust of Downing Street off his shoes and seen 'em for what they are. Ah, there you are, my boy.'

Max was eyeing me from my left side, and Fletcher from across the table, as I shrugged and sat down instead of setting the dog on Philpott. Max pushed the plate of roast turkey towards me with unprecedented goodwill, but it was burnt as usual, and I only pulled off a strip to feed to Mr Gibbs surreptitiously under the table.

I would keep looking for the Treaty. And if there was someone aboard – or yet to come aboard – as an *agent* for an as-yet-unknown power, I would find them, too. The crew, being regular packet men, were presumably above suspicion, and surveying the other passengers at the table it was hard to imagine that any of those present could be the agent either. There were only two men aboard I couldn't vouch for, but Max could have scant reason to undermine the Bourbons' English allies and Obadiah Fletcher had announced his dislike of us too roundly to be a dissembler – unless his dissembling was folded layer upon fiendish layer. Of course, such a thing was possible – I had learned to my cost things were rarely exactly as they seemed – but we were to stop off in Madeira and

Barbados on our journey, where other more promising suspects might yet come aboard.

I would be vigilant. I would find it all out. And you would be obliged to take me back, and restore my good name, whether you liked it or not.

NEVERTHELESS, YOU WERE right, My Lord, the report of my disgrace was useful. It was only a few days until Christmas, and the sea had picked up again after the brief lull, so that the piss pot in my cabin was now advancing to a count of three and was far too hazardous for actual use. We had made scarcely any progress, and a Christmas aboard without comforts seemed increasingly likely. I was on deck, conveying such gloomy thoughts to Peter Williams, when Obadiah Fletcher came waddling towards us, his eyes fixed on me.

'Looks like you're for it,' Peter Williams said, nodding at the squat approaching figure. 'Fraternising with a slave and a machine breaker at that.'

But Fletcher hardly seemed to notice Peter Williams at all and was, in fact, rather more friendly than was agreeable as he led me into a quiet corner where we might not be overheard. 'You could have knocked me down with a feather when I found out Mr Theodore Jay was aboard, after all that carry-on with the warship. Though I did suspect there was another American aboard, from the first night when I saw the darkie. Never thought it would be a Jay, by God!'

I grimaced what might pass for a smile, having nothing germane to say to this observation. Fletcher grinned gummily. 'Does he have the Treaty?'

'I've no idea.'

'I believe he has. Why else would he be returning to Philadelphia without his father?'

'He's called home for personal reasons, that's all I know.'

Fletcher shook his head. 'Well, there's a fascination in being at the thick of history, I must say. Where does he keep it, do you think?'

'Keep what?'

'The Treaty, of course.'

'I see you're determined it's aboard. But I know no more than you do.'

Fletcher was gazing out at the tumbling ocean, a look of calculation on his broad, smooth face. 'Aye, aye. But in any case, the Jay boy must know what's in it. And a man might profit a good deal from a foreknowledge of the contents.' He looked at me. 'How well do you know him?'

Hardly at all,' I said untruthfully, remembering the many scrapes Theodore had got himself into in London, and from which I had been obliged to rescue him. An image of the dark alley of Saffron Hill, a constable and Theodore escaping in my old hat came unbidden into my mind.

'Well, well. There's no point talking to Philpott, for he's mad set on supporting the elder Mr Jay. But you and I, sir, might make a dollar or two out of the business. I fancy they have agreed to open up the West India trade. If so, there's a deal of pent-up demand for American timber we might profit by.'

He had taken out another cigar, but a voice shouted down from the rigging to put the bloody thing out, and just then the bell rang for dinner. As I followed him down the companionway, I remembered that the Treaty had indeed opened up the Caribbean trade, but in name only. No American ship large enough to carry a profitable load of timber was to be allowed in British waters, and it was one of many ways the

Americans would be disappointed when Jay's handiwork was revealed to his countrymen.

Fletcher turned back to me at the bottom of the companion ladder and croaked softly, 'You've no cause to have scruples, if what Philpott says is true. And we are out here on the ocean, quite free from observation. If you'll help me, I'll invest your cash for you and we shall both be rich.'

8

With the legerdemain of latitude, the ship sailed suddenly back into summer. Spain lay to port, the cow ceased her doleful calling, and we were basking in sunshine, on a pleasant latitude with Gibraltar, Morocco, and eternal summer. Even Theodore Jay rose from his sickbed, for the sea settled to a corrugation of white-topped wavelets, and the ship scudded along swiftly at a steady angle that scarcely troubled his delicate digestion. I had made some further searches in the common areas – the water closet, the galley, the empty cabins between Jenkinson's and my own – but I was no further forward, and without help I feared I could do little more.

But the better weather made everything more cheerful. Having escaped the westerlies of the Channel, there was new hope we would spend Christmas in Madeira, amid delightful olive groves and vineyards and plentiful good food. I could smell pine tar and salt as I settled down on the warm planks of the deck to write an apprentice piece for Philpott. The canvas snapped above my head as the sailors tacked the ship, and I looked up from my paper, sucking the quill, to discover a foreign body in the rigging. A bulky shape perched in the maintop, waving its hat – it was Philpott, beckoning to me strenuously. I let my eyes slide past him, as though suddenly preoccupied by the network of ropes attaching the sail to the yardarm below him, and thence back to my paper. I myself was certainly not climbing half a hundred feet above the deck.

'You are wise.' It was the comtesse on her daily walk, pausing to look at me with a smile you might even have called kindly. Perhaps her bad temper of the past days had merely sprung from a troubled stomach, for in this sunny calm her face had softened.

'Am I?' I put down my paper, and, when she did not walk on, went to fetch her a chair which I set in the shade beside me. She sat down stiffly, with an arthritic groan, and leaned on her walking stick.

'To resist the calls from above of *Monsieur* Philpott, I mean to say.' She settled more comfortably and eyed Philpott again in his perch. 'Though I could 'ave done it, me, when I was young.'

'Then you are braver than I am.'

'Brave! I think we are all monstrous brave to risk this wide *océan*.' She was looking at me with candid interest. 'And why are *you* 'ere, young *monsieur*?'

My eyes slipped to my paper again. 'Oh – the need to escape a foolish past. Friendship for Philpott. The sheer excitement of a new world.'

'Ah – and the same for me, too. I am escaping the past, with Maximilien. 'Ow shall we find this new world, I wonder?'

I shook my head and looked back up into the tracery of the rigging. 'I suppose only time will tell.'

She looked pleased. 'Ah, but that is not so, I promise you.' She wagged her finger. 'The *tarot* can also tell.'

'The *tarot*?'

The tarot was a new thing, she explained at some opaque

length while I only half listened. A young woman in France had grown tremendously famous for her cartomancy, and was very popular with the rational Jacobins, if I could believe it. I wondered if the comtesse fancied herself in the same role, but perhaps she was merely bored and in search of novelty.

'You will let me read these cards for you?' she demanded, but Philpott was now also hailing me, having laboriously descended from his perch while I wasn't looking.

'God damn me, Laurence, you pale excuse for a human being. You have bowels of seawater, no manly courage at all.'

'I confess it. But I can't think the captain wants us clambering about in his rigging.'

'Quite the contrary, I assure 'ee. He was most pressing that I spend the afternoon in the maintop and enjoy the view.' Philpott pulled out a wad of papers and sat down. 'I never was so entertained in all my life. I call it *A Watch from the Rigging* and shall send it back to London from Madeira for Nancy to publish. 'Twill keep her in funds and myself in the public eye a few weeks yet.' He looked at me, suddenly the schoolmaster. 'Equip yourself with facts, then observe with understanding. How many pints of milk are drawn off the cow each day? How much water swills about in those casks in the hold, and how long until it turns stagnant and foul? How many bushels of flour are required to feed the crew, and how many hours of the cook's labour? How much grain for the turkeys, and what quantity of hay for the cow to keep her in milk? I have quizzed Captain Morris and have it all here.' He tapped his paper and I reflected that the captain had been wise to send him to the masthead.

'You have had us all in your eye, like Satan in his tree. Did you witness any misdoings in Eden?'

'Oh.' The hours in the maintop had darkened Philpott's always ruddy complexion to something approaching the colour of a beetroot. His face creased into a smile and his eyes disappeared as, in passing, I remembered my copy of Milton, which had been missing from the pile of books on the mess table when I searched it. 'Only a shameful flirtation between a young journalist and a beautiful noblewoman.'

At this, the comtesse blushed and smiled, and batted him away with a plump hand. He was undeterred. 'Also, that child Ben, the cabin boy, hopping up and down the companion ladder to the mess in some tomfool way, like as not to break his leg. I shouted out to him quite stern, but he only stuck up his fingers.' Philpott smiled fondly. 'A lad after my own heart. It took Peter Williams to dissuade him – I saw their heads together *most* earnest, and then the boy ran off.'

M R FLETCHER HAD found himself one friend aboard, as I discovered when I sloped off to the surgeon's cabin on the pretext of my painful knee for a refill of my little phial. The place stank of spirits, and Kidd himself looked pickled, wiry and swift in his movements as he slapped down a card on the trunk where he and Fletcher were playing Ruff for money.

'Join us, Mr Jago?'

'No thank you, sir. I'm no gambler.'

When I asked him, Kidd refilled my little bottle, while Fletcher, who had briefly turned his frog face up to me, went back to frowning over his hand. Unless I took him up on his offer regarding the Treaty, or consented to give him my money at cards, I was apparently of no use to him.

Another kind of card game was in progress when I returned aft to find Philpott in the comtesse's saloon. 'The Lovers?' He was turning pink with bashful excitement as I came in. 'And pray, what does that portend, *madame*? You'll not call me an unfaithful husband, I hope?' He seemed quite eager to think so. The comtesse had invited us into her cabin, to read our fortunes with her strange deck of cards, while Max had only sneered at such credulity and taken himself off on deck.

'Per'aps.' But the comtesse did not seem very likely to encourage Philpott's amorous hopes as she tapped the card. 'Per'aps not. See in the picture 'ow they meet *avec un justice*. It signifies friendship. Agreement. Per'aps an agreement of marriage; or per'aps a commercial venture.'

Philpott's head snapped up. '*Agreement? Commerce?* As if, you might say, A *Treaty of Commerce?*' He was suddenly even pinker, verging on puce. 'Good God, Laurence, it means the Treaty, I do believe!' He turned back to the comtesse. 'Quick, *madame*, does it say where it's hidden?'

'If it does, I'll swallow your encyclopaedia of superstition whole,' I said, but the comtesse was already shaking her head.

'*Non, Monsieur* Philpott, *je suis désolée …*'

'Ah, well, well, never mind. But still, I may be the one that's *meant* to find it.' Philpott looked satisfied by this flattering turn of events, and his future apparently a glowing one. Mine turned out to be beset with the Devil, the Fool and Death himself, though the comtesse assured me Death only really means change and rebirth.

'We will all pass through a veil into a new life, on this journey, will we not?' she said, suddenly as pensive as her nephew, chin on folded hands, gazing into the candle flame. 'Out 'ere on the sea we are between worlds.' And then, unexpectedly, 'A place *très bien* for a *séance*, I assure you.'

I shuddered at the very idea, but Philpott was getting to his feet again, hardly listening – perhaps he didn't know what the word meant – and preoccupied by a new thought. 'Now, ma'am, I wonder if you happen to have Peter Williams's suit of clothes still about you?'

She apparently did not recognise the name.

'Theodore Jay's man, you know,' Philpott added. 'Poor fellow, he possesses scarcely anything of his own, and I should be sorry to deprive him of what little he does have. Theodore calls him Peet, which I think a shocking insult to the man's dignity. Makes him sound like a child or a dog, when he's solemn as an owl.'

The comtesse blushingly produced Peter Williams's borrowed suit and thrust it into Philpott's arms. She looked pleased to be rid of it, as Philpott shook out the folds. She was likely quite unused to dealing with such practical matters, and unsure how to approach Peter Williams herself.

'Yes, yes, his suit, poor fellow,' Philpott said, smoothing the folds of fabric. 'But not this, I think.'

'The Englishman's wig?'

'Just so. Poor devil, he won't be needing it any more. And God damn me, I believe no other living man would consent to wear such a monstrosity.' Philpott studied Jenkinson's enormous hairpiece pensively for a moment and then, seized by a cheerful inspiration, set it with elaborate ceremony on the tattooed yellowing skull on the captain's table. It was hard to say whether the addition of the wig made it more or less macabre.

The Anatomy of a Ship

You can have no possible Conception, John Barleycorn, how neatly things are bestowed in a small Ship such as this! Having particular Reasons of my own, that need not be here explained, to search through all the various Arrangements of items both naval and personal aboard this Vessel, I find it an admirable Plan for all of Life, and I urge you to imitate the good sailors in their Customs.

All personal Belongings are contained in a Sea Chest, one for each man, that sits below his swinging Hammock and acts as Seat at Table, or Table itself just as circumstances dictate.

No Confusion of scattered Belongings here, such as Ladies in particular are wont to create. Children are still worse. Give them all a Box, John, and be done with Confusion. I dare say they will not like it but, being the Head of the Household, I should think your Word might be Law.

I have written home to Mrs Philpott on the Matter and will keep you advised of her Opinion.

9

'I SEARCHED HIGH AND LOW, with Peter Williams's assistance,' Philpott said, glumly chewing on his pipe. 'Not a sight or sound of the Treaty anywhere.'

Enlisting Peter Williams with his knowledge of steerage had been a good idea, and I wished I'd thought of it. But Philpott was shaking his head. 'And me foretold to find it by the cards! Well, it seems I'm not to lay my hand on it without further trouble and must use my wits. I have been to see the captain and represented to him that it's a matter of national importance. Persuaded him to search his men's dunnage, before we reach Madeira, and the papers can be smuggled ashore to wing their way to Paris.'

'He was willing?'

'Extremely unfriendly about the whole matter.' Philpott lowered his voice. 'He is a curious fellow.'

'A private man, that's all, and probably dog-tired of your questioning. And besides, for God's sake, he is the captain of a mail ship, carrying all manner of sensitive documents every day. He has enough to concern him.'

But I was glad Philpott had wrung a promise out of the captain to institute enquiries among the crew. Only men with far better knowledge of the ship's geography than Philpott or me would likely find Jenkinson's hidden papers. And though Fletcher's enquiries had made me a little less eager to reveal that the Treaty was missing and at large on the ship, the thing needed to be found, and frankly if anyone could find it for me, for whatever purpose, I would be grateful.

But it wasn't until the next morning, scarcely a day from Madeira, that the captain called an extraordinary muster on the main deck. I took up a station apart, watching the crew assemble in their Sunday best of white shirts and trousers. Even Mr Kidd had been roused from the seclusion of his cabin and looked as grey as a woodlouse prised from its cranny. I examined the other passengers covertly. Max was moody, Theodore apparently in a reverie. The comtesse looked ready to take charge of the whole business if the captain's method was not to her liking, and Fletcher – well, if the creator of the science of head bumps had happened to examine him, he would have pursed his lips. Very little development of good nature, he would have concluded, or of appreciation of finer things, in that cold-blooded, amphibian skull.

The crew had got wind of some trouble and looked uneasy under their cheerful straw hats. The captain came to the business of the missing papers only by degrees, perhaps reluctant to call his men outright thieves or, like me, doubtful of the wisdom of revealing that such a valuable item was missing at all. But he couldn't prevaricate for ever under Philpott's forceful gaze.

'It pains me that I must remind you of my instructions.' Even from where we passengers stood by the companion ladder, I could see that the captain's hand was trembling again as he waved a paper. The lines around his mouth were soft, and he seemed querulous instead of stern. I might almost have said he'd been drinking. 'If someone on this ship has been thieving, they'll not sail in a packet ship again. And, God damn me, if we come across another navy ship before we land, I'll hand him over without a qualm.'

'Thieving!' The carpenter, Mr Spiers, was small and quick, as befitted a native of Mousehole, whence he hailed. 'By Christ, Captain Morris, if any man touches my dunnage, I'll break his neck.'

'We are all sorry to believe it possible, Mr Spiers. A man's property is sacrosanct among us, I had hoped. But an item of great value aboard has gone missing.'

Gloom replaced anger in the carpenter's face. 'Missin'?' Behind him, a sudden grief seemed to be spreading rapidly through the assembled ranks. Even Ben looked anxious. 'Great value? You don't mean to say the *gold's* missin', Cap'n?'

'Gold? What nonsense are you drivelling, Spiers?'

'The gold yon young feller's taking to America. The gold what he's to bribe the Congress with.'

At this the captain frowned, more perplexed than ever, and Philpott laughed out loud. Peter Williams raised his eyebrows, and Theodore awoke from his reverie, apparently realising himself an entirely dispensable obstruction to this imagined Eldorado.

'I assure you, gentlemen, I've no gold,' he said quickly, horrified into speech. 'No gold at all. The missing item is, in fact, a paper – well, to be precise, a sheaf of papers, perhaps twenty in number – I assure you of it, on my honour.'

'Paper?' Even the generally sensible first mate looked disappointed, but then rallied with new hope. 'Paper money? French *assignats*?'

It was Max's turn to laugh. 'They'd be no use to you either. The Jacobins' money is entirely worthless.'

'Not *assignats*. But nevertheless, a document of great value,' Theodore insisted, with more honesty than discretion. I couldn't help glancing at Fletcher and saw beneath his usual oily gleam a richer glow of sudden satisfaction. He had been right in his guess that the Treaty was aboard, and now he clearly saw that the thing was in play for any man if he could only find it – or pay someone else to do so.

The crew began to cotton on. 'Value?' the carpenter ruminated aloud. 'You could sell it, like?'

'Yes, perhaps.' Whatever his qualms, Theodore was devoutly honest, and the crew cheered up considerably. I glanced again at Fletcher to see that he was eyeing the carpenter, as though weighing up a rival.

'But be this as it may, the vital document is missing,' the captain broke in again. 'And, therefore, of no value to anyone until found. I do not say any man is guilty of thieving, for there may be some other explanation – Mr Jenkinson had talked of hiding the thing before his untimely death. If the missing papers reappear, I'll ask no questions. I want a search organised of every corner, Mr Peters, excepting the passengers' cabins, which I will examine myself, with their permission. We'll be in Madeira by Christmas Day, and I'm determined no man jack will go ashore unless we've found the missing article.'

The crew's excitement dissolved abruptly.

'That'll put them on their mettle,' Captain Morris said as the men dispersed in low-voiced conclave. 'If it's to be found, they'll find it.'

'But Madeira ...' Peter Williams said quietly from behind us. 'You won't really keep us all aboard in port, sir?'

'That I will. The Treaty can come to no harm out here on the waves. If someone has taken it, which I still doubt, they must get it ashore, and I'm resolved they'll not do it on my watch.' But the captain himself looked chagrined. I didn't know it then, but I found out later that the crew had trunks full of items of their own, which they expected to sell to the Madeira natives, and then reinvest the profits in further purchases to be flogged off in Barbados. It made the packet crossing a far more profitable venture than their meagre wages from the Royal Mail allowed. Even the captain took a part and, as I would find out later, he had more reason than most to regret the loss of his own share of the profits.

10

THE SEARCH BEGAN at once, to pre-empt any subterfuge, and we were sent below to await the captain's investigation. Fletcher was brought up short, before he had quite hopped off the bottom rung of the companion ladder, by Philpott thundering down behind him. 'A devil of a business, ain't it, Mr Fletcher?'

Fletcher's voice was unctuous-smooth as usual as I stepped off the ladder in my turn. 'Indeed, it is, Mr Philpott.'

'The captain desires we stay out of our cabins until he comes down,' Philpott added, but the American ignored him, slithering into his own cabin with flagrant disobedience and shutting the door.

The rest of us milled about homelessly, like ants in a broken nest. Peter Williams appeared from the direction of steerage, with an unusually harassed frown, and made for Theodore's cabin. Max's mood seemed not to have improved as he took the comtesse's arm. 'The captain is quite welcome to search my cabin, but I'll take my aunt to her saloon, for she will not like to have her privacy invaded.'

She certainly would not, but neither did she see the need for it. 'Why search *our* cabins?' she was asking in French as he led her away. 'What possible reason have *we* to steal this Treaty?'

I sat myself down at the mess table with Philpott, Theodore and Peter Williams. After a moment or two Max returned from aft and joined us. We listened to the clanging of chamber pots and the slamming of drawers as the captain began his search of the cabins, ill at ease in his task, but determined to do his duty with a thoroughness that impressed me. We heard the low murmur of voices, first from the comtesse's saloon and then from Fletcher's cabin.

Peter Williams's dunnage would be searched by the crew, who had already begun ripping steerage methodically apart. He turned a troubled face to me. 'You don't think he'll really keep us aboard in Madeira?'

I hadn't seen him so put out since the day of the chase by the French frigate, and I didn't know why. Philpott's pen scratched away across the table, his face absorbed over some account – though whether it was of this search or some new nonsense of the gunner's I didn't know.

'You have a particular desire to go ashore?'

Peter Williams hesitated. 'It's a fine place. Stopped there on the way out, last spring. Hoped to see it again.'

Perhaps he'd had some assignation there, I thought. Some woman. Nothing but the thwarted promise of amorous congress seemed to justify his mood. I confess, it vexed me a little to see him returning to America when the English law would have allowed him to remain in London a free man. But he had a standing promise of liberty from Theodore's father, he had once told me, when the price of his purchase and education would be paid off. As Theodore had spent the previous summer trawling the backstreets of London, Jay senior had veered between promises of early release if Peter Williams kept his son out of trouble and threats of perpetual bondage if he didn't.

'Well,' I said, 'you may return to Madeira in 1805 if that's any consolation.' And at his frown, I added, 'When you are free, you know. You may go anywhere, then.'

'Free!' His fingers drummed on the table. His fingernails were short and neat, his long fingers made for holding a pen, not doing laundry. He seemed wary of speaking before Max and Philpott, seemed to be searching for words. When they came, they were ones meant only for me to understand. 'Saffron Hill was my undoing, sir. It was one thing too many.'

Again, the constable and the dark alley came to mind, with Peter Williams and myself chasing Theodore through Saffron Hill as he vowed to redeem the sodomites who frequented its shadows. Unknown to us, a French spy had alerted a passing constable and it had been a close-run thing whether Theodore would be arrested and his father blackmailed into abandoning the Treaty.

'But he came to no harm,' I said, in a low voice. 'You did your duty.'

'They said he should not have been there at all.'

'How were you to restrain him? He, at least, is free.'

'We are none of us free,' Max said, from Peter Williams's other side. He had understood the gist of the story, even if not the detail. '*Liberté, Egalité, Fraternité*, and here I am, exiled from my home. When I reach Philadelphia, I must take whatever work offers, though I have lands and titles and honours in France. I am a slave to another's foolishness on a path I have not chosen. And you?' He threw up his head and eyed me fiercely. I didn't know what he meant until he added, 'The tongue is tied, as you say in English? I have seen you, Mr Jago, at the surgeon's cabin door.'

Philpott's pen ceased scratching and I felt his eye on me. When he offered me a position in his employ, he had warned me against the Black Drop. *Seems to provoke a disagreeable mawkish enthusiasm,* he had said. *I should not like to have you jabbering about devils and angels amid a brisk Atlantic storm.*

'I consulted him for an injury,' I said hastily. 'An injury to my knee.'

Max still looked fiery, but Philpott's pen took up its scratching again.

'You are all of you free,' Peter Williams said. 'Free, at least, to make your own foolish choices between evils.'

T HE CAPTAIN SEARCHED my cabin, and then Philpott's. We neither of us had much and it was soon over. Captain Morris came back to the table, shaking his head. 'I'm sorry for this intrusion, gentlemen, but you know I'm responsible for the safe passage of all papers aboard.' He sat down, looking jaded. 'I represented to you from the first, Mr Jay, that the Treaty should go with the mail, under my own eye. But you would have your own way. A foolish proceeding, as it turns out.'

'Well,' Philpott said, placatingly, 'I wonder who the devil *does* have it?'

'I would wager my daughter's dowry that no one does,' the captain answered, drawing a hand across his hair. 'I am more and more convinced it went overboard at Mr Jenkinson's hand.' He sighed. 'But better safe than sorry. We'll keep every man on ship in Madeira and keep looking. After that, there'll be no more landfall until Barbados, and surely we'll know the truth by then.'

At supper, everyone looked pensive, perhaps reflecting that now there would be no escape from Mr Hind's idea of

Christmas dinner. But Theodore was probably still smarting from the captain's displeasure, and the comtesse from the search of her linen. Philpott and Fletcher were uncharacteristically silent. And yet, under the habitual frown that furrowed Max's forehead I thought he, for one, looked oddly relieved.

From the diary of the Comtesse de Salles

How disagreeable it is to be so confined, on this ship. I begin to see that, without knowing it, I have been free these past three years since the men went to fight. I ate what I wanted, wore what I chose, and no one questioned me. I even miss my servants who, after all, have been my companions these many years. We left so swiftly I hardly said goodbye. Did Max pay them? Did he dismiss them from my service? I dare not ask, for it would pain me to think of the tall echoing rooms empty, the fire in the kitchen cold. Christmas is coming, and instead I will imagine them all kneeling in the chapel for midnight mass. If I close my eyes, I can smell incense, and feel beneath my knees the hassock I embroidered as a young bride, long before the new rulers in Paris declared me, and God, both equally monstrous.

And still no coffee to be had, though the captain ASSURES me the box was brought aboard in Falmouth. Perhaps the dear Monsieur Philpott will remedy the matter for me. My nephew certainly will not, for he spends his days frowning into space and fancying HIMSELF the martyr, with his silly medal for mere brute strength, which is not what I would consider true courage at all when compared to my dear François.

II

I LINGERED ALONE AT the stern rail after dark, looking
out over the ship's wake, the water illuminated by the
spilling lantern light from the comtesse's cabin. The sea had
fallen since dinner, and the creaking and groaning of the
timbers had lessened. I could hear faint strains of music from
the crew's mess forward, and the patter of the deckhands' feet
as they came and went behind me.

If we failed to land in Madeira, the *agent* mentioned in Your
Lordship's letter to Jenkinson, and his unspecified ill doing,
might never materialise. Having grown hopeful about my
future, this was a circumstance as little pleasing to me as to
Peter Williams, for, in the continuing absence of the Treaty, it
was on the apprehension of this as-yet unknown fellow that
all my hopes depended. But there was still Barbados to come,
and not knowing the exact nature of this mysterious agent's
plans, he might just as well come aboard shortly before our
arrival in the New World as here in the Old. All I could do was
wait, and in the meantime continue my search for the Treaty. I
was stubbornly sure the captain was wrong, and the papers still
aboard, for I remembered Jenkinson's impatience the day of the

chase. *Whatever the Jay boy says, I'll be damned if I'll sink them and render our whole voyage useless.* But if I was right, Jenkinson had found a hiding place that had even fooled the crew. How I was to do any better was a question I couldn't answer.

Peter Williams found me. The dark outline of his head nodded a greeting, and then he leaned beside me at the rail. He never said much, but there were enough shared memories between us to make the silence a companionable one, with the dog asleep at our feet.

'What do you make of the Frenchman?' he said at last. His voice was soft, and his quiet hands were clasped together on the rail.

'Max de Salles?' I poked the dog with my foot, and he shifted in his sleep. 'Something of a curiosity, I suppose. He says he's running from some family trouble, but why he can't run to London instead of Philadelphia seems a mystery, especially since he drags his poor aunt along with him.'

'She has no one else. Her only son is dead.'

Peter Williams clearly had more access to gossip than I did, in steerage, and this might prove useful in any future enquiries of my own. 'I didn't even know she had a child.'

Peter Williams spread his hands but didn't elaborate.

'A soldier, I suppose, like Max,' I said. 'Killed in action.'

'I guess so.'

But now he was turning to me, holding out something that glinted gold in the lantern light from the binnacle. The topaz cross I had taken from Jenkinson's body was lying on his outstretched palm. 'I thought you'd want this back.'

I took the jewel from his hand, surprised, and weighed it in my own. 'Where the devil did you find it?'

'In Ben the cabin boy's pocket. He tried to run, but his legs were too short.'

'What did he say?'

'Nothing. I gave him the chance to clear himself – asked him if any of the crew had put him up to it – but he was as dumb as a doorpost.'

The cross was valuable, and likely someone had bid the boy steal it. I began to tuck it in my pocket, but then thought better of it and fastened it around my own neck. If there were thieves aboard it would be safest under my shirt.

Peter Williams was watching me. 'Will you tell on him?' He hesitated. 'I shouldn't like to see him put off on to some Royal Navy warship like the captain threatened. Should be sorry to see him a powder monkey adrift alone among three hundred men.'

'The captain would not do that, surely to God. Not to a child.' I fingered the unaccustomed gold chain under my collar. 'I dare say there's no need to speak. Not yet. You likely frightened him into good behaviour. But, if anything else goes missing, I suppose we'll have to report him.'

I had hardly been alone another minute before a new presence joined me. From its heat and nervous energy, I knew, even without looking, that it was Max de Salles.

'I'm sorry,' he said abruptly. 'I was unforgivably rude while the captain searched our cabins. I should not have mentioned the surgeon. Should not have betrayed your private habits in front of your employer. I embarrassed you. If you wish it, you may challenge me.'

'Believe it or not, there's nothing I'd like less.'

'But your future depends on *Monsieur* Philpott, *n'est ce pas?* You are a kind of apprentice to him?'

At my nod he smiled savagely. 'I envy you. For is it not "the finest profession in the world, sir?"'

I smiled reluctantly. 'So he says. At present, the whole notion seems entirely theoretical.'

'And so, as I guessed, you are not writing, when you shut yourself in your cabin for all these long, long hours?'

'You seem already well enough acquainted with my delinquencies that I need hardly confess them.'

He stared at me thoughtfully, as if he wondered how much to believe the lurid story attached to such a grey figure as I was. It occurred to me, then, that my retreat into laudanum might, at least, make the tale more credible.

'What do you think of Mr Fletcher?' I asked him. 'Do you think he is all he appears?'

Max snorted. 'He is *all* he appears. No gentleman. No *finesse*.'

'It does surprise me that his partners sent a man like him to England to represent them. But then, they are keen Wesleyans in Lancashire, and probably used to sanctimonious villains. His passion is for money, not God, that's all the difference.'

'Money, God and, worst of all, liberty.' He was gazing gloomily over the side down into the rippling water. 'Three deities that lead us to ruin.'

It seemed an opening to quiz him a little. 'And the rest of your family, *monsieur*? Where are they now? Are they still in France or do they also flee?'

He did not like that word, his mouth setting into a line. 'We are scattered, alive and dead, these many years.'

And his face blazed so hot, I found I was relieved when he said no more.

12

'Do I remember aright, Laurence?' Philpott had come upon me, bursting with a new idea. 'Did the comtesse mention such a thing as a *séance*, when we was in her cabin t'other day?'

I admitted guardedly that this might have been the case.

'Then let us put her on to it immediately!' He was pink and eager again. 'The captain's search ain't done no good, and no one wants to be kept aboard in Madeira.'

I was made slow by incredulity. 'You think a *séance* would help find the Treaty?'

'By all means! Recollect, now, the cards said I was the one to find it.' He was guileless and dreadfully reasonable. 'Who's to say the comtesse may not improve on her previous clair-voyance with a little other-worldly help?'

I couldn't tell whether he was serious. 'I thought you believed superstition all drivel. You scoff at the sailors' stories.'

'I do scoff, I confess. And yet – there is something to it, Laurence. Remember the cormorant – they said there'd be a death, and God damn me, there was one! Then, look at the way I whistled up that storm in the Channel! And now, with the cards pointing to me, the comtesse says I am a sensitive soul.'

I began to laugh, but then took pity on his innocence. 'Well, I wish you joy of your conversations beyond the veil. You must tell me all about it.'

His eyebrows shot up. 'Oh, but we must all be there. All the passengers.'

'All?' From what little I knew of *séances*, my mind baulked at the idea of Obadiah Fletcher's clammy hand in mine at the table. 'Well, I wish you luck with that. You'll never persuade Theodore to come. He'll think it ungodly.'

'Peter Williams is to come in his stead. As Theodore's possession, you know, it's all one.'

'Good God. You've asked him already?' I hadn't realised the thing had gone so far. 'You have all lost your minds. Can you not call me *your* possession, as I'm in your service, and leave me out of it?'

He frowned. 'You know very well that it is not the same thing at all.'

If we were to bring along all that belonged to us, I was even less eager. With old sins on my mind these past days, stirred by the presence of the French aristocrats, I shivered to think what souls might rise out of the shadows to condemn me. But, of course, it was all nonsense, Peter Williams and I agreed when we met in the mess that evening, before the others came in. 'You are no more one flesh with Theodore than I am,' I said. 'How can you let them talk such cant?'

'Well,' he prevaricated, 'do you really fancy Theodore there? Ten to one he'd have a vision, and there'd be another whole heap of foolery opened up for us to handle.'

I had to concede this might possibly be true.

'And I confess, I'm a mite curious,' he added. 'Only ever heard about such things in the papers.' He shook his head. 'Not to mention she's lighting a taper over a powder keg. That's another reason I'll be there.'

'What do you mean?'

But he only shook his head again, in his usual maddening way.

THE CANDLELIGHT FROM the table reflected off the small panes of the stern window and made the dark corners of the saloon glimmer, as we gathered in the comtesse's quarters after nightfall. The cabin had been rearranged, and, as I'd feared, we were to sit around the captain's table, hand in hand, in the middle of the room. The skull had been banished along with everything else, and frowned down at us from a high shelf, still wearing its wig, drawing my eye to the black rectangle of the skylight which, by day, introduced superfluous light from the deck into the already sunny cabin. There was a candle in the middle of the table, and behind it the comtesse was sitting, wearing an Indian shawl about her shoulders, her hair undone from its usual chignon and left to fall down her back in a girlish manner strangely at odds with her stern old face.

Even Obadiah Fletcher seemed momentarily silenced by this apparition and sat down opposite her with only a faint smile of derision. Peter Williams settled himself at the comtesse's left hand, Philpott was at her right, and, much to my relief, Max, looking all furious disapproval, plunked himself down between Fletcher and myself.

'Gentlemen – *madame* – we are gathered together tonight to ask the spirit world for guidance,' Philpott announced, looking terribly solemn. 'If Mr Jay's valuable papers are not found, we will be detained aboard ship in Madeira tomorrow, a circumstance unwelcome to us all, I imagine. And if they remain missing, 'twill be a nuisance from here to Barbados and beyond.'

I could see Fletcher's profile, still smiling and, remembering how he had sidled into his cabin before the captain searched it, I half-wondered if he had already found the Treaty and thought all this a most amusing joke at our expense.

'The comtesse has a rare gift for the occult, gentlemen, and has already intimated that the papers are willing to be found.' Philpott modestly forbore to mention that he imagined himself the one destined to find them. I still couldn't tell how much he believed any of this, a doubt bolstered when he added, 'I must confess myself hopeful of other visitors from beyond the grave. A word or two with the great men of the past, perhaps. Dr Johnson, now. I much regret I never met him. Oliver Cromwell would be an interesting fellow to quiz a little. Find out if heaven is the dull place he imagined it, with no singing or plays, or Christmas, God damn me. Or blind Milton …'

My copy of Milton had slipped my mind again. I still hadn't come across it in my searches. Perhaps someone had stolen that, too, though it was hardly a matter for the spirit world. Max was shifting irritably, and as usual he radiated heat, if little light. 'Believe me, Mr Philpott, we'll be lucky if my aunt raises the ship's cat.'

For once, the comtesse did not reprove him. She had been gazing into the candle flame all this time, and now closed her eyes. We fell silent, watching her. A breath of air found its way in through the skylight, and the flame flickered. I repressed an urge to laugh, out of apprehension as much as anything else. Peter Williams slid his eyes to me, and then the candle went out.

There was a little light remaining from the window, where the ship's wake gleamed, and from the skylight above us, where I thought I saw a movement – perhaps a passing crewman on his way to trim the sails.

The comtesse began the *séance* in her native tongue, which I dare say made it seem all the more mysterious to half of those about the table. 'Spirits, come if you are able,' she said in a dramatic whisper. 'If God permits you, come to give us counsel.'

On cue, there was a tremendous bang from above our heads that rattled the skylight. I leapt a yard in the air, my heart thrumming. Even Peter Williams stirred in his seat and frowned up at the darkness in the overhead window. But the comtesse was remarkably cool, and greeted this noisy visitor in English for our benefit and, it transpired, his own. '*Monsieur* Jenkinson, is that you?'

Of course, if any dead spirit knew where to find the hidden papers, it would be Jenkinson himself, but until now I hadn't imagined the disagreeable possibility of his appearing at this very table, and in the dark. The comtesse tried again.

'*Monsieur* Jenkinson. From the depths of the ocean, will you 'elp us?'

'*Notre père aux cieux*,' Max muttered irritably. He was right, it was all absurd, but the hairs on the back of my neck were already standing upright, and there was gooseflesh on my arms.

Another crash from above. Even Fletcher flinched this time. Looking up, I thought I saw faces at the skylight. Were they angels or demons? Or just some members of the crew she'd bribed to make the whole performance more imposing?

And then.

'*I am come.*'

For a moment I thought it another voice, coming out of the shadows to my right, but then I saw it was only the comtesse, husky, her voice an octave lower.

An impressive pause, then her voice changed. '*Enchantée, monsieur.*' I couldn't help smiling, despite everything, for all at once she sounded as if she were greeting our ghostly visitor at some spectral tea party. 'Now, *Monsieur* Philpott, will you be pleased to ask *Monsieur* Jenkinson your questions?'

'*Me?*' If the comtesse's voice had been an octave lower than normal, Philpott's had travelled in quite the opposite direction. He began to bluster. 'God bless me ... Well, I'll be ...' It was all more than he had bargained for, and his silhouette against the stern window flapped at me anxiously. 'Laurence – that is to say, Laurence – *you* will speak to him, my boy, I'm sure.'

Before I could formulate my thoughts, let alone a question, Mr Jenkinson's ghost interrupted us again in the comtesse's basso profundo.

'*I am come.*' Suddenly, his blood was up, talking rapidly, angrily. '*I will find the one that killed me. I will avenge.*'

'Good God,' Philpott said faintly. The comtesse seemingly hadn't warned him of what mischief she had planned. Peter Williams shifted impatiently in his chair, glancing up at the skylight again; then, suddenly, there was the sound of a tinder striking, and I blinked against the flame Max had produced and was setting to the candle wick.

Slowly, the room rematerialised. The candlelight gleamed off the medal at Max's breast. The skull, under its luxurious curls, looked fiercer than before.

'Enough, *Tante* Emilie.' Max stood up. 'It is a joke in exceeding bad taste. Forgive me, gentlemen, I had no notion she would say such dreadful things.'

For his part, Fletcher was quite unmoved. He stretched his arms and cracked his knuckles. 'Damn me, I thought we was just getting to the interesting part.' He stood up and slid out of the cabin without further leave-taking. Peter Williams muttered an excuse and followed him. Max shook his head at his aunt and went out in his turn.

The comtesse was unrepentant, taking the shawl from her shoulders and bundling up her hair into its usual low chignon with a hairpin. It was absolutely impossible to tell if she believed her own hocus-pocus. There were voices at the skylight. I heard Peter Williams's among them but couldn't catch anything of what was said. A patter of bare feet away across the boards, and we were left alone: Philpott, myself and the unfathomable comtesse, staring at each other over the candle flame.

From the captain's log

24 December 1794
Funchal, Madeira
In port

No trade to be done with the islanders, to my infinite regret, but the exigencies of the service trump all. Still, I had relied on good business to pay for Catherine's blue sprigged muslin and other things that grow more pressing to my mind by the day.

13

WE WOKE TO A celestial vision of green hills, climbing red-roofed houses, and the dark-paved streets of Funchal which we were forbidden to walk. The captain announced over breakfast that he alone would go ashore to see the shipping agent, to deliver the post and make his visits about the town as the King's unofficial ambassador. A trusted band of seamen – pockets emptied out beforehand – must also leave the ship, to organise the necessary replenishment of provisions, before a swift departure on the next tide to make up time lost in the westerlies of the Channel. But no passenger would be permitted to leave the ship. No bumboats would be suffered to come near, no visitors would be allowed. We were to be as effectively quarantined as if we had the plague. I felt sorry for Mr Gibbs, who must be pining for dry land under his paws, and I prevailed upon the landing party to take him with them. I watched him pull away from the ship's side in the small boat, his fur rippling in the breeze, with a little apprehension as to his safety and no small degree of envy. After depositing the seamen on shore, the boat turned back to the ship for the captain, who had now appeared at my shoulder, already sweating in full dress uniform.

'Fine morning, Mr Jago. Glorious prospect, ain't it?' He nodded to another ship presently docking – another packet, from the look of her trim. 'And there's the *Antelope*, on her way back to Falmouth, so I shall be able to send my report of all this business concerning Mr Jenkinson and the Treaty with her.' He shook his head. 'They won't be pleased.'

The small boat had returned for him and he touched his hat, before striding off towards the entry port, from where his privileged carcass was punctually rowed ashore.

The wind had turned around to the south, and the ship swung peacefully at anchor, bow turned to the open sea, stern to shore. I took up a position at the rail to watch the comings and goings of the town. After so many days of emptiness, the green hills seemed a miracle of colour, the waterfront an intoxicating bustle of life. A large merchant ship was taking on a prodigious number of casks from a convoy of small boats. I could make nothing of the calls and chatter of the boat-men, who were sun-beaten Portuguese with many an African among them, the legacy of the slaves and sugar that used to form the whole economy of the island before the West Indies stole their trade and they turned to wine. The docks were a muddle of ropes and broken crates, thronged with waiting harlots and rogues in expectation of new customers. They would be disappointed in us, I thought, as I peered among their ranks for any hint of a would-be passenger who might turn out to be the spy Your Lordship had anticipated.

Philpott appeared at my side, apparently irritated by the sight of so many pleasures debarred to him. 'Damned shame,' he said, leaning on the railing. 'I relied on a jaunt about the town, and an article out of it, to send back to England to keep Mrs Philpott and the children in funds another month or two. But the Treaty matters more, I quite see that, and we must resign ourselves to disappointment.'

'The *Antelope* returns to Falmouth, the captain told me.' I nodded to the other packet ship. 'Perhaps he'll let you send an article or two with his own papers.'

'Well, I shall ask him.'

But that would have to wait for the captain's return from his visits about the town. One by one every passenger appeared beside us as the morning wore on, to survey the forbidden delights of dry land. Only Max seemed uncharacteristically tranquil. The fires that raged inside him seemed momentarily quenched, and he was looking at the prospect measuringly, as a man might a gallows on which he was not obliged to swing. I realised then that he might not have felt safe from capture in Madeira, and in that case our enforced quarantine was a blessing, keeping the French along with the jostling bumboats away. But if an unusual inward peace had descended upon him, his body was still uneasy, and he turned away to exercise his restless legs up and down the length of the ship.

'A fine prospect,' Philpott said idly. 'Though I never reckoned to spend Christmas Day in my shirtsleeves. Ain't natural at all.'

The comtesse had just joined us from her own daily walk. 'At 'ome, the fields will be white,' she announced, her hands gripping the rail. 'The woods by the river a cathedral.' Her voice was melancholy. 'Quiet. Beautiful. And in the churchyard, the trees will be dark and green.'

'You leave loved ones there, I suppose?' Too late, I remembered her dead son, and as her eye filled with doleful feminine sorrow I saw I had distressed her. 'Did you spend much time there, or were you always at Versailles?'

'Versailles!' As ever, anger and sorrow jostled in her breast. The melancholy was abruptly gone, and she was scornful. 'I spent very little time in Versailles, *monsieur*, I assure you. Very few were welcome in Versailles, 'owever noble their birth.'

'You are an old family, then?'

'Tremendously old, *Monsieur* Jago. Older than most.'

But clearly not fashionable enough for Louis's court, and it rankled. I imagined some shabby old chateau with overgrown gardens and echoing stone-flagged floors.

The mighty Comtesse de Salles sniffed, and when we looked closer she was dashing a falling tear away with her sleeve.

'Why, *madame*, take heart, 'twill all be well, you know.' Philpott touched her gently on the elbow.

'I am not crying, *monsieur*.'

'Well, and why shouldn't 'ee? You'll miss your home, of course you will. But it's all in here, ma'am.' He tapped his own breast. 'All in here for ever, don't you fear, just as Nancy and my children are.' He laid a hand over hers on the rail, and she did not pull away. 'And tears are the shortest route to happy memories, oftentimes. No need to be ashamed.'

She was recovering herself, but it seemed her dignified carapace had yet to harden again, and she was unusually subdued. 'You spoke of your wife, before, I think. She is in London?'

'Aye, with William junior, and Margaret and the rest. They'll cross with Mr Jay in the spring, for Nancy does not like the storms in the Channel, and I do not like her to be unhappy, by God.'

'You miss her?' Her voice was still low.

'Of course.' Philpott hesitated. Cast me a sidelong look. 'Not to say that a little parting don't make reunion sweeter.' He looked out to the sea, somewhat sheepish. 'She is a woman very like yourself, *madame*, if you'll not take offence. Easy to aggravate quite without intending to. Yes, yes.' He was apparently lost in remembrance. 'A little parting now and then is—'

A good or a bad thing we would never know, for he was just then interrupted by a commotion at the entry port. The ship's tender had returned unseen amid the jostle of small boats which had swarmed about our sides all morning. A couple of the crew had been standing guard at the rail, in accordance with the captain's orders, to make sure nothing passed up or down. Mr Smith had been leaning on the side chewing tobacco and perhaps dreaming up more nonsense for Philpott, while the mousy Mr Spiers from Mousehole had been filling in his time by oiling the entry port's hinges. Now they both sprang to attention, the entry port was opened with some haste, and Spiers was climbing nimbly down into the boat. A moment later a recumbent form was manhandled up the side. More sailors hastened to help, and I caught sight of gold brocade. A bicorne hat. Captain Morris was being laid insensible on the deck, but though the crew were anxious and eager in their ministrations, they did not seem unduly surprised.

'What the devil is it?' Philpott asked Peters, the first mate, as he hurried past.

'Nothing to trouble about, sir. Captain's just had a bit too much brandy, seemingly. He's a hard-drinking man, that bloody shipping agent, and too free with his hospitality.'

I looked at the sun. It was not yet noon, and the captain had scarcely been gone ashore above two hours. If he had intoxicated himself to the point of unconsciousness in that short time, he had been quick about it. Peters directed the men to carry the captain below, while Smith and Spiers closed up the entry port again and advised the cluster of boats at our side to bugger off, for there would be no trade today. But the comings and goings were not finished, for over on the waterfront

I could see the landing party waiting with a procession of carts. Mr Gibbs was sitting at the bosun's heel, his nose raised to take in the multifarious scents that wafted down through the town. I was glad they hadn't lost him.

And there was even more excitement to come, for now Ben the cabin boy, who had been watching these affairs from atop a barrel, one bare big toe scratching the back of his other bare calf, raised an excited hand and called out. There was a new boat, arriving late to the party. It had no piled-up goods to offer, only two passengers: a slender brown-haired woman, wrapped in a sober shawl, and a small brown-haired bear cub sitting obediently beside her, paws folded in its lap.

The gunner and the carpenter brightened at this new development, and even more when the boatman pushed his vessel through the bumboats and announced his passengers intended to come aboard. During the ensuing lively dialogue, conducted in a mangled jumble of Portuguese and Cornish, the woman in the boat looked on, a pair of lively eyes under a rakish bonnet, while the bear cub nodded off, chin on chest, apparently well used to the excitement occasioned by its appearance. I glanced at the comtesse on my arm and saw her tears had dried, and there was even a gleam of amusement blossoming under her sorrow. For his part, Philpott was quite purple with excitement, and Max, coming up behind us, wore a look not of his customary bad humour, but of unaccountable alarm. 'What the devil?'

'The lady claims to have a berth booked,' I summarised. 'The sailors are astonished. The bear is unimpressed.'

'A berth! Nonsense! The captain said no one could come aboard.'

I was watching the careful, practical way the woman in the boat was gathering her skirts together, preparatory to climbing the side. She was younger than she'd seemed at first sight, and admirably agile. The comtesse was eyeing her nephew with surprise. 'If she does not mean to leave again, surely it is no matter?'

'No matter? With that – that *thing*?' Max was looking at the bear rather as he might regard a tarantula that proposed to join him in a confined space. The first mate had been called up from the captain's cabin, and seemed at first as little enamoured of the prospect as Max. But the woman was already climbing aboard, and a moment later she arrived on deck, removing her bonnet with a dazzling smile.

'Yer agent said t'would be all right,' she announced in a soft Irish brogue. 'Name's Lizzie McKendrick. I've an engagement in New York, and I'll pay handsome for a swift passage.'

'An engagement?' Peters was looking from her to the bear and back again.

'A performance at John Street Theatre.' She jerked a thumb cheerfully. 'Bruin does a fine routine. I'll give ye a free show while we're on board, if ye'll have us.'

After his momentary alarm, Max's face had now darkened to fury, and he hastened to the first mate's elbow to voice his objections. 'The *capitaine*, he said he'd take no one else aboard. That *créature* infallibly has lice, or the *rage*, or worse.' It seemed hardly credible, but the craggy soldier was apparently afraid of a tame bear cub, even after facing down the armies of the Revolution in the fields of Flanders.

'God bless me, it's manna from heaven,' Philpott was saying from the first mate's other elbow, rather like the bad angel to Max's good. 'What a story! "All at sea with Lizzie McKendrick and her bear". You must take them aboard, Mr Peters; by God, you must.'

'Where do you propose it sleeps?' asked the first mate, ignoring both his counsellors, and looking at Bruin, who was yawning in the boat. Unimaginatively named. Patently not rabid. And as to the lice, that would only be proved by experience.

'Oh, he's admirable housetrained, sir,' the woman Lizzie said, with another smile that lit up her brown eyes. 'A passenger cabin would do fine.'

'Good God,' Max said, and flung away. His aunt glanced at him a moment but couldn't keep her eyes from the enthralling entertainment.

Peters was also brightening. 'You propose to take two cabins? Do you have the wherewithal for it?'

'I do, though I'm afeared to open my purse here among strangers.'

Peters led her below, to see the captain, he said, though I could hardly imagine he would be in a fit state to decide the matter. The crew joked among themselves almost as cheerfully as they had at Mr Jenkinson's extinction by the falling spar; and the cabin boy jumped up and down on his barrel. The look of interest had softened the harsh lines around the comtesse's mouth as she peered down at the boat where the bear was now peacefully slumbering.

'And the creature won't bite?' Peters was asking as he returned on deck with the girl in due course.

'He will not, sir, never in life. Not unless he's provoked.'

The first mate was apparently content with this rather unsatisfactory pledge, and the bear was suffered to scramble up the side, their luggage thrown up after him. At close quarters Bruin was small, but his experiences seemed to have left him serious-minded. He snubbed the cabin boy's eager advances and allowed himself to be led to his cabin, perking up only at the novelty of the ladder down into the mess, a thing he apparently had not encountered before. I watched the woman follow him. A glimpse of laced boots, a knitted stocking and a grimy petticoat.

T HE SHIP SLIPPED anchor at dusk. I stood at the rail alone as the crew put out the sails to catch the light breeze, and we crept after the pilot boat out to sea. Behind us, the lights were coming on in the town. The festival lights for Christ's nativity were also blinking into life: myriad candles in small earthenware pots, illuminating the whole hillside in a wide arc like tiny beacons, winking one to another and reflecting off the still water of the harbour.

14

THOUGH IT WAS Christmas morning, there was much activity on deck before breakfast, with the stowing of the casks brought aboard in Funchal. Miss McKendrick's bear cheerfully dived into the hold headfirst to assist in this deep realm hitherto unknown to him. As I came up the ladder from the mess, he was clambering back up, tugging something behind him, in a way that rather reminded me of Mr Gibbs, when his enthusiasm to carry home a dead tree trunk overcame his common sense. The bear had already obligingly produced the comtesse's coffee, Philpott told me with some amusement from where he was watching by the rail, unearthed from a spot in the hold the cook swore he had searched a dozen times before.

Now Bruin was using his mouth and paws to manhandle the new, much larger, object out of the hatch, while the sailors below shouted reproaches and bade him desist, probably fearing he'd drop it on their unprotected heads. Philpott wandered over and I followed. Mr Gibbs was already there, hunkered down, his paws over the edge for a better look, and as I joined them Philpott called down into the dark hold, 'What the devil has the creature found?'

'Just an old spar, sir,' one of the men answered. 'But it's heavy. He'll do us an injury if he don't leave off.'

'An old spar?' The captain had joined us, too. 'I thought we cleared the hold in Falmouth.'

Philpott had been squatting, peering down into the dark, but now straightened. 'I'd get that thing out for a closer look, Captain, if you'll take my advice.' There was something new in his tone. The captain looked at his uncharacteristically serious face and nodded. After another moment's hesitation, a couple of the crew jumped down into the blackness of the hold and began to heave the heavy timber skywards. The end nearest to us had a short length of frayed rope attached to it. It took a good deal of panting and shouting, but eventually the thing was pushed up out of the hatch and rolled across the deck in a way calculated to knock the dog off his feet if he hadn't had the presence of mind to scamper back.

'What is it?' I asked.

'A piece of the rigging, I believe,' Philpott answered, sounding grim. 'With a good deal of gore attached.'

Down in the cool, dank hold, Mr Jenkinson's blood, hair and brains had not yet dried beyond all recognition. The captain frowned, looking alternately from where we stood in the waist of the ship to the forepeak thirty feet forward, on the far side of the ship's boat in its cradle, the foremast, and innumerable other obstacles, and then back to the spar at his feet. 'How in God's name did it get all this way from the heads into the hold?'

'It has obviously been carried there,' I said.

There was a moment's silence, as we all contemplated the import of this discovery.

'Carried there! But who by?'

'By the murderer, of course,' Philpott answered, 'and God damn me, did not the comtesse say so, after all? This blessed spar did not fall from the rigging at all, or it would have lain where it fell, or tumbled into the sea. Someone wished to hide it, after they bashed Jenkinson's brains out with it, and they threw it in the hold out of sight.'

'Impossible,' I said. 'It took three men to lift it out of the hatch. We have just seen it.'

'There's no limit to the strength of a madman,' Philpott answered darkly. Lizzie McKendrick came up behind him in time to hear this pronouncement, and looked rather alarmed.

It was perplexing. Even if Jenkinson had indeed been killed by this spar, at the hands of a supremely strong man, why hadn't the culprit left it lying beside the body? No one would then have suspected it anything more than an accident. And yet, it had fetched up in the hold, and there was no other possible explanation except that someone had dragged it there, and tipped it in.

The captain was fingering the frayed ropes. 'A trace of powder on this one,' he said, holding up one blackened end to our examination. 'But not on the other.'

'Powder?'

'The rope took the force of a shot, but there's been no firing this voyage, except for the *Brunswick*'s warning cannon, and the poor gentleman was already dying by then.'

I looked around at the curious faces. Whatever the cause, someone had been eager to hide the evidence. But then why not throw it overboard? I looked around again. The sides were high; the only easy access to the sea was by the entry port, but that would need opening, and would be sure to be noticed even in the dusk of that early-morning watch when Jenkinson was killed. Perhaps the villain involved had reckoned carrying the weighty spar to the hold an exercise marginally more secret.

It was all a puzzle, but one thing was clear: if our discovery in the hold meant Jenkinson's death was not natural, then it struck me that nothing other than the pursuit of the Treaty could possibly have motivated a man to murder the inoffensive old official. Jenkinson's instructions rose before my inward eye. *We know the agent is to come aboard the* Tankerville, *and we are certain of their intent.* With a shock, I now saw that Jenkinson's *agent*, a strong man, with an overpowering desire to get hold of the papers the official carried, had not planned to come aboard in Madeira: he had been among us all the time.

'WELL THEN!' PHILPOTT rubbed his hands, his eye hectic, and I was glad to be spared the full force of his enthusiasm, which was now turned on the comtesse. We had clattered down to her cabin to convey the astonishing news. 'You perceive the ghost was quite right? You do see it, do you not? There *was* a God-damned murder, just as Jenkinson's poor old spirit said there was.'

I perched on the table and examined the comtesse's tarot pack, turning the cards over, one by one. The Devil. The Fool. The two of cups. The latter was a love card, I remembered the comtesse had told us. I looked up. 'But I don't see how it can be murder, sir. That spar was too heavy to wield, unless the man was a colossus, and there's no colossus aboard. Except you.'

Philpott smiled sunnily at this compliment. 'And some of the crew are hulking men. Well, well, I dare say it will all come out in the end.'

For my own part, I thought it safer to discover the murderer as soon as possible, and the comtesse seemed of the same mind. 'Let us consider the circumstances, dear *monsieur.*

Jenkinson was murdered on the day we met the British war-ship, *non*? Mr Theodore Jay, Mr Peter Williams and Mr Jago. You and I. Max. And Fletcher, just come aboard. These were the only passengers beside Jenkinson.'

'Well, it can't be Theodore, o'course,' Philpott said, looking out at the morning sun on the water, 'since he had the Treaty already in his possession. Peter Williams is tall and vigorous and might fetch a fellow a stinging blow if he had a mind to do so, but he has no more reason than Theodore to steal something he's already got. I can't suspect myself or Laurence. And your nephew has no reason to help the Jacobins. Which only leaves Fletcher, but he is quite feeble. He could not pick up that spar, let alone use it as a weapon.'

'Unless he 'ad someone do it for 'im. Some member of the ship's crew, per'aps, in return for this imaginary gold they speak of. It is a certainty that *Monsieur* Fletcher is also in pursuit of the Treaty.'

I looked up, surprised to find her so well informed. 'What makes you think that?'

''E came to quiz me about it, and I 'ave seen 'im whispering about it to the slave.'

Though we were so confined aboard ship, I had known nothing of this. It was therefore quite possible that Fletcher had been bribing members of the crew, equally unseen. I remembered his excitement on finding that Theodore Jay was a fellow passenger. It had seemed genuine enough, but per-haps he'd only gulled me with this pretended ignorance, and had in fact come aboard already quite well aware the Treaty was here. Was it possible that, while we were busy escaping the French frigate, he was already persuading the crew to make the attempt on Jenkinson? It seemed the comtesse had come to the same conclusion.

'*Monsieur* Fletcher paid someone to find it, mark my words. They killed Jenkinson, and yet still Fletcher searches. Therefore, Jenkinson did not 'ave it. When Fletcher stops searching, we shall know he 'as found it.'

Philpott was all admiration at this incisive reasoning but, after all, she had likely been judge and jury on her own estate and heard many a petty case of thieving or poaching. Of any of us, she was the most likely to be familiar with the shifts and equivocations of the guilty.

'Well,' he said, 'I suppose we shall. And then?'

'Then we will take *Monsieur* Fletcher to Captain Morris. We shall demand of 'im which man among the crew found 'im the paper. For whoever did so is infallibly also the murderer who wielded that 'eavy spar.'

From the captain's log

25 December 1794
Latitude 31° 49' N and 18° 19' W
Fair winds: made 30 leagues from Madeira by the noon
observation

All Christmas rites observed. Mr Theodore Jay preached a sermon at the noon muster. New passengers came aboard in Madeira, to wit: an Irish actress and her performing bear which, God willing, will not destroy my ship. Wrote a dispatch home regarding this troublesome development with Jenkinson.

15

OUR CHRISTMAS BREAKFAST was very little improvement on Mr Hind's usual efforts. What the sailors ate beyond the bulkhead I don't know, but their riotous cheerfulness at the prospect of extra rations, and a tot of rum on top of their daily gallon of beer, had a hectic edge to it. Coming after the discovery of Jenkinson's murder, it made me look at them afresh, thinking again, and anxiously, of pirates.

Things were quieter in the passengers' mess. The bear cub had tolerable table manners, sitting meekly between Lizzie and Philpott, quite taken up by the porridge that the cook had ladled out for him. Bruin used a surprisingly long tongue rather than a spoon to clean out the bowl and Philpott watched admiringly.

'What a creature! Where did you discover him, Miss McKendrick? Was it you that taught him his manners?'

She had been dipping her spoon, somewhat disconsolately, into her own bowl of congealed oatmeal, and seemed not at all displeased to be distracted. 'Me? Oh, I did not, sir. I had him from a fellow in Kildare. Sure, he's only a cub, but he can already dance, and has learned a whole piece, called "A Bear's Tea Party" where he comes by his marvellous table manners.

There's nothin' an audience likes so well, ye know, sir, as a bear that can behave like a man.'

'And what possessed you to buy him?'

'Oh …' She paused, her spoon at her mouth. Her teeth were good, only a little stained with tobacco, and her parted lips were soft. She saw me watching, and I dropped my eyes. 'Times are dreadful hard in Ireland, Mr Philpott, as I dare say ye know, being a political gentleman.'

'I know there's agitation for reform, just as in England. And a wish for independence like the damned Americans.'

She looked at him, apparently surprised, while I quietly admired the scatter of freckles across her nose. She was as much of a contrast to Anne Bellingham, the under-secretary's cool and elegant stepdaughter in London, as could be conceived. She was much more like my sister, and the other country girls of my childhood.

'I thought ye supported the reform, Mr Philpott?' she said, softly but reproachfully, and opening her eyes very wide. 'Did ye not assist that Thomas Hardy, the shoemaker, just now, in his trial for treason?'

'I did, ma'am. But his demands were reasonable. I'm afraid your own radicals are turning a deal more fanatic.'

'Well.' She cautiously licked the porridge off her spoon with a pink tongue. 'At all events, sir, the theatre trade is shocking bad at home.' She slid me a lively look. 'And I did fancy an adventure, I confess.'

She pushed the bowl away from her and wiped her hands on her gown. 'Will ye watch me put him through his paces, before the Christmas service? 'Tis a marvellous amusement.'

As Philpott followed Lizzie and Bruin up on deck, Max emerged from his cabin and began to pick at the remains of the food at the table, with a look of extreme bad temper.

On deck, Bruin was already dancing to a tambourine with some nervous energy, while Mr Gibbs barked at this astonishing occurrence even more persistently than he had done at the turkeys. Lizzie was dancing, too. Though she held the tambourine above her head rather awkwardly, she looked extremely pretty, her hair flying, and her slim figure swaying. The crew, at Christmas leisure, perched in the rigging, clapping along as the pair below them twirled and stamped. What lascivious thoughts possessed their minds, as her skirts flew and showed her comely calves and ankles, I could well imagine.

Bruin was certainly a first-rate clown, though whether he was meant to be one was another matter. 'Up!' Lizzie shouted, whereupon he collapsed on his back and studied his toes. 'Down!' she commanded, whereupon he swung himself into the rigging beside the gunner, who looked as astonished as if one of his own stories had turned out to be true after all. Mr Gibbs leapt at the mainmast, looking up at the bear as he might at a squirrel up a beech tree, gazing longingly into the forest of ropes above his head.

'I hope it stays up there all day,' Max said behind me, having emerged from the hatchway to the mess with a look of caution.

''Ow 'igh it climbs,' the comtesse marvelled, as Bruin hopped up from the main shroud to the topgallant, apparently for a better look at us all.

Captain Morris was at the wheel, seemingly recovered from his intoxication of the day before, and now rather apprehensive for his rigging. Meanwhile, Lizzie was laughing immoderately, and demanding Bruin descend at once, and do as he was told. He turned upside down and hung from the ropes by his hind toes, fifty feet above our heads.

'Good God!' Philpott said cheerfully. 'If he falls, we'll be as flat as poor Jenkinson.'

''E will not fall,' the comtesse replied. 'See 'ow content 'e is! If I was 'im, I would stay there all day and never come down at all to that cruel woman.'

'Cruel!' I said. 'She seems quite an amiable person to me.'

'Amiable! Ah, yes, because the poor thing will make 'er money. Do you not know 'ow they teach the bears to dance, *Monsieur* Jago? It is 'ot coals they use; that is why 'e lifts 'is feet so 'igh. The little drum with bells reminds 'im.'

I had heard some such story before, but the bear, like its mistress, seemed cheerful enough. Now it craned its neck, peering at the comtesse as if it had heard her, and then tumbled down the rigging so fast the crew whooped and Mr Gibbs fell into a yapping frenzy. Once on deck, Bruin scampered directly towards us, fur bouncing, and sniffed the hand the comtesse reached out to him with all the gravity of a small and rotund suitor.

'Well, this will cheer us up,' Philpott said, his eyes also fixed on the bear cub. 'We was all a bit glum, what with the Treaty missing, and being stuck aboard ship.'

'And Mr Jenkinson's death.' I couldn't believe the grim discovery of the morning had already slipped Philpott's mind.

'Mr Jenkinson? Nonsense. My dear boy, it will be a positive delight to investigate the matter, now we know it was murder.'

WE MUSTERED ON the quarterdeck at noon for Christmas prayers and another reading of the captain's instructions, which seemed to be a kind of naval creed. After that, Theodore presented himself at the captain's shoulder, and the dismal news soon percolated through the assembly that he was to give us a sermon of his own devising. We had been at sea too long, without diversion, and it seemed the vice of idleness took men in different ways. Fortunately, we were in fact spared any notion of Theodore's religious views, for he commenced his sermon in such a breathless undertone that his remarks were entirely inaudible to anyone. Only Lizzie seemed inclined to listen and crept a little closer to hear.

My mind wandered away from Theodore's monotone almost at once and, with the discovery of the spar in the hold and all it signified, I found myself looking at the crew afresh. How small the ship was, like a planet in the vast universe of the ocean, and how was I to know what – or who – was true or false? The cause for the murder had surely been the Treaty, but the ship had been searched and nothing found. Nothing *to my knowledge* found. I had discounted the Cornish crew as possible agents, but if someone had acted for Fletcher, as the comtesse guessed, then among them was Jenkinson's killer.

I furtively examined the captain's men, one by one. Mr Smith, the gunner, was singing what seemed a mournful song quietly through his beard. The carpenter, Spiers, had wedged himself into a shadow and was apparently asleep on his feet. He resembled every joiner I had ever known – nimble, quick-witted and prone to complaint. The first mate was supervising an urgent change to the rigging, which could not wait for the end of Theodore's remarks, urging on his men in a polite undertone. The ship heeled as she came closer to the wind and surged on a shade more briskly. Trevenen, the young second mate, seemed to be in mourning for his hammock, where he should be catching some sleep before his next watch. The surgeon, Kidd, was absent, probably slugging brandy in his cabin with Fletcher, who was also missing. Rogers, the scowling third mate, was at Peter Williams's elbow again and, though I wasn't sure, I thought I saw his lips moving, and Peter Williams's head imperceptibly bent to listen.

Of the twenty or so other crewmen, three had begun surreptitiously playing cards, out of the captain's sight. Ben had tired of Theodore's drone and was peering in at his turkeys, his hand on Mr Gibbs's fur. Beside him was the sailmaker, and with a shock I saw he was glaring at me with a look of utter loathing. Surely to God he wasn't still angry that I'd taken old Jenkinson's topaz cross? As our eyes met, he dropped his gaze and fumbled in his pocket for his pipe, which he clenched in his teeth unlit, and commenced to chew vigorously.

But there were other, pleasanter distractions to console me. My laudanum, waiting for me at bedtime, and now Lizzie McKendrick, who was still listening dutifully to Theodore's wisdom. Philpott saw me watching her and smiled significantly. I frowned.

Theodore came finally to the end of his homily. He was blushing, folding the sheet of paper into his pocket with a misplaced self-congratulation. The meeting scattered with relief, and the crew took to their recreations more openly. On the surface, at least, it was a peaceful picture, the smell of roast turkey already wafting from the direction of the galley, while Peter Williams had hastened below and re-emerged with a basket of Theodore's shirts, which he was about to lay out to dry in the sunshine.

'Laurence?' Theodore had appeared at my elbow. 'Would you call that woman an actress?' He was looking at Lizzie, who was alone by the rail, her hair lifted by the breeze, and her expression thoughtful.

'I hardly know. She's on the stage with the bear, at least.'

'It's a terribly corrupting profession, I gather.' He looked more anxious for her soul than seemed entirely necessary, but this was nothing new. I could see the familiar wheels turning in his brain, wondering if Lizzie needed his ministrations.

'I dare say it's not a regular life,' I answered. 'But she herself may be a paragon of virtue.'

'It would make an interesting sermon. "The Temptations of the Stage", you know. Perhaps I shall consult her. She asked me about my work this morning. Said she'd like to hear more sermons if I'd spare the time. Says she goes to Church every Sunday, ashore, and misses God's word.'

'Then she's clearly no need of your attention.'

'On the contrary. I fear from what she said that she's a papist.' There was no arguing with him, and either he'd not yet heard of the gruesome discovery in the hold that morning or he was remarkably callous.

As the sailors improvised a hammock for the bear in the rigging, and Bruin described slow circles as he failed to climb in, Theodore was hastening over to Lizzie's side. I watched as she turned, her lips parting into a smile, and then compressing again to sober humility, as Theodore no doubt began his enquiries. She was amenable enough, and allowed herself to be steered along the quarterdeck towards the ship's boat. Another moment, and I saw them sitting in the boat, heads bent close together over a Bible. I caught her eye as she shifted uncomfortably on the wooden bench seat, and I almost thought she winked at me before she turned back obediently to listen.

The winds were growing warmer by the hour as we slipped down the coast of Africa, looming somewhere out of sight over the larboard horizon. I took off my coat and for a moment contemplated removing my shoes and stockings and going barefoot like the crew, but the comtesse was strolling towards me across the quarterdeck on Philpott's arm, and she would think it a shocking breach of decorum. Philpott's large broad-brimmed hat shaded his face and offered some protection to her own, as he walked between her and the sun. Above us, Ben and Bruin were skylarking through the rigging, the boy apparently determined not to be outdone by the bear's gymnastics, and Mr Gibbs was barking with increasingly hoarse excitement as they climbed ever higher.

'Yes, I fear it's a cruel profession,' Philpott said regretfully, as they paused at my shoulder. 'I confess I've never heard a good word about these bear-keepers.'

'But Miss McKendrick is extremely agreeable,' I objected. 'Perhaps she meant to rescue the poor creature and give it a better life.'

'Do you think so?' Philpott brightened. 'I shall quiz her directly, the moment she escapes Theodore's clutches.'

'Poor woman,' I said. 'Between the two of you, she'll find herself quite persecuted.'

'Aye, aye.' Philpott leered at me somewhat horribly. 'I saw your face, just now, when you looked at her, my lad. I dare say you'll be doing a little *persecution* of your own.'

'Nonsense. But I still say she seems kind enough to the bear.'

The comtesse sniffed. 'Me, I would not trust such a one. The man or woman who cares not for animals cares not for anything. The stables at the chateau were finer than the tenants' cottages, I assure you.'

I forbore to observe that this misplaced bounty was exactly why the French had overthrown their aristocracy, the comtesse among them. Philpott had no such scruples.

'And a shocking disgrace it is to you, ma'am, I cannot pretend otherwise. Am I the only man aboard to have noticed that the bear, however agreeable, has a cabin to himself, while

Peter Williams slings a hammock among the crew? Not that it won't make it a better piece for the *Cannon* when I write it up. Being a political paper, 'twould be whimsical to write a story about Miss McKendrick and her bear entirely devoid of a moral. As it is, I shall have the full decay of nations and the inhumanity of man to conjure with.'

The comtesse chose to ignore his reproaches, only putting out a hand to Bruin, who had descended from the rigging again, and come up as if eager to contribute to the conversation. He evinced much delight as she stroked his muzzle and attempted to embrace her. She put him off with a gentle hand and he contented himself with rolling on his back and chewing at the beading on the hem of her heavy skirts.

16

LIZZIE FOUND ME by the rail at sunset and leaned beside me quite companionably, though we had as yet hardly spoken, only exchanged glances. 'Well, I'm fair jaded,' she said, twisting her hair into a pigtail and pulling it over her breast against the stiff breeze. 'My soul has been saved entirely, and I find it's a taxing business. Has Mr Theodore Jay ever preached ye a sermon, Mr Jago?'

'I'm afraid not.'

'Sure, I'm surprised, for I hear from all quarters that ye are quite the sinner, too.'

'I wouldn't place too much reliance on ship's gossip.'

I wondered exactly which part of my reputation she had heard, but the question was soon answered for her smile broadened. 'Would ye not? Then I'm rare disappointed. But perhaps Theodore Jay accounts ye quite beyond redemption.'

'I am,' I said. 'But, in any case, Theodore chooses more beautiful creatures for his ministry. He doesn't mean to, but it's a sad fact.'

'Oh, I think ye're handsome enough,' she answered lightly. 'And will take the compliment, myself, if that's what ye intend.' She turned, leaning her elbows behind her on the rail, the setting sun full in her face. The rosy light gave colour to her milky skin and illuminated faint lines coming at the corners of her eyes and either side of her nose. I reckoned her only two or three years younger than I was. Unmarried, for so she must be in the life she led, and apparently alone at large in the world, without the protection of father or brother or any other man.

She seemed unperturbed by the macabre discovery of the morning, but in truth there was little reason she should care. She had never met Jenkinson and could hardly grieve for him. In fact, it was a relief to speak to someone detached from the business, I told myself, though in this, I confess, I was probably quite as self-deluded as Theodore. 'You certainly don't seem much in need of rescue to me.'

'As I tried to tell Mr Jay, but he seems dreadful certain that females are full of sin.'

'The old Eve,' I suggested.

'Just so. But there are God's laws and man's laws, Mr Jago.' She looked at me coyly. 'And I don't even like apples.'

I said nothing, only turned my head to watch the comtesse and Philpott taking their evening turn together on the quarterdeck. They were becoming inseparable, no doubt still earnestly discussing the ship's manifold mysteries. Now a third figure joined them at a scamper, fur catching the dying sun like a halo.

'I reckon Bruin thinks that woman's his mother.' Lizzie had followed my gaze with a mischievous smile. 'She's as wide in them hoops as a she-bear and looks just as fierce.'

'Perhaps he does. Should you mind it?'

'Me? Mind it?' She looked a little puzzled. 'Bruin can do whatever he pleases, Mr Jago.'

'You don't fear for his safety?'

'He's scarce tall enough to fall overboard, and he can climb like a cat. A bloody duchess will do him no harm, I assure ye. Perhaps she'll improve his manners.' She smiled at the idea. 'But I declare I was surprised to see yer Mr Philpott so snug with her. He seems muddled in his loyalties, so.'

'Muddled?' I answered, perhaps more seriously than she expected. 'I don't think so. He's a traditionalist at bottom, but wants the best for all men, which is why he supports reform. And takes people as he finds them. We are all mere sinners after all, as Theodore has been telling you.'

'You're fond o' the man.' It was an observation, not a question.

'He's the North Star in a shifting world, even if his own compass spins a little.' I looked at her sidelong. 'He wants to ask you about it all. The life of the bear-keeper, you know. For his newspaper.'

'Does he?' She turned her head towards me. 'Sure, there's not so very much to tell.'

'It might give you some welcome publicity in New York. For your performance, you know.'

'So it might.' She tilted her head thoughtfully. 'I shall think over what to say, then. Thank ye for the hint, Mr Jago.'

When I had anticipated the likely passengers to come aboard in Madeira, I had hardly imagined this. I had spent too long among spies, murderers and the grey men of Whitehall, but even in Cornwall she would have been a rarity, an emissary from another more captivating world. Did you ever meet a woman, My Lord, whose smile shattered your heart with its sudden radiance? The wind was in her hair again, the setting sun turning the loose tendrils ruby red. Her eyes were dark pools, lit with an inward gleam. Her soft Irish voice was like a spell. She had been aboard scarce four and twenty hours, but I was already fascinated, and though I had thought myself as angry and cynical as Max de Salles, already halfway to being in love.

I HAD PRIDE ENOUGH not to dog her footsteps about the ship too closely the next morning, though I felt a twinge of jealousy when I saw her smile into Fletcher's oily face, or converse with the handsome second mate, who was probably boasting of his ambitions for a ship of his own. At six bells in the morning watch I followed Philpott down to the comtesse's saloon, to take a cup of her new-found coffee and seek respite from these new and surprising sensations.

Bruin was already there when we entered, sitting on the faded velvet of the window seat, eating a crust, and watching the porpoises gambol in the ship's wake. Philpott settled himself beside the bear while, as usual, I perched on the corner of the table. I took one mouthful of the syrupy black brew the comtesse poured for me, and almost spat it out again. Burnt and bitter. If I'd remembered the fact it was Mr Hind the cook who'd made it, I should have taken a more cautious sip.

'Aye, aye.' Philpott sighed noisily and put down his own cup untouched beside the grinning skull, which had now been restored to its proper place. He was eyeing the bear with speculation. 'As a newspaper article it will do. But though I kept her in the mess a half-hour after breakfast, Miss McKendrick is mighty unforthcoming. She would not explain her method of instruction, which I dare say *is* a secret of her trade, but she would not even tell me the creature's favourite pastimes neither, though I quizzed her as close as a God-damned lawyer.'

I had seen Max come through during this interrogation as

full of unreasoning hostility as ever. 'I wonder why Max is so afraid of the creature,' I said. 'It's only a cub. Full of mischief. Not fierce at all.'

'A quite inoffensive beast, bless its whiskers,' Philpott agreed, and on a whim plucked Jenkinson's wig from its place on the skull and settled it suddenly on the bear's head with a chuckle.

Philpott's whim had consequences that came one upon the other as swiftly and destructively as toppling dominos. Bruin, taken unawares and temporarily blinded by this new append-age, bounded down from the window seat with sudden alarm, and scampered for the door. The comtesse raised her voice in remonstrance. 'Come back, *Monsieur* Bruin. You are mon-strous naughty!' But the creature was already scurrying along the corridor into the mess, whence we heard a stifled yell of alarm from whoever was then occupying it.

Philpott and I chased after, but by the time we'd climbed the ladder to deck, Bruin was cavorting through the rigging with the cabin boy, snorting, swinging from one sheet to the next, a laughing Ben on his heels. As I put one calming hand on Mr Gibbs's hackles and shaded my eyes against the blinding sun with the other, the bear presented a small, round, bewigged silhouette to the company fifty feet below him.

'Jesus Christ,' Mr Spiers the carpenter said with some wonder. 'Smithy's right. It's the man himself.'

Max was standing at the forepeak in conversation with Lizzie and turned to look. Another unreasonable stab of jealousy shot through me, but Max was already leaving her, striding towards us across the sloping deck. He was just pass-ing the ship's boat, when there was a scream from above us. The bear had turned on Ben, perhaps meaning to reverse the chase, and in his surprise the boy had lost his grip. Now the child was sliding down the sail, frantic for a handhold, but the canvas was too smooth and taut under the pressure of the spanking breeze, and he only tumbled faster and faster towards the deck.

I found myself hurtling towards Max and the point where the boy was falling. We crashed together, all three of us, in a tangle of limbs, among a nest of coiled ropes which thanks to providence broke our mutual fall, and saved Ben from smashing his head open on the unforgiving planks.

PHILPOTT'S NAVAL SUPERSTITIONS

C

The Ship's Cat is a venerated Personage, and never to be harassed by Dog, Man or Bear. Not only can she keep the Ship's population of Mice and Rats to acceptable Numbers, she can also predict the Weather, tell when Land is near or raise a Storm if she is displeased.

F

It is absolutely necessary to defer Departure, if the Day of sailing happens to fall on a Friday. Whether they imagine Judas Iscariot to be lurking in the Rigging on such a Day, or merely fear the touch of Death's brief Ascendancy on that long-ago Hill in Golgotha, I know not.

J

A Jonah is never to be tolerated aboard Ship. They will not absolutely confess to tossing unlucky Passengers overboard, but by the d—l, I'd not put it past them.

17

I GATHERED LATER THAT, while I carried the boy to the surgeon, Peter Williams apprehended the ursine culprit and divested him of his wig, returning it to the skull in the comtesse's cabin. Meanwhile, Ben perched on the surgeon's bunk, looking pale, his sleeve stained dark red with blood. Kidd commenced cutting off the boy's shirt to reveal a jagged wound down his skinny forearm. The comtesse, who had followed the procession to the surgeon's cabin, clapped her hand to her mouth, while Lizzie, who came in a moment later, looked pale and vexed.

'A very pleasant Christmas gift, confound it,' the surgeon murmured, though it wasn't clear if he was addressing us or himself. 'Clean it out. Sew it up. Infection from the air.' He was searching for his instruments. 'If one of you will hold him, I'd be obliged. Painful process ...'

We all hesitated, and in the end it was the comtesse who came forward, sitting down gingerly beside the boy and encircling his thin shoulders with her arm. His dirty hair brushed her cheek, and as the surgeon came back with his needle, the boy flinched away. '*Non, non.*' The comtesse tightened her hold. 'Now, attend. It must that you begin to count, as soon as ever the surgeon comes near.'

'Count?' Ben's voice was only a hoarse whisper.

'Start at one, and never stop. It is a certain cure for 'urts, I assure you. Come now. One, two, three …'

For once her imperiousness was a virtue for, over-awed, the boy counted along obediently, tears running down his hot face on to her neckerchief as the surgeon wielded his needle deftly.

'A drop of laudanum for the pain,' the surgeon went on, 'and a cupful of blood to prevent a fever.'

Kidd opened his locker and poured out the tincture of opium into a small glass for the boy as Captain Morris came in, looking rather ill himself. 'Now, Ben, for God's sake be more careful next time. I'll not be the one to tell your mother you've broke your neck.'

''Twas all the bear's fault.' The child was offended as he took the laudanum from Kidd's hand and swallowed obediently. 'I never fell before.'

'Well, then, don't go chasing with the bear in the rigging again. You're no match for him.'

'Gunner says that un's the ghost of that dead feller.' The boy's lip had begun to tremble again.

'Stuff and nonsense,' Kidd said, even as Philpott's eye brightened with its usual curiosity. 'That man talks ballocks from dawn till dusk. Don't mind him, Ben.'

'He was only playing, you know,' I added, glancing at Lizzie's face to distract myself from the warm suffusing glow of well-being contained in Ben's now empty glass. 'The bear, I mean. There's no malice in him at all.'

'Malice!' The comtesse drew herself up, quite ready to expound for the dozenth time on his afflictions. '*Au contraire*, 'e is the one who suffers, 'im, I assure you.' She curled her lip.

'Forced to dance by a *monstre*. It boils my blood.'

Lizzie was no longer pale, but had flushed a deep red, and was looking at the comtesse with an expression somewhere between offence and dislike. I couldn't blame her, but if she could only overcome the noblewoman's prejudices, she and the comtesse would learn to like each other eventually. Kidd fussed about with his lancet and brass bowl. 'A white lead plaster, and a bandage. Yes, yes, you will do, young man, I dare say.' The boy winced again, but more feebly under the effect of the laudanum, as the small blade cut into his forearm and blood dripped into the bowl, bright red in the sun coming through the surgeon's skylight.

MAX CAME UP quietly to where the dog and I were dozing in the shadow of the ship's side, sheltered from a noonday sun suddenly and preposterously hot. I had, by now, defied the comtesse's disapproval and removed my stockings. The sun was directly behind the Frenchman's bent head, shading his face as though he were an angel of unbearable brightness. I squinted up at him, until he sat down beside me and resolved himself into a human being once more. 'How fares the child?'

There was a change in Max's manner that I couldn't quite make out, as I sat up. 'Tolerably well, though he won't be climbing the rigging or fulfilling his usual little duties for a while.'

'We did well, between us, *n'est ce pas*? Any bruises of your own?'

'My neck aches. I think it was my damned head that broke his fall.'

I also had a graze across my cheek from Max's infernal medal, but I forbore to reproach him as he nodded and grinned. He was suddenly cheerful, that was the difference, and I wasn't sure that his dazzling smile was less alarming than his usual scowl. 'And I, too. I shall be blue and black, as you English say, by morning. But honourable wounds in a dishonourable flight, *hein?*'

If I was ever going to satisfy my curiosity, it was now, while he was so strangely sunny. 'But if you are to leave France, why go so far? Why America, and not London?'

'My aunt asked me the same question.' Max absently ran a finger down the scorch on his cheek as though it still smarted. 'I told her, "The war is lost. The Jacobins cannot be stopped, and there is no hope for us. In London we will starve. In America we can make a new beginning."' He looked at me ruefully. 'But it is not true, Mr Jago.'

I opened my mouth to say something comforting, to remind him of Philpott's confidence that in Philadelphia we would all find a new life in the anonymous crowd, but Lizzie was coming up, her feet also bare and her hair lifting in the breeze, freed from all constraints, in a manner that would have troubled Theodore and only confirmed him in his opinion of her lax character.

'The gunner has been telling me a tale and I don't know if it's true,' she said without preamble. I glanced at Max to see if he was still unaccountably angry with her, but then I remembered they'd been talking earlier, before the boy fell, and their differences seemed resolved.

'If the gunner told you, I'm afraid it's certain to be false,' I said, as she sat down cross-legged beside us and swept the hair out of her eyes.

'Somethin' about a great dreadful important paper, that Mr Jay was carryin' to America, and was lost. A treaty, of all articles.'

'In this case the gunner is quite right, and I'm only amazed it's taken you these days to learn all about it.'

'And how was I to know it, being just arrived, and no Government personage at all?' She blinked at me, reminding me, perhaps, that my own reputation was better known. Max was watching us, a very faint frown on his forehead. No longer dislike; I rather hoped it was jealousy.

But old habits made me cautious. 'Well, for your further information, there was another Government fellow came aboard in Falmouth.'

'Mr Jenkinson, so. The poor man who died.'

I nodded, deciding to play down the exact nature of his death, which seemed to have escaped her, or the consequent implication that the Treaty was now in the hands of a murderer. Partly I wanted to protect her; partly I still didn't know what I thought of Max, who was listening attentively. 'Before his death, he undertook to hide the Treaty in a safe place against the French. Unfortunately, he chose his hiding place so well that no one's found it since.'

'Dear me, how very aggravatin'.' Lizzie turned to look out over the receding ship's wake and wound a stray lock of her hair around her finger.

'MAX DE SALLES is a man transformed,' Philpott remarked, when I met him by the rail an hour or so later. 'I was just now obliged to advise him against whistling. But his spirits were quite irrepressible, and he positively laughed in my face.'

'Saving Ben's neck does seem to have cheered him up.' I looked around for the Frenchman, and then, as ever, for Lizzie. Bruin was tapping politely at the third mate's backside, in hope of a bite to eat, but the third mate did not seem to have forgiven him for the frights of the morning and drove him off. 'Perhaps, to Max's mind, saving the boy atones for fleeing the battlefield.'

'Hm.' But Philpott wasn't really listening. 'Well, well, whatever the reason, I shall act without delay while he is still amenable. After all, it must be undertaken by *all* or *none*.'

'What must?'

'For God's sake, Laurence, have you forgot there is a murderer among us? You are rather too cool about the matter, I must say. Fortunately, I have contrived a plan to move our enquiries forward, even if you have not.' Philpott looked impressive. 'You recollect the spar in the hold?'

'Of course I do.'

'You recollect the question of its immense weight?'

'We discussed the matter, yesterday, at some length.'

Philpott nodded. 'And we agreed that only a handful of men aboard could manage the thing alone. Well, then, I have devised a stratagem to test the matter beyond doubt. A Boxing Day recreation is a thing quite customary, you know, and no one can possibly guess my true purpose.'

I remembered the St Stephen's Day amusements of my home town and thought I should dislike to see the *Tankerville* crew in such a state of pagan excess. 'What are you thinking of? Dancing?'

Philpott snorted. 'Dancing! Are you out of your mind?'

'Wrestling, then?' The Cornish dances had often enough descended into drunken scuffles.

Philpott had been about to scoff again but cocked his head momentarily. 'Not such a bad idea, my boy. But no, no, my own plan is vastly superior. The best way to discover the relative strengths of those aboard is a weightlifting contest.' He nodded at Peter Williams, who was passing purposefully towards the foredeck where the crew were taking their festive recreations. 'That dear fellow is to test the crew, and ourselves the passengers.'

I had to concede this was clever.

'Look about you,' Philpott went on. 'Everyone is at leisure, everyone a trifle bored, and I don't doubt every man will consent to the amusement. Go and fetch Fletcher, for although he seems a weakling, as our chief suspect he must be tried with all the rest.'

WHEN I BROUGHT Fletcher back to the quarterdeck, Philpott had been busy. There were items from the galley – firkins of ale, brimming pails of water – and a number of cannonballs had been brought up from the gunner's store and were rolling about with black malevolence, intent on bowling us off our feet or cracking our anklebones to splinters. Philpott was supervising the lashing of a long spar to the side, to prevent a more general obliteration if it were left to roll about like the cannonballs, and after a moment I realised it was the same spar Bruin had discovered in the hold yesterday.

Lizzie had now appeared, watching with interest, while someone else had fetched the comtesse a chair and an umbrella against the sun. Bruin was scampering with excitement between our party on the quarterdeck and the other one forward of the mast, where Peter Williams and the third mate were in discussion and the rest of the crew were larking about.

Max now also appeared among us, looking positively eager. He removed his coat and folded it carefully, his medal for bravery upwards, before flexing the set of very striking arm muscles bulging at the fine linen of his shirt, and stretching

143

his back in preparation for the contest. Fletcher wore his usual look of contemptuous amusement and Theodore – I had forgotten that Theodore would also be summoned – looked vague.

'Will you not warm your body a little, Mr Jay?' Max asked him. 'Being such a studious fellow, and unused to manly exertion, it will save you a sore back tomorrow.'

Theodore cautiously bent to touch his toes in imitation of the Frenchman, a proceeding which provoked Mr Gibbs into an anxious paroxysm of astonishment. Max beckoned me peremptorily. 'And you too, *Monsieur* Jago. Your long limbs are also in need of exercise before such a prodigious trial.'

I had forgotten Theodore was to be tried; I had also forgotten that I would be required to participate. I had carried the milk churns for my sister during my brief stay in Cornwall before this voyage, but even that had been a struggle and she had laughed at me. I bent, unwillingly, and my spine protested, but before I was obliged to repeat the effort, Philpott called me over.

'Do you see my stratagem?' he asked in a low voice and with some rather irritating self-congratulation. 'I shall distract them with these baubles of water pails, barrels and cannon shot before proceeding to the nub of the matter.' He gestured to the spar. 'Max, at least, will not shirk the trial, I am certain, for he is as vain as a peacock, especially with the young lady watching.'

I now saw with some gloom that while Max displayed his impressive physique, I would be obliged to demonstrate my own feebleness to Lizzie's laughing brown eyes. But at least I would not be called upon to compete with the crew, who had thought of a simpler method to display the prodigious strength of their arms. Just now they were all hanging, one-handed, from the rigging, while Peter Williams tried in vain to imitate them.

Fletcher pushed forward and snatched up the pails of water, perhaps meaning to impress while he might, for there could hardly be much strength in his amphibian arms. But, in fact, being squat and wide, he looked more comfortable at the business than I had supposed as he bent his elbows and raised the pails to his middle.

''Igher,' the comtesse called from her chair. '*Monsieur* Philpott decrees the weight must reach the shoulders to be counted.'

This was also clever, for it was one thing to lift a heavy weight a little way off the floor, but quite another to raise it high enough to fetch another man a hard blow to the head. Fletcher gave the comtesse a rather unfriendly look, and his wide mouth squeezed as he spread his arms like wings and brought the brimming buckets perpendicular to his shoulders.

'Too easy,' Max said. 'Far too easy, *Monsieur* Fletcher.' He bent to the firkin of ale, which weighed easily half as much as himself, and with the sinews standing out in his neck he hoisted it first to his knee and then, with something of a flourish, to his shoulder. His face was red, but he was grinning again as fearsomely as ever, while sweat trickled down his cheek.

'*Alors*,'ow he preens,' the comtesse observed acidly from her chair.

Max set the barrel back down on the deck, and invited Lizzie to take a seat upon it, apparently meaning to parade her about the deck on his shoulder, atop the firkin. She demurred, laughing, and then blushed as he flexed his powerful arms for her inspection and assured her she would be quite safe in his hands. Annoyed, I glanced forward to the foredeck again, where the sailors were now running up the ratlines without deigning to use their feet, thereby proving themselves all equally capable of Jenkinson's murder, while Peter Williams was following them more sedately, using all his available limbs like a sensible man.

Thwarted of Lizzie, Max turned his eyes on his aunt, his face still red and sweating. 'Well, Aunt Emilie,' he said, breaking into excitable French. 'I think *you* are the most ponderous burden here, having drowned all your boasted griefs in butter. But how will I grasp such a gelatinous orb as you?'

He approached. She fended him off with the point of her umbrella. Everyone else laughed for they had not understood him, and thought her playful when she was really offended – or perhaps even a little afraid. I was sure Max cared for her, even if he was often impatient, but now he was in a strange, wild mood. Fortunately, before he could seize her up, chair and all, and distress what little remained of her old dignity, there was an angry shout from the masthead. The captain had been up there all this time with the lookout, and it seemed he had only just noticed the proceedings below.

'Where's Peters? Where's Trevenen?' he shouted. 'God damn it, who permitted this uproar on my quarterdeck?'

Philpott did not seem to register the captain's displeasure and looked up, beaming. 'We are having a trial of strength, Captain,' he replied, cheerfully, at a bellow. 'Will you join us?'

The captain snapped shut his telescope and stormed down the rigging. Peters and Trevenen came running from where they had been laughing at the crew's antics with Peter Williams, now looking harassed.

'Quickly, gentlemen,' Peters said. 'Clear away this muddle. The captain is vexed.'

The cook hastened away with his pails, rolling the firkin

along ahead of him with his feet. The gunner nimbly descended from the rigging at the forepeak and hurried aft to retrieve the cannonballs.

'We must clear that thing away at once,' Peters said, pointing to the spar, still lashed to the side. Peter Williams had just then joined us, and Max nodded to him. 'Come, Williams.' Even now, he was in a state of baffling excitement. 'A hand if you'll give it.'

The spar was scarcely unlashed before Max hoisted one end and waited for Peter Williams to take the other. The thing was long and unwieldy, but at that moment I would have bet my mother's farmhouse that, still glowing with the same strange elation that had gripped him all day, Max could have hoisted it to his shoulder just as easily as any brawny sailor.

From the captain's log

26 December 1794

These four and twenty hours since leaving Madeira we have been kept company by a brig, lying far astern at the range of an eyeglass. Her rig puts me in mind of the Lovely Lass, *but that ship could hardly be here when she is notoriously confined in port at Baltimore. It is a troubling fancy and one I will not share with the passengers or crew. God knows, my judgement may be faulty with all the circumstances lately weighing upon my mind.*

18

'WELL, IT SEEMS we're none the wiser,' I said to Philpott, when the deck had been cleared and the competitors were gone about their ordinary pursuits. The comtesse had returned to her cabin, looking suddenly very old, and we had taken ourselves out of the captain's way, for he still seemed peevish.

'We now know that any one of the crew could have done it,' I went on. 'Did you see the sinews in their arms, thick as the ropes they swung from? And they had a motive for murder, too, for we know they believed the Treaty valuable as *gold*.'

'Or they could have acted on Fletcher's orders, as we have already surmised.' Philpott had been chewing the stem of his pipe like a pensive sheep, but now looked mischievous. 'Whatever else, we may at least be pleased to find three men cleared of the crime by today's business – if there could ever have been any doubt.'

I looked enquiring.

'Since Theodore Jay seemed uncertain where to find his toes in order to touch 'em, and Peter Williams proved as handy as a haddock in the rigging, neither can be our man, I suppose.'

These shortcomings weren't exactly a disqualification for murder, but Philpott was amusing himself. I sighed, for I knew what was coming. 'And the third?'

'Well ...' He looked as sympathetic as a doctor with bad news. 'You must confess, my boy, you did not cut a very manly figure at the trial yourself.'

'That's hardly fair. I never got the chance to try.' But I gloomily foresaw that to Philpott's florid fancy I would be now, and for ever more, marked down as a physical weakling.

'Max de Salles was in a strange mood,' I said. 'Didn't you think so? I must say I shouldn't fancy meeting him alone in a dark alley in that humour.'

Philpott looked dismissive. 'He can have no interest in the Treaty.'

'Of course not. No more than Fletcher does,' I answered. 'But we know Fletcher thinks it a valuable document to make him money, for he told me so and offered me a share if I would help him.'

'And you think Max de Salles equally mercenary?'

I remembered the Frenchman's offer of a duel merely for offending me. If anything, Max was rather too honourable for comfort. 'No ...' I was casting my mind back to previous days. 'But he did hear Theodore talk about the Treaty, I'm certain, the day of the French chase, for he was scarcely an arm's length away and I couldn't induce the lad to shut his mouth. Jenkinson was no better, broadcasting the affair about the ship. And then later, after Jenkinson's funeral, I think Max may have heard me say I knew the Treaty's contents.'

Philpott shook his head and turned for the companionway. 'The Treaty is intended to prevent America from taking the side of those damned Jacobins ruining his country. To steal it would be a strange act for a Royalist officer, I think.

Besides, his only hope of returning home and taking possession of his landed estates is if those devils are driven out.' He
stopped me at the top of the ladder. 'For pity's sake, mind
your tongue, Laurence. The Comtesse is a very admirable
woman in a difficult plight and has troubles enough without
suspecting her own nephew of a crime he could not possibly
wish to commit.'

WHEN WE PASSED through the mess, Obadiah Fletcher
was at the table, gleaming damply, his large blank eyes
fixed on the disaggregated pieces of his model cotton gin,
which Max de Salles was holding up to the light filtering
down through the hatchway. Fletcher was apparently a
businessman, not an engineer, for his own stubby fingers
flapped helplessly as he watched. Hitherto I had never seen
Max speak more than two words to the American, and to
see them comfortably employed together was rather odd,
especially in light of the new, half-formulated thoughts I had
just communicated to Philpott.

'Is it broken beyond saving?' I asked, as Philpott bustled
away in the direction of the captain's saloon, perhaps for a
less perplexing discussion about his ingenious test of strength
with the *admirable* comtesse.

Max looked up at me, his mad glow only a little faded.
'I have mended many guns, many cannon, *Monsieur* Jago.
Monsieur Fletcher is good enough to allow me a look.'

'Very kind of you, I'm sure.' Fletcher was eyeing Max cautiously, apparently also wondering what this show of friendship meant, while the Frenchman turned the handle of the
little machine without looking at him.

'My aunt says you visited her in her cabin,' Max said,

squinting at the mechanism sidelong, so as not to bring the shadow of his head between the model and the light.

'Oh. Ah. Indeed.' Fletcher was wary.

'She is old and bewildered, *Monsieur* Fletcher. I think she did not quite understand you.'

'An easy mistake.' Fletcher squirmed. 'But I assure you, my questions were kindly meant.'

'If you say so. But why an old woman would have the American Treaty about her person, I do not know.' Max laughed shortly and offered a broken piece up to the main body of the model, to see where it might fit. 'Still, your offer of help to her in Philadelphia was most kind.'

'Ah.' Fletcher sounded relieved, though his frog eyes turned in my direction to see if I had registered this hint of a bribe for information, if she had had any to give. 'Yes, yes, your aunt seemed to think you had no fixed plans, that was all.'

'We will go ashore in Philadelphia, for there are many Frenchmen there.' Max nodded as he found a small piece of metal that consented to slip into the turning mechanism. 'But you are right: after that I do not know, *monsieur*. I am a soldier. Not fitted for work with pen and ink.'

'You would prefer a more – physical – occupation?'

'I think I would.' Max inserted another spindle but found it would not turn. 'Fetch me some grease, will you, Ben?' he asked as the boy came through, looking a little pale but otherwise recovered, his left arm in a sling. A minute later the boy was back with a tub of goose fat and, apparently having nothing else to do, settled himself at Max's elbow to watch.

'In the South we are farmers, managers, constables on our own plantations,' Fletcher was saying, his eyes also following the movement of Max's capable brown hand.

'That sounds more agreeable than sitting at a desk.'

'I think so. And the life is more wholesome, in the country-side away from the pestilence of the cities where yellow fever destroys so many every season. Good air, good food, a moderate exercise, lightened by the labour of our many Africans.'

'There is no sickness among *them*?'

'Oh – hardly to be concerned about, *Monsieur* de Salles. And one need not venture into the stews of their camp, you know, unless discipline is to be administered.'

Max was still having trouble with the spindle, and found it taken out of his grasp by Ben, who deftly slotted it home with his good hand. 'Bravo,' Max said, sitting back. 'You like this kind of work?'

Ben finally smiled, showing a gap where his front teeth were growing in. 'Like to be a chippy like Mr Spiers when I do grow, sir.'

'Would you now?' Max held up his hands. 'Then I shall leave this entirely to your cleverer fingers.'

Max took his leave while Fletcher stayed at the table to watch the young boy's earnest face for a moment before sliding off to his cabin with some muttered excuse about letters to write.

I wasn't sure, but just then I thought I heard a woman's voice raised in laughter from Theodore Jay's cabin further along towards the stern, and my interest in the dance I had just witnessed between Max and Fletcher abruptly waned. I found myself gravitating inexorably towards Theodore's cabin door, which was ajar, perhaps as a concession to decency, for I was right: Lizzie was in there.

They seemed to be reading a treatise on the conduct of young women together, and as I paused to listen, their voices were so low I judged their heads almost touching over the page. 'Women in various stations of life are misled, by the desire of renderin' themselves agreeable, into dangerous freedoms with men they can scarcely know,' she was reading quietly. Then added, with a demure sigh, 'What freedoms does he mean, Mr Jay? Ye don't think he'd disapprove of *us*, do ye? I guess I don't know ye so very well.'

Theodore sounded nervous. 'I believe he is speaking of conversations far more indecent than this, Miss McKendrick. And of men less scrupulous than myself. We are innocently enough engaged, I think.'

'Oh, that's certain. But supposin' you weren't that kind o' man, Mr Jay? Suppose ye lured me here for your own purposes?' She sounded a little breathless, and I pictured her breast heaving. 'What then? What might ye do to me?'

For a moment I was jealous, but there was something in her voice – a trace of amusement, I thought – and I perceived she was merely making mischief. In this she seemed to be successful, for there was a sudden clang and the chamber pot came careening out of the door, propelled by the foot of a man leaping anxiously to his feet, and I could hear Theodore rummaging vigorously through his papers.

'Well, well, Miss McKendrick. I think we must leave it there for today. In fact, I must be calling Peet, for it is well on to dinnertime.'

I retreated a decent distance to the mess table as she came sauntering out of his cabin, her hands deep in the pockets of her skirt, from which she retrieved a small plug of tobacco, preparatory to tucking it in her cheek. When she saw me, she hesitated, desisted from her chewing pleasures, and grinned.

'Are you tormenting that poor lad?' I couldn't bring myself to pretend I hadn't been listening.

'Deserves it, don't he?' For her own part, she seemed pleased enough to share the joke. She came up and brushed my sleeve lightly. 'Tell me, does every Englishman think every unwed female a doxy?'

I thought back across my male acquaintance. 'I suppose most do. Of your unfettered type, of course.' I smiled. 'I'm hardly speaking of a woman like the comtesse.'

The flash of her teeth in another grin. 'And what do *ye* think, Mr Jago?'

I considered all the independent women I had known. 'Decidedly not. Murderers maybe. But not whores.'

Her eyes widened and she laughed aloud. 'Lord, Mr Jago, I should like to meet them, I should so. Who is it exactly that the ladies have murdered?' She tucked my arm in hers and led me towards the ladder. 'Come and tell me all about it.'

YET AGAIN I visited the surgeon's cabin for my dose, and yet again Fletcher was with him, but this time they were hard at the brandy, and well past any attempt at cards. Kidd was unsteady on his feet and feeling confidential as he refilled my phial, while Fletcher lay prostrate on the surgeon's bunk.

'Remarkable business with this bear, ain't it?' Kidd swayed and a precious drop ran down the side of the bottle, which he licked off in apparent thrift. 'Ever seen such a creature before, Mr Jago?'

I confessed I hadn't, as he tried and failed to push the cork home in the bottle, and I took it from him to do it myself.

'A very hungry animal, it seems, always bothering the crew for ship biscuits. But then, there is always something new. A million things I've seen on these ships – a million million.'

I feared he was going to emulate the gunner with some preposterous story, but I felt obliged to listen, for he was, after all, my only route to laudanum. In the end his observations turned out to be less good-natured and a good deal more prurient. 'Many a female we've carried aboard this ship, sirs, though the crew don't like 'em aboard. Think 'em unlucky, and I dare say they're right from the state of their pricks. If the women ain't spreading their legs, they're on the lookout for a steady berth and a husband.'

'And which do you call this Lizzie McKendrick?' Fletcher raised his head and leered, looking more than usually disgusting.

'Ain't sure yet. Shall reserve judgement.' Kidd plumped back into his seat and closed his eyes. 'But I should say the latter. She don't look well used, I'll give her that much, and I saw her snub young Trevenen last evening, like one used to it.'

'I thought she was on her way to New York, for a show,' I said. She would probably rather be called a husband hunter than a whore, but it seemed hard that, as she had observed, no man could think of her in any other light.

'That's what they all say.' Kidd was growing drowsy.

'I don't suppose they all have a bear to bear out their tale.'

'Bear – bear out – very good, very good.' His voice was fading. 'Millions and millions. Carried that Thomas Jefferson once, on his way to France. A red-faced fellow, but at least he had some manners. Fine fiddle player too ...'

His head fell back and without further ado he began to snore loudly. I made to leave, but Fletcher sat up with an effort and detained me with a sticky hand. 'You'd best watch out for that God-damned Frenchman,' he said, in an under-tone unnecessary in the circumstances. 'Been asking all sorts of questions about you.'

'Questions! Such as?'

'What position you held in the Foreign Office. Whether you ever saw the Treaty before it was lost. I told him I had asked you that already, and you didn't even know it was aboard until the thing went missing.' He worked his lips. 'Pound to a penny he's decided to go after it, too, wherever it's hidden. He and his old aunt may be nobility, but I believe they're broke.'

Perhaps he was right. If so, it solved Philpott's objection to Max as a suspect. Abject poverty was surely the only possible reason Max would consider taking a position on Fletcher's plantation, and another solution – even murder – might have seemed a preferable enterprise to his warlike temperament.

'We all need money,' I said cautiously.

'And none more than Captain Morris.' He nodded at my look. 'Dead drunk in Madeira my ass. He was taken ill – very ill – but they don't wish to let on, for fear we'll take alarm and demand a refund on our passage for the risk of sailing under a dying man.'

'Where in heaven did you get this tale?'

'No tale, Mr Jago. The solemn truth. Kidd has just found a tumour in his belly as large as a goose egg.'

From the diary of the Comtesse de Salles

A fat woman can never be an object of pity. No matter how she weeps or sighs, men will find her only a figure for jest, thinking sensibility incompatible with fleshly padding, and that the soul of a poet cannot co-exist with a hearty appetite. Aboard this ship, only Monsieur Philpott truly sees me for who I am.

The same thing holds true, by analogy, for my birth. Men find it just as hard to see that deep feeling is also compatible with rank and a privileged existence. If I am taken, they will see only pride and hauteur. If tears come, they will account it a victory, and mock me for being only a human creature after all. Yet when did I ever claim to be more? We are all of us descendants of Adam and Eve. All stained with original sin. Why am I to account for the transgressions of my fathers, more than they for the crimes of theirs? We come into this world naked, and I chose my station no more than those ragged men who work the guillotine.

And now this business with the murdered Jenkinson makes me see we are never safe. Moreover, Max grows stranger to me every day. There is a hot passion about him, as though fires rage inside his mind. He is angry that his cousin placed us here. He rages to be free of all bygones. I understand him less and less by the day.

19

PHILPOTT SAT ON his usual seat under the window in the comtesse's cabin, while Bruin slurped from the cup of tea the comtesse had poured for him. I was still pondering Fletcher's words about Max, but I would tell Philpott about it later when we were alone. Besides, the saloon showed no sign of the poverty Fletcher ascribed to the de Salles, and I remembered the comtesse's expensive coffee – which had been banished again, without comment, for we were back to Mr Hind's more practised tanniferous brew.

I examined the skull on the table beside me, its macabre gaze now putting me in mind of Captain Morris. He was almost always sallow, always trembling, and I had uncharitably put these appearances down to too much gin.

'Lizzie McKendrick is a comely lass, but she has no common sense,' Philpott was saying. 'She leaves poor Bruin to run wild about the ship – cheerfully enough, I admit it – thundering about the decks and the mastheads. But the boy's accident makes the crew nervous. I have seen them shrink from the creature. Perhaps you should warn the girl, Laurence, while you're a-wooing.'

It was certainly pleasanter to think of Lizzie's face than Fletcher's or the dying captain's, even if Philpott was teasing me. 'She has no fear for him, she says. He is too short and stout to fall overboard and can climb like a cat.'

At this juncture there came a tap at the door, and, rather to my surprise, Ben was admitted. He looked alarmed to see me there – probably thought he was finally to be arraigned for stealing Mr Jenkinson's cross – but in fact I still hadn't passed on the story of his thieving, and I was as ignorant of the reason for his presence in the comtesse's saloon as he could ever be.

'Ah, *très bien, très bien*,' the comtesse said, beckoning him vigorously and gracing him with her most authoritative glare. If she had any tender feelings towards him after tending him in the surgeon's cabin, they were very well hidden. 'Now, *mon garçon, écoute-moi très bien.* The men in the ship. They look for the Treaty, *n'est ce pas?*'

'Eh?' The boy looked entirely stumped by this mangled French and English.

'Someone searching for the missing papers?' she prompted him. 'Among the crew?'

I had thought Philpott oblivious to all my suggestions after the trial of strength, but he was also nodding at Ben encouragingly and it seemed he and the comtesse were pursuing their own enquiries after all. Perhaps the comtesse had also watched the crew swinging easily through the rigging and drawn the same conclusion I had – that they were quite as suspect as anyone else.

Ben seemed eager enough to please. 'There's *gold* missing, ma'am. Ain't there?'

'Ah, yes, gold you call it, I remember. Ben, you must tell the truth.' As any man among the crew got the *gold?*'

The boy's ears turned red, and he licked his coming front

teeth. For the first time I remembered the words Jenkinson had said to the boy in his dying confusion. *Thou art naked.* The boy had passed on those words with a good deal less prevarication than he was showing now, and I couldn't help wondering if his bafflement was feigned.

'If you know who took the papers – the *gold* – you must tell me,' the comtesse persisted. 'Or *Monsieur* Philpott, or *Monsieur* Jago 'ere. No one else.' Only then did she soften. 'And, if you do, I'll give you a slice of the cook's cake, at the table with Bruin. It is *sa gâterie favorite*, I assure you.'

This was a dubious inducement for any self-respecting human animal, and for his own part Ben looked rather trapped, an impression confirmed when he pointed suddenly at Bruin, in an apparent attempt at distraction. 'Going to dance on New Year's Eve, ain't he? Been teachin' my birds.' His eyes widened with sudden animation. 'When you do bash a bucket, they do bobble and yap fearsome.'

The comtesse had no idea what he was talking about, nor any desire to find out. 'Well, well, boy. Come back to me tomorrow. You understand? With any news you can find.'

She was quite as much a mystery to the boy as he to her, and exactly what impressions he retained in his eight-year-old brain was uncertain as he pattered off back to the deck.

'The boy clearly knows nothing,' Philpott observed. I wasn't sure I entirely agreed, but there was no time to discuss it, since a tremendous lovers' quarrel was about to blow up between my companions.

'Between teaching his birds to dance and helping your nephew mend Fletcher's model,' Philpott went on, 'he is quite taken up, I assure 'ee.'

The comtesse turned slowly, like a majestic three-decker. 'My nephew? Mending *Monsieur* Fletcher's model?'

'Yes, indeed. He seems quite eager to help him. Does he really propose that you join Mr Fletcher on his plantation in Savannah?'

'Join him!' First, surprise made her bad-tempered. But then as Philpott's meaning sank in, she was aghast. '*Mon Dieu*! 'E will not bring me down to such 'orrors?'

'I don't know exactly what he intends, ma'am, I confess it. Just overheard a word or two. But you know, it might suit you. Country air. A grand mansion, just as you are used to.'

'With *Fletcher*?'

'Beggars can't be choosers, ma'am.'

Philpott was thoughtless and too cheerful, and she dismissed us at once, in a terrible rage.

I MET LIZZIE COMING out from steerage, banging a bucket against her leg with a purposeful step.

'What are you doing?' I asked.

'Milkin' the cow, amn't I?'

'Why in the world are you doing that?' I followed her up the ladder, wondering if her purse had proved shorter than she admitted, and she was working for her passage. Max, the captain, the crew and now Lizzie, all possibly in need of money.

But in her case, I soon found I was wrong, for she had merely been dragooned to fulfil Ben's tasks while he recovered from the depredations of her bear. 'Cabin boy's still too feeble to milk her,' she said. 'And it's my fault, o' course.'

The cow was tossing her head and showing the whites of her eyes as we came up.

'Do you know how to do it?'

'Sure, I've seen it done. It can't be o'er hard.'

The gunner proffered her the milking stool with a flourish,

and she gathered her skirts, thanking him, before sitting down at the cow's flank and rubbing her hands resourcefully. She glanced at me, hair falling in her eyes, and then bent her head to look under the cow's belly and reached tentatively for the udder.

The cow's side twitched, and the animal put back her ears. 'Careful,' I said. 'She'll kick the bucket if you don't hold it. She's well past her milking time and getting sore.'

Lizzie wedged the bucket between her feet and fumbled for the teats.

'Don't tickle her but draw her off quickly. She'll not stand much dithering from a stranger.'

From where I stood, Lizzie's mouth was a firm line. 'Ye're quite the expert, so.'

'I was born on a farm. Milked cows since I was ten years old.'

She pulled at the teat, the cow groaned, the bucket turned over, and Lizzie was on the floor beside the stool, her hair in her face, and a hoof print of cow shit on her skirt.

'I told you so.' I feared she might be vexed, but as I pulled her to her feet, she only returned my grin and pressed against me for a moment, all lithe warm softness.

'Perhaps ye'd better do it.' She proffered me the bucket by its handle. 'Occupy yerself with something useful, instead of amusin' yerself at my expense.'

I took the bucket gladly, quite willing to show her I was handy at something. Lizzie stood at the animal's head and watched as milk began to spurt into the pail. For all my boasting, my hands were unused to the task, and would soon be tired.

I raised my eyes to her face, to find she was watching attentively, though it was my face, not my hands that preoccupied her. 'You don't come from the country, then?' I asked. 'A town girl, I suppose.'

'Just so.'

I laid my cheek against the cow's warm side. I could hear the creature breathing, and the gurgle of her many stomachs as she chewed the cud, placid now.

'Bejesus, I hope the boy soon mends.'

'It wasn't your fault.'

'Oh – 'tis not *that*. I'd not have ye act the farmhand for me too many days, that's all.'

'Come, then,' I said. 'I'll teach you.'

She settled obediently back on the stool at my bidding, resting her cheek against the cow's flank as I had done, and taking hold of the slackened teat. 'There's plenty more milk there to be taken. And plenty of time to take it in, for she's easy now. You'll soon get the hang of it.'

In truth, there is no great mystery to the process, and she soon had the milk spurting into the pail as well as I had done. I stroked the cow's damp nose and watched until the steady flow faltered and the udder was almost empty. I laid my hand on Lizzie's shoulder, the fabric of her dress smooth under my palm, and took her place on the stool again, to strip the cow dry.

Lizzie stretched her back, hands on hips, and then ran her finger around under her neckerchief. Kidd might have thought it the brazen assurance of a whore; in fact, it was like nothing so much as the ease of a man. 'How warm it is! Almost like a summer's day. How can such a thing be possible at all, in December? I even think the days are longer.'

'We are going south,' I answered. 'And, therefore, they are indeed lengthening, contrary to all the pronouncements of the calendar. I thought you a seasoned traveller. How long is it since you left Ireland?'

'Long enough.'

Her face was closed, and I suddenly fancied that she was as new to all this as I was. Partly to test my theory, and partly out of sheer mischief, I added, 'Yes, the world is a tremendously curious place, Miss McKendrick. Did you know, the moon we left behind us in Madeira is quite another than the one we shall see in Barbados?'

She had taken back the bucket and turned to go, but now looked back at me, arrested. 'Quite another?'

'Yes, indeed. When we cross the Tropic, we shall leave one behind for the other. For how in the world could we see the same celestial body from two such far-flung points on the globe?'

She studied me. 'And the same, I dare say, goes for the sun, now?'

'I imagine so.'

'And the pole star, and the planets, and all the constellations?'

I began to wish I hadn't started the subject. She shook her head, pityingly. 'Ye've been talkin' to the gunner, I perceive.'

From the captain's log

31 December 1794
The Tropic passed at Latitude 23°
A New Year, God help us all

All crew to be bleeded. Mr Kidd prescribed me a greater quantity
of Epsom Salts, but I find they give little relief.

The ship I feared the Lovely Lass is gone, and I was therefore
wise to doubt my judgement. The cabin boy seems none the worse
for his mishap in the rigging. The Third Mate represents to me that
the bear should be confined, but, having scarcely room enough for
the cow and turkeys, I am at a loss to know where it might be kept.
Certainly not in its cabin, for I have seen it secretly chewing on
the flock mattress, and, after missing our trade in Madeira, I am
too penniless to replace it.

Some men seem made for money-making. I perceive now that
Mr Fletcher is certainly such a one, and believes I am to be bought.

20

FOR SOME ARCANE CUSTOM, quite beyond the understanding of we landsmen, the naval new year occurred at noon on New Year's Eve, but as far as the crew and the passengers were concerned, the proper turn of the year would come at midnight in its regular fashion. The entertainments planned would include a performance by Bruin, and another by Ben's dancing turkeys. The cow would have a crown, and Mr Spiers announced his intention to juggle. Late in the afternoon I left the others picking over the dubious New Year dainties the cook had provided. Theodore had blushed at the very sight of Lizzie, who was dressed in a becoming gypsy costume for the performance to come, while Bruin chewed doggedly on an unyielding turkey wing, oblivious of his impending celebrity. I went on deck and joined Philpott and the comtesse at the rail. As we quietly observed the last sunset of 1794, the third mate passed us, talking to another crewman.

'He's to do it with tankards, like the cup and ball trick, do you see? Says the extra bit of conjurin' will help it all along.'

'Ah,' replied his interlocutor, with what sounded like fascinated unease. Just then, a low but audible hiss came from behind us. I glanced back, expecting to see the ship's cat, who had a propensity to address Mr Gibbs in a similar manner, but the source was in fact the sailmaker, who had turned to find the bear at his shoulder, in cheerful pursuit of the comtesse. The look on the fellow's face was the ugliest I had ever seen aboard ship, and for the first time I truly felt our total isolation. Had the packet not been in the service of the Royal Mail, a good number of these men would be as happy aboard a privateer, so long as their wages were as regular. And somewhere among them might be a murderer.

Peter Williams seemed to materialise out of the setting sun like a genie from a bottle. He was holding three tankards from the galley in one hand, and a ball in the other. I hadn't known he had a talent for sleight-of-hand, but then I reflected that I knew very little of anyone. We had all come here from lives elsewhere, full to the brim with friends and family, pastimes – and secrets – from which we had been severed the moment we boarded the ship.

'Come,' he said to the sailmaker. 'I have the trick to show you.'

The fellow turned away from us reluctantly, still scowling, and Peter Williams frowned at the comtesse. 'You'd be wise to be careful.'

'*Comment?*'

'Don't raise no more ghosts.'

I remembered seeing the crew's faces at the skylight during the comtesse's *séance*, eavesdropping on our goings-on. I remembered Spiers's cry of wonder at the sight of Bruin in Jenkinson's wig. *Smithy's right. It's the man himself.* I hadn't understood him then, but now I remembered what Ben had said while the surgeon stitched him back together after his fall from the rigging. *Gunner says that un's the ghost of that dead feller.* All in all, it seemed Bruin had fulfilled Mr Smith's foolish fantasies quite admirably, not least, I now saw, by producing the murder weapon from the hold on his first morning, in true avenging fashion. If it hadn't been for the sailmaker's scowl and Peter Williams's frown, it would all have been quite amusing.

But then Mr Smith was himself upon us, waving his spy-glass at Philpott and full of good cheer. It was to be a particularly propitious New Year, he announced, as it coincided with our crossing the Tropic of Cancer. He thrust the spyglass into Philpott's hand, and Philpott raised it obligingly to his eye.

'You'll see the *line* in the telescope, sir.'

'Line, Mr Smith?'

'Almost like a hair, sir. Do you see it? Bang across the middle.'

'Oh, yes, yes, I see it now.'

'That's the *line*, sir. The Tropic of Cancer, its very own self.' The gunner reached out his hand to take the telescope from Philpott and raised it to his own eye. 'Ah, and there it is, gone. We're over it now. You was exceeding lucky to see it. Not many do.'

'Well, I'm highly obliged to you, Mr Smith. A wellspring of information as always. I shall go directly to write it up.' Philpott held out his hand for a second look, but the gunner shut the telescope with a click, and returned it to the grinning third mate.

'And don't forget the mermaids what I told you of. With them breasts.'

'No, no, never fear, dear sir. It shall all go off to the press as soon as ever we land.' Philpott hesitated, his rubicund face just a particle less silly. 'But while I have 'ee here, Mr Smith, what can you tell me of that business with the spar? The one that killed poor old Jenkinson, you know?'

'Spar, sir?' Mr Smith only looked puzzled. 'Oh, the article in the hold, I dare say you mean. Yes, a devil of a business, weren't it?'

T HE SHIP'S GLASS turned for six bells – eleven o'clock by common time – and almost as soon as the bells rang out, the music started up on deck – a reel, played on a fiddle – and a moment later the deck resounded to the slap of bare feet. There was singing, too, though I couldn't make out the words. Lizzie was swirling about in the slender arms of that damned second mate, Trevenen. As I watched, she relieved herself of him with some dexterity, and the next moment had Peter Williams in her grip, who had been watching them all cavort about as elegantly as a herd of heifers. She had not yet seen me. Would she choose me next? Or take her pick elsewhere? I remembered Kidd's gossip the other night in his cabin. What was she really up to? The story of her engagement in New York must be true, for Bruin was proof enough. But was she, despite all appearances, a whore, or a woman alone in search of a husband as the surgeon said? If so, she had picked the wrong ship, for the captain was both married and dying, and would never dress her up in silks and satins, and call her his dear, as the old song said. In fact, just now she was laughing up at Peter Williams, and he was hardly material for a husband either, being as married as the captain, and entirely ineligible in any case, in his own difficult circumstances. It was all nonsense.

Theodore was at my shoulder, his eyes as wide and exasperating as ever. 'You should take a turn, Theodore,' I said. 'Ask Comtesse de Salles for a dance.'

He smiled, guileless as an infant and about as useful. How

Peter Williams could tolerate him was beyond my imagination. I would have long ago knocked the boy on the head.

'Christ in heaven.' Fletcher had come up behind us, unseen. 'You show no authority at all over that animal, Mr Jay. Are you quite content to have him scatter a trail of mulattos in his wake?'

Theodore turned to him and frowned. 'I beg your pardon sir, I don't quite—'

'Giggling and mooning in each other's arms that way. They'll be off into the shadows for a jig before you know it, mark my words.'

'You mean Peet?' Theodore was catching his drift at last and was as floored as if Fletcher had accused his own father of fornication. Fletcher put out a hand to grasp at Lizzie and Peter Williams as they passed and drew them to a breathless halt.

'Unseemly,' he grunted at them, more pig than frog just at this moment. 'Get your hands off the wench, Williams, and go about your duties.'

I hoped for a moment that Peter Williams would thump Fletcher and ease both our feelings. But with a self-control no doubt born of a thousand such insults, he only stiffened, bowed his head a fraction, and turned on his heel. Lizzie relieved the moment's awkwardness by seizing a startled Fletcher by the hand and pulling him into the throng.

Rogers, the third mate, was hailing Peter Williams vigorously, and with no more than a cursory nod to me he hastened over to where a crowd had gathered about the scuttlebutt at the fo'c'sle, with a lantern and what looked like the same three tankards I had seen him holding earlier. Ben was also arriving, pale with excitement, Mr Gibbs skipping at his heels. The boy flung himself on Peter

Williams's back, who gently extricated himself and squatted down among the group.

The eighth bell was tolling – midnight – and the very turn
of the year was upon us. I could see Philpott out of the corner
of my eye, gallantly kissing the comtesse's hand, their earlier
quarrel apparently forgotten. Inside the huddle of bodies Peter
Williams had been shuffling the three upturned tankards and
now lifted the middle one to reveal a crumpled, papery sphere.
He passed it with some ceremony to the gunner, who then
lit it at the lantern. The gunner held it aloft for a moment,
until the flames reached his fingers and he dropped it in the
brimming scuttlebutt where it was extinguished at once. Their
drinking water would be faintly ashy tomorrow but, having
been exposed so long to Mr Hind's culinary creations, their
taste buds were doubtless blunted, and there was at present an
appearance of general satisfaction among them. Eyes raised to
the rigging in pious praise. God alone knew what they were
up to.

A hand on my arm. Lizzie, gazing up at me, the delicate
planes of her face lit by the ship's lantern. 'A happy New Year
to ye, Mr Jago. Lord, what a solemn face ye have, to be sure.
You look like God in judgement, frownin' down on all our
little doings.'

And then, without warning, she kissed me suddenly, on the
mouth, her breath fragrant with tobacco. Her hands came to
my shoulders, mine went to her waist. Do you want the details,
My Lord? I promised you your money's worth, I recall. Her
mouth was soft, wet; our lips slid together.

'Not here,' she said in my ear.

'Then come to my cabin.'

'Nor there neither.' She laughed, breathlessly. 'Sure, will you
scandalise Mr Jay entirely?'

'Where, then?' I was enflamed and elated all at once. Above every other man aboard, she had chosen me at the midnight hour. Whatever she was, I wanted her.

'The boat.'

THE PLANKS OF THE ship's boat were still warm from the day's sun, and we were out of sight from every point on board save for the crow's nest at the top of the mainmast, whence a small, round figure was looking down at us by the light of the fattening moon.

'The bear!' Lizzie laughed again into my shoulder, as I untied the strings of her bodice with shaking fingers. Found the warm, round softness of her breast.

'He's your chaperone. Will object if I get too familiar.'

She arched her back for me to pull up her skirts. 'Then he'd best do somethin' now, Mr Jago, for otherwise ...'

We heard voices approaching from the direction of the forehatch – a couple of seamen, seemingly off for a companionable shit at the heads. We froze in exquisite eagerness as their voices rose and then fell again to a distant murmur. She was looking at me full in the eye with her steady brown gaze.

I will not confess how long my abstinence had been, My Lord. You know well enough that I could never have tasted such freedoms with the under-secretary's daughter, and the clean London whores were much too far above my purse. Some of the other clerks kept a mistress in cheap lodgings – country girls, adrift in the city – but I had never relished the idea of such subjugation. Laudanum and treason had been distractions almost enough, but to run my hands up her bare arms and bury my face in her hair – to smell the scent of her unwashed body and taste the salt on her lips – was a miracle to me at that moment, greater than any in the Bible. She gasped, and then laughed again, as from the crow's nest above us Bruin snorted audibly with what seemed like disapproval.

Afterwards, we lay in the boat for a long time. As the night cooled, I wrapped her in my arms, though in truth it was her own effervescent body that warmed us both. I had been the unrequited suitor for so long, I could hardly believe how easy it all could be. *Between worlds*, the comtesse had called our state at sea, and indeed we were all of us stripped from our old lives, and nakedly awaiting the new ones, which lay over the western horizon, as yet unrealised.

M

Mermaid. I beg you to dismiss all your prior Notions of this glamorous Creature. She is not comely, with a Comb and a Mirror, singing innocently atop a Rock. No, her Teeth are sharp, and her Song only beguiles a Ship to its Ruin. Sir Patrick Spens had the right of it, and a Mermaid is never a thing to be welcomed, despite being, I am informed, tremendously voluptuous in Bodily Charms above her Fish's Tail.

Which leads us on to:

W

Women are never to be permitted aboard, unless absolutely necessary, and then only as Passengers. Their involvement in any part of the Ship's building or sailing is a Recipe for Doom. A pity, I think, as the Cook's cooking puts me very much in mind of my Wife's, and I believe she would make a splendid Ship's Steward.

21

It was almost dawn when we crept back to our separate beds undetected. I dozed on my bunk through the morning, dreaming intermittently of Lizzie in her cabin nearby, and then of Anne Bellingham in London. My dreams, in either case, were not particularly creditable. After I woke, I lay abed for an hour reading Gray's *Elegy*, for I still hadn't found my copy of Milton. When a shadow fell across the door, I looked up, hoping to see Lizzie's figure, but it was only Captain Morris peering in at me. I couldn't see his face in the gloom, but his posture spoke of harried impatience.

'You'd oblige me by keeping this door shut, Mr Jago.'

'It lets in some light, sir.'

'Aye, aye, but it will come off its hinges if left to roil about in this manner. There is light in the mess if you must have it.'

He was more trembling than usual, edgy and vexed, and as I dressed I wondered if it was the after-effects of the New Year revels or a further accession of illness that bothered him so.

Out in the mess, Peter Williams was ironing, while a low murmur of familiar voices came from Theodore's cabin, the door wedged open with the chamber pot again. I had lain abed too long, and Lizzie was back at her mischief.

'I'm mortified, Mr Jay, to be sure I am. But I can't help it. Havin' been raised to it, ye see.'

I paused to listen, unashamedly now. Peter Williams raised his head and saw my smile.

'Raised to it!' Theodore's voice approached a bat-squeak of mixed surprise, gratification and alarm.

'Oh, from ever so young, sir. I hardly dare tell ye.'

A silence, while Theodore apparently groped back to steady ground from this unexpected confession. 'Prayer is the best healer, Miss McKendrick. I promise you faithfully, you will feel so cleansed, the moment you repent.'

'Oh,' she said again, 'but I do repent most dreadful, Mr Jay. And will never try my arts on ye again, I swear. It was only that …'

A pause. A cough. My eyes met Peter Williams's across the room. I was still smiling, but Peter Williams seemed in as black a mood as the captain.

'Yes, Miss McKendrick?' Theodore was husky.

'Only that …' Her voice dropped to a whisper, and I held my breath to listen. 'Only that ye are so handsome, sir.' A pause, just long enough to let this register. 'And call me Lizzie, do. I don't deserve no better.'

'Then, Lizzie, shall we defeat Satan together? Shall we pray?'

She was hazy on the words of the 'Our Father' – probably more used to them in Latin – but repeated 'amen' obediently at the end, and then, after the briefest pause, added, 'And how you must miss yer *own* father, Mr Jay.'

'I beg your pardon?' It seemed that Theodore had never before thought of the deity and his own parent in the same breath, and he sounded so stunned at this new idea that I almost laughed aloud.

'*He*'s the great man, too, ain't he? And did terrible important work in England, or so I hear? Ye must be so proud to carry his Treaty home to President Washington ...'

Though Theodore was a fool who deserved all he got, it was cruel of her to remind him that, on the contrary, he had no treaty to bear on to the President in Philadelphia at all. She was incorrigible and was mightily enjoying it.

I retreated to the mess table and the pleasant smell of hot linen, and took up a book at random from a pile in the centre of the table.

'Good God. Look at this, if you please!'

Here, at last, was my very own Milton, fallen open in my hands at the verses I had been reading before I lost it. That seemed strange until I saw that the previous page had been ripped out, creating a lacuna as evident as a gap in a shining set of teeth. As I lifted the volume up, the mirrored sheet, from somewhere much later in the book, fluttered out, set loose from its moorings. On closer inspection, there was a cut along the sewn seam, a careful slit, which rather put me in mind of Jenkinson's neatly torn instructions.

'Why the devil would anyone act the vandal in this way?' I asked, holding it out for Peter Williams's inspection. He glanced up briefly from his ironing, but he was still moody and didn't seem much interested. 'And to the mighty Milton, too!'

I had lost the book the day we were chased by the French warship. The comtesse had come out of her saloon, demanding to be taken on deck to watch Obadiah Fletcher come aboard. Max had been cleaning his pistols at the mess table, and I had laid my Milton down beside them, open at the page

I had been reading, before following the pair of them up on deck.

Had the book still been there when I came hastening back down into the mess later, to find Jenkinson and ask him for his advice? Philpott and the comtesse had been arguing about her clothes, and Kidd had been setting out his saws and drugs on the table. I had only had eyes for the laudanum, but perhaps he had tossed the books to one side to make room for his surgery. After speaking to Jenkinson, I had gone back up on deck. Had anyone else subsequently gone below? Dozens of men, no doubt, for the ship had been in uproar, and any one of them might have seen the volume and ripped out the sheet, if they had been so inclined. But why the devil should they want to?

'Ye are very solemn.'

Lizzie had come out of Theodore's cabin unheard and hovered at my shoulder. Out of Peter Williams's sight, I put a hand on her waist and she came to me willingly, resting her hip against my arm.

'Just a curiosity. I lost this book weeks ago, and see, it's reappeared, all spoilt.'

'That's a fret, to be sure.' She took the volume in her hand and turned it over, but without much more interest than Peter Williams had shown. I spoke low enough that he would not hear.

'I'm thinking it's a dreadful long time till dark, Lizzie.'

She twinkled at me. 'And why else do ye think I pass the time teasin' poor Mr Jay, than to hurry the hours along?'

Blind Milton!

After an unaccountable Absence, my Apprentice Laurence Jago's copy of Paradise Lost has been found aboard. God send that some other MISSING ITEMS might turn up with as little Fanfare!

But perusing the battered Pages of the little Volume, which has passed through a dozen Hands in its lifetime, I dare say, and illuminated a dozen Minds with its Grandeur and Solemnity, has set me thinking of the Temptations we all are prey to. Yes, John, you may as well settle yourself comfortably, for I am embarking on a Sermon!

They call Superstition a Sin, but I could never see much Harm in it, and have relished passing on to you my Discoveries among the illiterate Crew. It is not entirely due to Ignorance, neither, that some find Comfort in such things. I suppose a hundred and fifty years ago we should have prayed to our Saints, or the blessed Virgin, ourselves, if you can imagine such a Heresy, and found much Comfort in that too.

No, I can wink at any Nonsense that gives us Consolation in a wicked World. But there are other kinds of Credulity I'll not condone. First there is the foolish Dependence of the unthinking Man, who never questions his own Persuasions – but such a man is only to be pitied. Worse is the Scoundrel who exchanges God or Providence for the worship of Reason or of Man himself, as the French have done. It is a bad Bargain, for that Deity will always fail him. Last, and worst of all, is the Worship of Money, which turns a sound Man to an odious Reptile, slithering his way through Life over the sticky Residue of his own Greed.

22

THE MOON HADN'T YET risen and it was darker in the
boat, Lizzie only a breathing shape beside me, the touch
and earthy scent of her flesh even more present to my mind in
the absence of sight. She wriggled one booted foot between
mine, and flung the other across me, swathing me with her
coarse linen skirts. A strand of her hair lay across my face, and
I smoothed it away. I took her under my arm, rested my chin on
her head. The warm glow of relaxation was leaving my limbs,
and if we stayed here a while longer, I thought luxuriously, there
would be yet more pleasure to come.

'You are lovely, Lizzie.'

She nuzzled her head under my chin by way of answer.
Something like peace whispered through me. Whatever her
past, and whatever rogues like Kidd might think, she was as
cool and immaculate as crystal. 'Are you a fairy, Lizzie? I think
I've heard Ireland is awash with them.'

'I am, so.' Her voice was bright. 'And I have put a spell on
ye, to serve me for ever.'

'In that case …' I shifted my arm, for the weight of her head was
deadening sensation in my shoulder. 'What are your commands?'

She raised her head. 'Oh, not so many. Only to love me for eternity, and tell me every last thing about yerself, so that I might possess ye entirely.'

'It will be a long tale, then.'

'Will it, so?' She sounded content.

'But no longer than yours, I fancy. What are *you* doing here, Miss McKendrick, so far from home, and possessed of a wild animal over which you seem to have no authority at all?'

She laughed. 'Oh, see, it's a regular man ye are, to be catechising a poor female, as bad as Mr Theodore Jay. Will ye cast me off if my tale proves unsatisfactory?'

'How can I? You have put a spell on me, remember, and even if you are as heartless as a Fairy Queen, I remain a helpless knight in your service.'

'Like *Tam Lin*? How grand.' She leaned up on an elbow and looked down at me. The moon was suddenly risen without my noticing, and by its light I saw her bodice was still untied. In the moonlight her skin was milk. 'But come, I asked first. Is it true you were a Government man in London, before you came to sea?'

I smiled at her apparent awe. 'Are you teasing me, like Theodore? I was only a clerk, you know.'

'But ye was acquainted with all those great gentlemen.'

'I served Lord Grenville, the Foreign Secretary, if that's what you mean. Met Mr Pitt once or twice.'

'Did ye so?'

'Don't gawk like a kitten, Lizzie. They're only men. And often foolish ones.'

'Foolish, how?'

'To believe they can control everything. Hang a shoemaker on doubtful evidence, for instance, without considering the views of a common jury.'

'Common people are a force to be reckoned with, truly.'

'And Mr Philpott a greater man than most of them in Downing Street.'

I THINK, FOR ALL HIS oiliness, Obadiah Fletcher enjoyed the idea of munificence, or at the very least found Kidd an insufficient audience for his vast cunning. He held me back at the mess table the next morning after breakfast, when everyone else had dispersed about their business. He spoke low, as usual. 'I have more news of the Treaty, Mr Jago.'

'News?' My eagerness was only half feigned. 'You know where it is? Can I help you?'

'No need.' He took out a cigar and rolled it between his fingers, as pleased as punch, I could tell. My heart quickened.

'No need? You've already got it?'

'As good as.' His wide mouth smirked. 'And without the aid of the spirit realm, or that damned fool of a woman, Mr Jago.'

I let this pass, only looked enquiring.

'You mind the matter of Morris's illness? Well, I've been mulling the thing over in my mind for a time, and it seemed to me there might be a deal to be done.'

'A deal?'

'I went to the good captain yesterday, in his cabin, and told him I'd had the whole story from the surgeon. "I am dreadful sorry to hear this is your last voyage," I said. God damn me, he wasn't pleased. Spoke quite sharp. "I would be obliged to Mr Kidd if he had kept his mouth shut. What else did he tell you?"

'"That you have a wife and children in Falmouth will be left quite destitute 'pon your death." Well, at that he turned puce. Thought I might have killed him then and there with an apoplexy, so I spoke on, quite hurried. "You must be worried about 'em," I said. "A windfall of cash might be of benefit to you. I could arrange such a thing, in return for a sight of that *missing* paper." I spoke with a good deal of significance, God damn me, and he took my meaning pretty quick. Was tempted, too, I could see. "Careful, sir," he said, as sharp as a razor. "There are many ears about a ship like this.'"

Fletcher nodded at me. 'We have all been casting about in search of Jenkinson's papers, thinking some devil among the crew or passengers has snaffled 'em. But such a story would be mighty convenient to the captain, would it not, if all along Jenkinson had given him the Treaty that day, to put in the mail for sinking?'

This, I confess, had never occurred to me. I had believed the captain implicitly and, if counterfeit, his search of our cabins had been well feigned. But there was a simplicity to Fletcher's theory that impressed me. As the captain of a packet ship, discretion would be worked into Morris's bones as deeply as veins in marble, and how better to protect the Treaty, after all, than to deflect attention from its true whereabouts with a meaningless search? But this didn't explain Jenkinson's death, and I said so. Fletcher only shook his head.

'Too many God-damned rogues aboard to know what happens under cover of darkness.'

'You think he argued with a crewman?'

'Or that darkie of Jay's. If a murder happened on my plantation, Mr Jago, I would know where to look, and it wouldn't be among white men, I assure you.'

It was, when I thought about it, a minor miracle that no one else had raised this disagreeable suspicion. 'Well,' I said, sitting back, 'do you think the captain will come to terms?'

'Men always come to terms for money, Mr Jago.' His wet lips smiled. 'It's only the required sum that is unknown.'

'When will you hear from him again?'

'I await the upshot. But if he's tempted, I dare say he'll do it before I change my mind.'

Fletcher was right in one thing. It was not absolutely certain that Jenkinson's murder had been over the Treaty, and I couldn't help remembering how the captain had discouraged me from enquiry and had spoken only reluctantly to his crew. In the end, it was perfectly plausible that Jenkinson had entrusted the vital documents to him after all, and that the captain had gone through the charade of a search to throw us all off the scent.

Could Fletcher possibly succeed with his bribe, against all the discipline and honour of the Royal Mail? With the lump growing in his belly, how easily the captain's disgust at Fletcher's bribery might turn to temptation, and then to something perilously like hope.

'S OMETHING'S BOTHERIN' you, so.'
    'I deny it. How could I be troubled, here with you?'

'Ye've worn a frown all day. Ye'll not be foolin' me.'

'Just Mr Fletcher and his usual manner.'

'What an animal he is, to be sure.'

'Does he not put you in mind of a frog, Lizzie?'

'He does.' She snorted a laugh. 'I declare, this very minute he's sittin' on a lily pad, singin' with his friends.'

'Paddling about the boat, with only his eyes above the water?'

'Ah, for shame, the poor wee creature.' She sobered. 'But what in the world has he done to offend ye, now?'

'Just harping on about Mr Jay's Treaty, that's all. He longs to find it and make his fortune.'

'That's scarce a surprise.'

'He believes the captain has had it all along, in the mails. That the search has been a wild goose chase, to distract attention from its true whereabouts.'

She stretched. 'I suppose it's thinkable.'

'But then, for what possible reason was Jenkinson killed? Fletcher blames Peter Williams for it, of course, with no evidence at all. And he hopes to bribe the captain to part with the Treaty and dishonour his profession, the scoundrel.'

She slipped her hand down my chest. 'Which is why you're frettin'. 'Tis all very aggravatin', I agree, but there's time for work and time for play, my dear, and 'tis a blessin' I'm here to divert ye, else ye'd have no peace at all.'

23

L IZZIE FULFILLED HER intention to bring me peace so well that I watched Fletcher less keenly than I should have done over the following blissful days. In the end, it was the *fool of a woman* who found him out.

'*Ce connard, Monsieur* Fletcher, 'as outdone 'imself,' the comtesse announced when Philpott and I came into the saloon for afternoon tea. I was there reluctantly, for Trevenen, the second mate, had volunteered to teach Lizzie the mystery of measuring the ship's speed with the knotted log line, and I didn't trust his arm not to come about her waist in the process.

'*Vous comprenez*, I do not try to 'ear what passes yonder.' She meant the open window, which was only a man's height below the stern rail where so many conversations were wont to be conducted. 'But it is impossible to close my ears, especially when I am already 'alf asleep. I was reading on the seat there, this afternoon. *Comme d'habitude* it was noisy – the 'elmsman, the officers, the crew running about with their dreadful bare feet slapping. But at dinnertime, it comes quiet. Only a voice or two. I think to sleep.' She looked at us defiantly, as if we would disapprove of such weakness.

'Yes, *madame*?'

'A tap at my door wakes me. But by the time I rouse myself to open it, there is no one there, only 'eavy footsteps climbing to the deck. Then I 'ear voices at the rail. It is Captain Morris and *Monsieur* Fletcher. "Don't fear, Captain," Fletcher is saying. "The men are too far away to 'ear us, and the old woman downstairs is not in 'er cabin, I checked."' She nodded at us. 'You see, it was *Monsieur* Fletcher that knocked. But 'e was too quick in thinking I was not there. "Well, Captain?" *Monsieur* Fletcher asks. And then 'e says 'e will pay good money for the Treaty.' She frowned. '*Voyez*, that rascal, 'e even tries to bribe the captain! Can you believe it?'

'Stuff and nonsense.' Philpott wasn't greatly troubled. 'As if the captain could have the Treaty at all! God damn me, we've searched the ship from stem to stern, ain't we?'

'It is the *effronterie* of the man that never ceases to surprise me.'

'But what did the captain say?' I asked. 'How did he answer?'

'Oh, some laugh. Some talk of falling apples I do not understand, and then they walked away.' She nodded. '*Monsieur* Fletcher, 'e is lucky that the captain laughs and does not lock 'im up.'

I was sorry to believe it, but what else could possibly make the saturnine Captain Morris laugh, except joy at the delivery of his *windfall* of cash, and relief from anxiety?

And so, My Lord, I am happy to inform you that the matter is almost settled, at least as regards the whereabouts of the Treaty, which I firmly believe is now, or soon will be, in Obadiah Fletcher's possession. I can hardly go to the captain for help, of course, but I will keep Fletcher in my eye until we reach Barbados, and will there have him taken up, and the Treaty recovered. The document will be delivered to President

Washington in Philadelphia, and I hope the outcome will satisfy you.

One or two questions remain. Fletcher is certainly the *agent* Jenkinson wrote of, and came aboard with the full intention of stealing the Treaty. But he would never have been capable of wielding the spar that killed Jenkinson, and probably did find a member of the crew willing to do so on his instruction, as the comtesse supposes. When that proved fruitless, he turned his formidable mind to the actual whereabouts of the Treaty and found it out while the rest of us failed. The man who killed Jenkinson on his behalf is a murderer, of course, but that is thankfully a matter of naval discipline, and not one I am required to solve.

I have done my utmost to serve you, My Lord. Please give my regards to Sir James and Mr Aust – and, while I am unlikely ever to meet her again, ask the old man to convey my regards to his stepdaughter, Anne, of whom, as you know, I often think.

I am, as always, your humble servant, etc. etc.
LAURENCE JAGO
6 January 1795

PART TWO

Earth trembled from her intrails, as again
In pangs; and Nature gave a second groan;
Sky lour'd, and, muttering thunder, some sad drops
Wept at completing of the mortal sin
Original ...

John Milton, *Paradise Lost*, Book IX

From the captain's log

8 January 1795
Latitude 23°: 37' N and 31°: 38'W

Cape Verde and its pirates less than 200 leagues eastward. An extra watch at the masthead. The trouble I feared from one of our passengers has come to pass, just as I knew it would. God damn me for being so soft-hearted.

REPORT OF LAURENCE JAGO

For the attention of Foreign Secretary Lord Grenville,
Downing Street, London

My Lord

Affairs aboard this ship have gone worse than I could ever have imagined when I accepted your commission, and set sail upon her, on 10 December last. From the captain's papers, sent home on the *Antelope* packet from Madeira, I think you will, by now, have heard of the death of Mr Jenkinson of the War Office and the loss of Mr Jay's Treaty, guarded so jealously by his son under Jenkinson's eye and my own. I am sorry to inform you that a second death has occurred, and that I fear this death is by no means unconnected with the first, or with the loss of the papers you bid us guard. Were it not for the laudanum I would be ready enough to throw myself overboard after the poor devil who now brings the total of murders aboard this ship to two.

I thought myself cynical and hard to fool after my experiences in London, but that has proved far from the truth, and over the past four and twenty hours I have undergone something of an education in the brute realities of secrets and lies that your agents must evidently often navigate on behalf of King and Country. I made up my mind, far too quickly, as to the fate of Mr Jenkinson and the Treaty. I even wrote a report,

which I meant to send to you, explaining all my vapid reason-
ings, and which I am now tempted to file away in Davy Jones'
locker. But I will resist the promptings of injured pride and, on
reflection, I will enclose that report with this. If nothing else,
it is a bare account of the facts, with the dates and times of the
affair set down for our mutual convenience.

24

THE SQUALL BLEW up before dusk on 9 January, coming out of a sultry blue sky that had seemed to grow more airless all afternoon. There were a few moments of mad activity as the crew scrambled to lash down the hatches and secure anything loose to prevent it flying off into the darkening sky. I took a sharp blow to the head from the comtesse's sewing basket, as it crashed down from its overhead locker with a tremendous heel of the ship. The rain had started, and water was pooling at the bottom of the ladder, so that Theodore skated rather than walked to his cabin with an armful of papers. Philpott wrestled with a volley of books, flying at him from all directions out of unseen cubby holes. The ship heeled dreadfully, there was a shout of alarm from the deck, and then what seemed like half the ocean came flooding through the hatch. I thought we were all going to die. Bruin seemed of the same mind, for he burst from his cabin with a woof of alarm and hurried down the corridor to the comtesse's saloon, perhaps thinking she was the only one who could save him. I hadn't seen Lizzie all afternoon, but she was probably prostrate in her bunk, for this was the first bad weather we'd had since she came aboard, and she was likely seasick.

She reappeared at what passed for supper in these difficult times for the cook. When I came out of my cabin to the summons of the bell, she was sitting beside Philpott, who had recurred to my chequered past in misplaced good humour, as if he thought to distract her from the shuddering blows that assailed the ship with every passing wave.

'They are doleful creatures, those Ministry men of Laurence's,' he was observing, catching an errant knife out of the air as it flew from the table on an upward slant and aimed directly for his own throat. 'Shocking hypocrites, too. Lord Grenville, with his flowers, and Sir James with his poetry, while they seek to hang men on a whim, young woman, I assure 'ee.' I sat down beside Lizzie and she smiled briefly before turning her head back to Philpott, who was still rambling on. 'And old Aust, the permanent under-secretary ...' He winked at me. 'Well, well, perhaps we might let him off, for though he's as bloodthirsty as the rest of 'em, he has a pretty stepdaughter young Laurence has fancied these ten years. Hey, hey, my boy, ain't it so?'

Despite his jokes, my success in wooing Lizzie had either passed Philpott by entirely or else he thought to cement her regard by making her jealous. She was still smiling, but she had dropped her eyes to the cloth. I squeezed her hand under the heaving table as I said, 'Lizzie McKendrick also leaves a dozen disappointed suitors in her wake in Ireland, I don't doubt.'

IT WAS TREMENDOUSLY HOT. I fancied the equator a great wall of fiery air somewhere to the south of us, gusting its devilish heat at the ship as it laboured in the gale. I was bruised from the flying debris in the mess, but I wasn't tired or sick when I came into my cabin to find it lit by forbidden candlelight and Lizzie there, her back to me at the bunk, dressed only in her shift and her hair loose over her shoulders. In our hurried meetings in the ship's boat, I had not yet seen her so naked, and desire flooded me at once. I shut the door again, so quietly she didn't hear above the roaring waters. The cabin was so small I was practically touching her, and I slid my hands around her waist. She startled, with what seemed intense pleasure, and I buried my face in her neck, breathing her in.

She turned to me, wound her arms around my neck, and we fell back against the bunk as the ship heeled. I put my hand on the mattress to steady us and felt paper under my fingers. She was kissing me, and I tossed the thing away, before helping her up on to the bunk ahead of me with one hand while fumbling at my breeches buttons with the other.

Afterwards, we lay sprawled together naked on the narrow bunk, my arm bracing us against the violent action of the ship, her toes stroking my calf, her hand on my chest.

'You are shameless, Miss McKendrick,' I said. 'But you were certainly wise to come here or we should have drowned in the ship's boat.'

She didn't laugh, though she nestled closer. 'And I fear ye are as much of a rake as they called ye. What was she like, at all? The girl in England?' She had plainly been thinking over Philpott's words at dinner.

I wished I could tell her how very much my reputation was the reverse of the truth; but my own pride, as well as some vestigial discretion, kept my lips closed. How could I convey to her that Anne Bellingham had always been beyond my reach? And how might she take the implication that she, Lizzie, was not?

I moved my foot, and the paper I had felt under my fingers before crackled under my heel. I sat up, glad of any diversion from the need to answer, and took the paper up. Jenkinson's coded instructions.

'What the devil …' I swung my legs over the side of the bunk and held the paper to the light. Yes, it was definitely the torn letter I had been keeping among the papers under my bunk.

Lizzie spoke from behind me, hurriedly, as if she thought confession might avert my wrath. 'Oh, faith, ye'll hate me now.'

I turned to look at her, the paper loose in my fingers. She was staring at me, eyes wide in the candlelight.

'I was pokin' through yer things, Laurence. I never meant fer ye to find me here at all.' In the midst of her confession, she still dimpled. 'Though it's been grand, o'course.'

'What in God's name—'

'I just wanted to see. Wanted to find …' She dropped her eyes. Her voice faltered.

'Find what?'

I was shocked, I confess it, and, as she evidently feared, a little angry. She turned her face to the pillow, her shoulders shaking. 'A letter,' she said, muffled. 'From *her*. I couldn't bear it if ye was still writin' to her while we was …'

I smoothed Jenkinson's letter and slid down from the bunk to return it to its place among my belongings in the drawer under my bunk, which I saw now were disarranged. After the first flash of anger, I was only puzzled. 'Lizzie, I'm quite done in England. Anne Bellingham is likely engaged by now. I'll never see her again.'

'But ye've loved her this ten year. Mr Philpott said so.'

I neatened my books into a pile on top of the coded paper,

and slid the drawer closed. What was the puzzle? That she had searched my belongings, or that she cared enough to do so? I looked at her long, milky back, naked where she lay face down, her head turned away from me in shame. It was impossible to imagine any part of this scene with Anne Bellingham in it. 'I did love her, after a fashion. But never like this, Lizzie. Not real and solid and happy. Never happy. It was all just a dream.'

She stirred, and a lock of hair fell on to my hand, where I gripped the edge of the bunk. I took it between my fingers and wrapped it around my thumb. 'Shall I come with you to New York when we land?'

She was silent for a heartbeat, then lifted her head to look at me, wide-eyed, by the light of the illicit candle. 'Will Mr Philpott let ye come?'

'I'm not indentured to him, you know. My apprenticeship is voluntary. He'd give me a few days' leave, to see your show.'

'Oh.' She laid her face down on the pillow.

'What?'

'Nothin'.'

'What is it?'

'Nothin' at all. Only I thought …' Her eyes were oddly sober. 'I thought you meant *come with me* to stay.'

I was silenced for a moment, Kidd's speculations apparently answered. She was tired of her itinerant life and sought a marriage. Now I thought about it, in all our lovemaking she had feared no intimacy, nor paid any lip-service to avoiding the possibility of a child.

Searching my papers and now this. I saw she really cared for me. A room rose before my eyes, somewhere in a bustling American town. Lizzie in my bed, smiling without shame as I untied the strings of her shift and pulled it aside. If we lived together – if we married – such would be a joy to be savoured every morning and every night. Her mischief and liveliness every day, to shake off the black misery of the past years. And I had left England with so little hope.

'I'll ask him.'

She had begun to smile at me, tremulously, but now it faded. 'Ach, ye worship the man, sure. You'll never come to New York at all.'

'I swear I will. But then, afterwards, you must return to Philadelphia with me. There must be theatres there, too, where Bruin can display his talents, and we can be happy for ever.'

25

LIZZIE SLIPPED BACK to her cabin unseen, for decency's sake, but I felt disinclined to lie in my own bunk just now. I was in a curious state, fizzing with the confidences of the past hour, but uneasy, too, for the storm was still wild, rain slamming on the deck above, and I had no desire to be alone.

I had seen Philpott gravitating as naturally as Bruin had done towards the comtesse's saloon. When I followed them in, I saw that the extremity of the weather had wrought some changes to the apartment. Philpott was clinging to the bucking window seat, but the large windows had been shuttered, and only the ship's lantern shining through the pane in the roof cast any dim illumination over the comtesse's writing desk, where she sat turning over a spread of tarot cards. Prominent among them was Death again.

She raised her head as I came in, nodded, and tapped the ominous card. 'Well, *regardez, messieurs.*'Eaven calls us at last. We shall infallibly sink, and I am glad of it.'

That was all very well for her to say, but, naturally, it was just her usual drama, for hadn't she already told me the card meant only change or rebirth? And equally naturally, Philpott could not exercise his brains to see it, but sprang to his feet in an excess of concern. 'No, no, my dear Emilie. Never say so! There is always much to live for.' He was leaning his earnest pink face close to hers, and she put out a hand to grasp his own.

'For you, per'aps, my dear Philpott. But for myself, I will be glad to go to my son.'

If Philpott had been shot with one of Max's pistols, he could not have recoiled with more exaggerated astonishment. It hadn't occurred to me to tell him what I'd heard of the comtesse's past, and whatever other organs of intelligence he thought he had aboard had apparently failed to keep him informed on matters so close to his heart. 'I never knew you had a son, my dear.'

'Nor do I,' she answered with tremendous dignity. 'Not now. I 'ave not even 'is body, for the victims of the guillotine 'ave no tombs.'

Now I was also surprised. I had pictured her son's death a military one, on some distant Flanders battlefield, not under the blade in Paris. And yet it made a sudden sense. I had asked Max what happened to his family, but he had been evasive, angry. And hadn't I heard him say to his aunt, the day of Jenkinson's funeral, that there was *all this against us as a family?*

The blood began to thrum through my temples quietly, like a distant drum. 'When did your son die, *madame?*'

'In '92. Before what they call *la Terreur* even began.' She was holding her head erect, determined not to cry, and spoke raspingly. 'My son was one of *Monsieur* Guillotine's first victims, and a 'ero, *messieurs.* 'Ow much more a 'ero than 'is cousin Max, for all 'is little medal, which 'e only won for lifting a cannon off a wounded officer, a cannon which barely weighed a ton. I say to Max, *Be proud of what your cousin did*, but 'e will not see it so. Always so angry, as though it was François ruined our fortunes, and not the Revolution itself. As though there is any going back, when all that is gone, for ever. I say to 'im, *Even the odious Fletcher looks to the future, with 'is bribes and tricks. Be a man.* But 'e is so caught up in 'is own affairs, 'e does not see what goes on around 'im. Only looks at me and says, *Fletcher! What 'as Fletcher ever done?*

'*Only got 'imself the famous Treaty*, I say, and at that 'e stares at me as if 'e thinks I am out of my mind.'

'But your son's crime?' Philpott had not followed any of this diatribe, and to be truthful, neither had I, for the beat in my head was more insistent now and drowned everything but the growing sense of foreboding, gathering at the corner of my mind. 'What the devil did he do?'

'My son was a 'ero,' she said again. 'For many, many others, 'e 'elped to flee the blade.'

'Others? Aristocrats like yourself?'

'Excuse me,' I said, for the drum was now a din in my head, and any lingering new-found happiness with Lizzie abruptly banished. I dared not stay, or I would be driven to ask, with even more urgency than Philpott, what exactly her son had done in France. Whom exactly he had *helped to flee*. And above everything else, I desired not to know the answer.

26

I NEEDED AIR. Holding on tightly to the rope at the top of the companion ladder, I breathed in the salt wind that was blasting across the deck like heat from a furnace. The boards were bright in the moonlight, scrubbed clean by the rain and tossing waves as effectually as the crew could ever have done it with the severest application of elbow grease. But despite all the evidence, the sea must be falling, for there were other passengers on deck, and perhaps I was only dizzy from the shock of the comtesse's tormenting words.

I made my way to the capstan with something of a lurch, and caught hold of it for safety. The deck was striped with moonlight and the shadows of the rigging, and two figures were standing by the mainmast, barely ten paces ahead of me in the gloom. Lizzie, whom I had thought returned to her bunk, and the broad, strong figure of Max de Salles. Silhouetted against the silvery sea, the strong wind whipped Lizzie's words back to me.

'*Tu es sûr qu'il l'a?*'

I could feel the smooth wood of the capstan under my hand, while the deck planks lurched under my feet. Max said something I couldn't hear, and then she nodded.

'*Le-feras tu? Ou moi?*'

She called him 'tu'. How could they be so intimate when I had scarcely ever seen them together? First, I felt a stab of animal jealousy. Then a crashing wave of fury followed at my own idiocy for not registering at once the far graver trouble that she was speaking French at all. Fluent French at that, if with a soft Irish lilt, as charming in that tongue as in my own. And what possible construction could I put on the ominous words themselves? *Are you sure he has it? Will you do it, or will I?*

She was moving away from Max now, turning towards the companion ladder. I shrank against the capstan, but she had seen me. Her face lit up in a sudden smile, and she dropped the guide rope the crew had strung up around the deck and allowed herself to be blown into my arms, laughing.

I could have let her go. Watched her fly off into the howling darkness. But my arms caught her, my hands steadied her. 'Jaysus,' she shouted in my ear. '*Monsieur* Max thought 'twould be amusin' to see the storm. It's cracked, he is!'

I looked past her. Max had gone away, forward. *Will you do it, or will I?*

Her fingers were clutching my arms, hotter even than the wind that lifted my shirt, and her eyes were sparkling. 'Bless ye, Laurence, you're as solemn as a judge.' Her lips on mine, her hands in my hair. Was it possible that all these past days had been a mere simulacrum of happiness? Was it possible that she would lift up my head by the hair from the basket of the guillotine and show it to the triumphant crowd with equal joy? She had laughed when I had called my previous female acquaintance murderers, not whores, and here was another, seemingly, to add to my dismal tally.

I have thought myself wise, My Lord, and cynical enough,

at least when it came to politics. I think I even observed earlier in these papers that *nothing is ever as it seems*. I vowed, at that moment, that I would never make the same mistake again.

From the captain's log

10 January 1795

A troublesome squall last night, but now I detect the true Trades from the east, at last. Cloud prevented an observation this noon, but by yesterday's reckoning, Barbados is only 700 leagues distant, which is good fortune, for after our financial disappointments in Madeira, we are tolerably well provisioned, but there is no plenty. Six salt beef barrels remain, and sixteen of water.

My Complaint only worsens, and I am hippish.

27

I WAS THERE WHEN a water barrel came up empty, shortly after dawn, for I'd been awake all night, watching as the squall blew itself away off our starboard quarter towards Europe and home. The captain only tutted at this inconvenience and ordered up another. When the second barrel also came up empty, he was vexed.

'Good God, Mr Peters,' he said to the first mate. 'Did you not lash the infernal things in Madeira? You should know as well as I that a squall can come on us at any moment. We've scant provisions enough without mishaps such as these. Yes, yes,' to the enquiring look from the third mate on the pulley. 'Try again.'

Five more barrels were tried, and five more came up empty. Captain Morris was no longer angry, but suddenly anxious and sweating. His fears were justified. The casks had come adrift from their moorings in the storm, the men in the hold reported, and had smashed about like ninepins, heavy enough to crush an arm, a leg or a head, if any man had been unfortunate enough to be down there. Heavy enough, at least, to spring each other's joints on impact. Moreover, there was only a little left in the scuttlebutt for drinking. Captain Morris closed his eyes for a moment, before glancing up to the rigging and the snap of the sails.

By now, the news had spread throughout the ship, and Philpott arrived at the captain's elbow, clucking his tongue. Max had also appeared, leaning on the rail, his hand wrapped in a bandage, and Peter Williams was beside him, wearing an expression I could hardly fathom. Lizzie was still below, probably sleeping peacefully in her cabin, but for the first time I was relieved by her absence.

'We're making good speed,' the first mate was reassuring Philpott, as the sailors in the hold delved deeper in search of undamaged barrels. 'Ten knots, according to calculation – and if the wind keeps up, we might be in Barbados within the fortnight. Fourteen days, at short rations, and we could do it on half a dozen casks.'

Philpott was aghast. 'Six barrels of water, to last near two thousand miles! And what if the winds fail us?'

'Then we'll be looking out, uncommon anxious, for another ship or a good rainfall.'

'Is there land near?' Max asked. 'Could we re-provision ourselves?'

'Only by beating back into the wind, eastwards to Cape Verde.' Captain Morris had rejoined us from a brief reverie. 'An undertaking which has its own hazards. Not to mention that the islands are lawless and infested with slavers and French privateers. No, Mr Peters is right. We have finally caught the trades, good and proper, which are reliable so long as we don't run into a hurricane.'

Philpott's unruly mind scampered off directly. 'Hurricane! And did you not get blown into the Sargasso by just such an article last voyage? The gunner told me all about it.'

'The gunner is prone to exaggeration, Mr Philpott.'

'But it is possible? To be blown about by another squall, or becalmed? In other words, to be delayed beyond the compass of six barrels of water?'

'All things are possible at sea, Mr Philpott, as I dare say you have noticed.'

'And how close is Cape Verde, with all its delightful streams?'

'If we turn now, we might be there by morning.'

Max stepped forward from his place at the rail. The bandage on his hand was dark with dried blood. Not fresh, but rather a wound sustained some hours ago. 'Then I beg you reconsider, *Capitaine*,' he said, with his usual saturnine fire. 'Cape Verde cannot possibly be more hazardous than the gamble you propose. For my aunt's sake, I insist that we turn for land at once.'

The captain frowned, but all these remonstrances proved needless in any case. Only three barrels contained any water at all, and even they were leaking badly as they were lifted up through the hatch and stood hastily on end. There was no choice remaining but to beat back to the islands as Max, Lizzie's partner in subterfuge, had so peremptorily urged.

THOUGH THE SQUALL had passed, the sea was still rough as the ship turned back into the brisk following wind and began to shoulder aside the waves, striking manfully back towards Cape Verde, which lay directly to stern. I followed Captain Morris to the wheel and requested a private word. Under the general racket of wind and waves, I told him all the new suspicions that had come upon me since the previous night.

'It don't surprise me you're in Grenville's pay,' he said, taking out his pipe thoughtfully, 'being always on the watch, as you are. But your reasoning is mighty conjectural, sir. Max de Salles strong enough to kill Jenkinson with that spar? Well, it might be so, but why should he? Lizzie McKendrick inveigling herself into all men's confidence? She's a chancer, I can see that much, but it don't mean she's a spy.'

'I heard her address him in French last night. I saw him go towards the hatch to the hold. The water casks are broken, and he has an injury that he might have sustained in loosening the ropes to set them rolling.'

More conjecture, no doubt, and the captain wasn't listening. 'You saw him? In the full dark?'

'I saw him venture forward from the mainmast.'

The captain tutted at such poor evidence. 'We may encounter the French with or without an agent's help, sir. And the squall was quite enough to break the casks without human aid and injure a man quite innocently.' He looked at me. 'But supposing all this is true, what would you have me do?'

'Lock them up, so I may deliver them to justice either in Cape Verde or Barbados.'

'And where do you propose I confine them, aboard this small ship? There's scarcely room to pen up the livestock. Besides,' he had broken his own rules, lighting his pipe and puffing vigorously, 'Max de Salles is a French nobleman. I can't submit him to such indignity without much better reasons than you've given, Mr Jago.'

'He helped Fletcher mend his model – accepted his offer of a position in America. Don't you think that strange in a proud French nobleman?' I was in earnest. 'If Lizzie is the agent I was bid to find, and Max somehow in league with her, it would be convenient to be forced back to land where the Treaty might be sent on its way to Paris.'

'The Treaty! And what in the world makes you think they've got it, after all the infernal trouble we've had?'

'I'm afraid Max knows about Mr Fletcher and the papers, sir.' In my wakefulness I had finally remembered the exchange with her nephew that the comtesse had described to us last night in her saloon. I found myself apologetic. 'The comtesse heard you talking of it, and unfortunately told him. I'm afraid he'll try to get them. And after Jenkinson—'

'A deal of gossip aboard this ship, seemingly.' The captain's expression was hard to read, but he sounded professional and self-confident enough. 'And why Max de Salles should thereby conclude Fletcher has the Treaty I don't understand.'

He turned away, the matter closed. But his puzzlement was surely feigned, I thought, as I walked the sloping deck back towards the companion ladder to the mess. I had lost faith in everyone aboard, except for Theodore, Peter Williams and Philpott, who I knew as well as myself.

THE SUN BLAZED OUT as the clouds dispersed westwards, and the passengers emerged from their cabins, all except for Max, who seemed to have taken himself off to nurse his wound in solitude. Lizzie followed me about the ship, chattering breezily, while I shadowed Fletcher, so loyally that he began to shrink away from me. At least while I had him under my eye I knew he was safe. For even if the captain wasn't lying, Max *thought* Fletcher had the Treaty, and I feared he would try to take it from him, whatever the cost.

And the cost might be high. I remembered Max's strange elation at the weightlifting competition, which had made me think him capable of anything. I remembered the extraordinary physique he kept hidden beneath his coat. And only the previous evening, I had learned that he won his military medal for a feat of strength beyond imagining, however his aunt might belittle it. Philpott had dismissed my growing suspicions after the trial of strength, but then Fletcher had told me Max was indeed interested in the Treaty. Fletcher had put it down to the Frenchman's poverty and that had seemed possible, even if it went so much against his honour and the interests of the Royalists. But now Lizzie's inexplicable involvement – and this strange, French exchange between them – left me newly baffled and frightened.

'Ye do be quite the quiet one, today,' Lizzie observed as I failed to match her cheerfulness. In fact, I distrusted it, as more evidence that she was close to the fulfilment of her wicked intentions, and I only shook my head. Unlike her, I was no actor, and couldn't hide my unease.

At sunset, the ship was all scarlet light where the dying rays slanted, and deep crimson shadow where they could not reach. We were scudding across a wine-dark sea, Ben helping the third mate sing out the knots from the trailing log line to the captain at the wheel with a minute-glass. Lizzie had abandoned my unsettled company and attached herself to Theodore, whom she presently followed below. I took my chance, crossing the deck to Fletcher, who only grunted a reluctant greeting. He looked downcast.

'How does your search prosper?' I leaned on the rail and glanced at him sideways, feigning an eager, conspiratorial air. Fletcher's large eyes slid towards me, but he didn't answer. 'Has Morris succumbed to your proposals? Has he given you the paper?'

Fletcher swelled slightly, but it was a shadow of his former bluster. 'If he has, I ain't obliged to tell you.'

'No, indeed.' He was shifty as the devil of a sudden, all

friendliness abated. Had he got wind of his danger? Was he, somehow, afraid of me, too? 'But if the paper's still missing, I could help you find it.'

  "Fraid I'm out of the game, Mr Jago.' Fletcher deflated suddenly, as shrivelled as a flattened toad. 'I wish you luck in your hunt, if you choose to undertake it, but I can't be a party to it any longer.'

28

I WATCHED EVERYONE go to their cabins before I lay down on my own bunk, with Mr Gibbs on my feet. I hadn't slept the previous night, and now my scalp crawled and my eyes itched with exhaustion, but I must stay vigilant for Fletcher's sake.

I stiffened as somewhere out in the mess a door creaked. I half rose to investigate, but a moment later there was a tap at my door. It was Lizzie, in her shift again, and she brought the scent of cologne with her as if she had been bathing to please me.

'Jesus, Mary and Joseph,' she said as she came in, 'Theodore Jay has had me in his cabin again, this past hour, full of preachin'.'

Mr Gibbs grunted, and leapt down from the bunk stiffly, sloping out into the mess as she closed the door behind him. The comtesse had called Lizzie a *cruel woman* when she first came aboard with her dancing bear, and later Philpott had grumbled when Lizzie left the creature to wander the ship alone. I had disregarded them – even defended her – but now I remembered how Bruin was always hungry, begging biscuits from the crew. Had I ever seen Lizzie feed him? Had I ever seen her tending his cabin or grooming his fur? I had never even seen her stoop to scratch Mr Gibbs's ears. She had no natural sympathy for animals at all.

Had she come aboard with the bear, then, only as a distraction from her true purpose? A creature she did not care for, and whom she could neither train nor control? I was sure she was Irish – that much was not feigned – but where had she been before we met? If her fluency was any indication, she had been in France a good long time.

She came to my arms as soon as the door closed, with a comfortable laugh of pleasure. It was pitchy dark, with no candle lit, and the only sound our breath as we kissed. If she sensed reluctance in my embrace, it only urged her on, and she pressed me on to the bunk eagerly, pulling at my shirt.

I submitted to her caresses – what man could not? – but all the while I was listening for sounds outside in the mess. The labouring sea made it hopeless, the timbers all around us creaking and groaning, and even as she took me, I was remembering the blow of a spar on a man's defenceless head. The spatter of brains and blood.

THIS TIME, SHE DID not leave me for her own bunk, but curled into my side on the narrow mattress, yawned as prodigiously as Bruin, stroked my cheek, and seemed to go directly to sleep. I stared into darkness and wondered what to do. Was she instructed to keep me here, while Max went to Fletcher for the Treaty? If I confronted her with my suspicions, would the next defenceless head be mine? Another death might stir the captain into action, but it would be scant consolation if that death was my own.

I lay frozen into indecision, her warm breathing on my neck. The pleasure and the peril of our lovemaking had spent me, and, despite everything, I must have dozed, for the next thing I knew I was alone in the dark. I sat bolt upright and listened. Further off, I thought I heard another door slam. I pulled on my shirt and breeches, opened my own door with the utmost caution, and went barefoot out into the mess.

Water was swilling around the decks as the ship laboured, and had seeped down through the hatches, lying in puddles outside my door. I listened for a moment. Philpott was snoring in his cabin, and there were no lights anywhere. I checked the water closet, which was empty, and then knocked softly at Fletcher's door. No answer. I knocked again, more loudly, and then pulled at the handle. The door opened easily, and the cabin was so small that, even without the candle lit inside, I could see at once that it was empty.

Yes, my eyes were growing used to the darkness. Mr Gibbs roused himself with an irritable groan from under the table and followed at my heels as I went to the companionway and climbed up, rung by rung, into faint, silvery moonlight gleaming off the sails, the spars and the brass trimmings along the rail. The wind was hot as it lifted my untucked shirt and sent it flapping.

Obadiah Fletcher was standing on the quarterdeck, a small squat silhouette, one hand clutching the rail, alone but for the silent helmsman at the wheel. The rest of the watch were invisible, perhaps dozing in the shadows at their duty. Even in the dim light I could see that Fletcher was holding a bundle of papers rolled up in his fist. If I hadn't known better, I would have sworn that he was about to throw them overboard, but that would make no sense at all.

I started towards him, and perhaps he heard me, despite the loud sea, for he span about. But the next moment I saw that it wasn't me that had startled him, but the dark figure at the wheel. I thought I saw Fletcher's lips move, as if in answer to an unheard question, and the next moment the helmsman let go of the spokes and dived across the short space between them.

Helmsman? No, the wheel was lashed steady with rope and the figure who had pretended to hold it was someone who seemed much more familiar than one of the crew. It must be Max, I thought, struggling with Fletcher at the rail, but however strong the Frenchman might be, Fletcher gave a convulsive heave and managed to break free, still in possession of the papers. His coat flapping, he bounded for the stern, the other figure in close pursuit.

'What in Christ's name is going on?'

Max was at my shoulder. And Lizzie beside him, her face equally amazed. For a moment I couldn't make sense of it. But here they were and had only now come banging up the ladder from our quarters.

'It's Fletcher with the Treaty,' I said. 'You're – that is, *someone*'s after him.'

There was no time for more, for on the deserted, moonlit deck the chase was still in motion. I could see Fletcher again, now at the stern rail, once more locked in an embrace with his much taller pursuer. Slippery as ever, he writhed, then punched the other figure squarely in the guts. The shape doubled over, and though it wasn't Max it was certainly a man whose manner I knew just as well. Fletcher ran forward at a loping pace, against the bucking of the ship. Perhaps he had lost his bearings, for he didn't turn for the companion ladder. He didn't see us standing at the top of the steps, and he was still out of hearing as I shouted for him to come to safety.

The following figure was still after him, and behind them

I could now also see the dark shape of Mr Gibbs, ears flopping in pursuit. There was nowhere left to go but the forepeak and the heads. The deck was slick with water and the squat Fletcher was more sure-footed than his adversary. Meanwhile, Max slithered behind me, reeling with every punching wave, as I fought my way after the two men who were now gone into the shadows beyond my sight.

When I passed the ship's boat, Fletcher's flapping coat revealed him balancing precariously on the swooping grating of the heads, above the churning sea. Mr Gibbs had him cornered, and was barking persistently, but the shrill edge to the dog's cry was drowned by the roar of wind and waters and still the sailors slept on, the scene unfolding in eerie solitude. I hastened my step and clutched at the following figure, only a fraction beyond my grasp. I knew him now as well as myself, the cool tilt of his head as he hesitated before launching himself forward with uncharacteristic passion – and Fletcher let go of the papers.

They flew directly towards me, caught in the roaring trade wind that battled the ship for forward motion, white as doves in the darkness. I almost thought one sheet grazed my fingertips, but they were flying too high above my outstretched hands, out into the sparkling blackness of the moonlit ocean.

When I turned back towards the bowsprit, the two figures were locked together for a third and final time on the lurching grating. Fletcher once more freed himself with a convulsive heave which, this time, sent him windmilling back towards the grating edge and the open sea. He held out his hands in terror, and his pursuer lunged after him. There was a brief confusion of wrestling bodies, and then, as only one dark shape came staggering back from the edge, I saw that Fletcher was gone. Another moment's hesitation, and the remaining figure was scrambling up into the rigging, using his hands and feet in the careful way he had done among the sailors at Philpott's trial of strength. He was silhouetted against the pale canvas sails for a moment, plain to my vision, one white sheet of paper clutched in his hand, before he vanished out of sight.

I ran to the side, where Max and Lizzie were gazing down into the water, straining to see movement in the waves. But there was nothing. Not even two eyes, in a green head, emerging from the deep. Max roused himself and cried out, '*Man overboard!*' but his voice was hoarse with exertion, and the ship was bucking so violently that, even if Fletcher were alive, we would never retrace our course to find him. Max leaned over the rail and was suddenly and violently sick.

The rigging was empty now, Fletcher's murderer melted into the night. 'Did you see who it was?' I asked Max anxiously.

He wiped his mouth on his sleeve and looked at me. 'No,' he answered, to my relief. 'Only a shape in the darkness.' He was already moving away, Lizzie beside him.

'Where are you going?' I pulled myself to my feet and followed. His voice came back to me faintly, against the wind.

'To tell the *capitaine* about Fletcher.'

And again, as before, the wind whipped Lizzie's words back to me.

'*Quelle absurdité est-ce que c'est, que ça?*'

We alone had witnessed the fight and Fletcher's murder, at the hands of a man I had first thought was Max but was not. A man who had chased Fletcher into the sea, and who had climbed the rigging to escape. The man who had not been Max but had indubitably been Peter Williams.

A Misadventure aboard Ship

A Pound to a Penny, John Barleycorn will think himself very well situated where he sits by the Fireside when he has read this Letter, the latest from the Tankerville, as small a Dot in the wide Ocean as a man might possibly conceive.

What a Storm we suffered! Not quite a Hurricano, the Captain tells me, and from this I can confidently aver, dear John, that a Hurricane is a thing to be as greatly feared as a Fire in a Hay Barn. For even the Squall we suffered was enough to make a man think himself drowned already. How the Ship groaned! How she sprang with a thousand leaking joints and tumbled about in the Waves like an Apple in a vigorous game of bobbing!

Thank God she did not founder, and William Philpott remains to you, only a little bruised and stunned. But we have lost a second Passenger – a worthy Gentleman from Savannah, Georgia, swept overboard by a tremendous Wave. An Accident, the Captain calls it, and perhaps it was, but infected by the Crew's dark Superstitions I almost think it an Act of vengeful Providence against presumptuous Man, who dares confront the almighty Power of His creation by venturing out on to this monstrous wide Ocean at all!

29

'*LAND HO!*' jerked me out of a laudanum stupor the next morning. I had been dreaming of Peter Williams, and now I could hear his voice out in the mess, in conversation with the captain. By the time I came out of my cabin, however, he was gone.

'No one knows anything more,' Captain Morris was saying sombrely to Philpott and the comtesse, who were together at the table alone, while Mr Gibbs snaffled up their bountiful leavings. 'But Max de Salles saw the poor devil fall. Fletcher was not a pleasant man, but it's a damned bad way to go. Alone, and in the dark.'

'Poor creature,' said the comtesse, with an absolute absence of sympathy or sorrow.

We were already coming into Praia harbour, heeling into a stiff breeze that carried us quickly past the headland, the low bare hills emerging from shadow into substance. I needed to determine a course of action, and quickly.

Peter Williams had pursued Fletcher around the ship, Peter Williams had wrestled with him at the bowsprit and sent him plunging to his death, and Peter Williams had clambered away through the rigging with a page of the Treaty in his hand.

It was at that moment I knew my first report to you was useless, My Lord, and even my subsequent reasoning had been faulty. It was Max and Lizzie I had feared would hurt Fletcher, but now how obvious it seemed that, despite appearances, Peter Williams had every reason to wish Theodore and his father ill and be willing to sell the Treaty for his own reward. Even one page would be worth a good deal, and Cape Verde, haunt of pirates and privateers, would be a fine place to sell it and disappear. We had all disliked Obadiah Fletcher, but who could have hated him more than Peter Williams? Fletcher had insulted and demeaned him. It wasn't hard to conclude that the slave might have had scant compunction in pushing the slave-master overboard, for the sake of his own freedom, and in moral retribution for the countless others who would never taste it.

I was in a fever of mixed emotions, I confess it. If the paper would buy his freedom then why should I not stand aside and let him go? I might pretend it was loyalty to you, My Lord, that decided me, but that would be a lie. The truth was that I had spent so long in pursuit of the Treaty I couldn't bear to see it gone and all my own pains for naught.

I am not proud of this, but at least I never thought of betraying him. Peter Williams might be a thief and a killer, but he was my friend. Nevertheless, I told myself that the enterprise he had embarked upon would infallibly lead him to ruin. He would never see his wife or children again and would live out his life a hunted man. If I could only retrieve the page he had taken, before he could seek to use it, I could quietly conceal the evidence of what might have amounted only to momentary madness.

Under the influence of these pious convictions, so convenient to my own interest, I looked for him in steerage, but he wasn't there. His hammock was stowed away with the rest of the crew's belongings; his dunnage was in its usual place. After a swift glance around me I fumbled with the buckles of his portmanteau, swaying as the ship tacked and there was a volley of shouts from deck.

His shaving kit came first to light, neatly stowed in a soft leather pouch. Then a quantity of clean shirts, then a spare wig and a stock or two. I recognised his second-best suit from the comtesse's spell inhabiting it, and a pair of buckled shoes suitable for Whitehall. Under them, at the very bottom of the portmanteau, was a large sheet of paper – probably twice the size of our ministerial Demy. It was certainly not a page from the Treaty, but I looked at it with swift curiosity, for I'd seen nothing like it before.

The sheet, unfolded, was covered in diagrams, drawn in faint lead pencil with inked annotations. Letters and numbers. Something about a mule. Something about a jenny. A name: Arkwright. It meant nothing to me. I folded it away, replaced the shoes, and as I did so something else rustled and, thank God, from one of the shoes I drew another sheet of paper.

A hand on my arm made me startle. It was Ben, frowning slightly. 'Why you do be fossickin' in Mr Williams's things?'

I shoved the paper hastily in my pocket without looking at it, and began stowing the slave's possessions away again. I thought of pretending he himself had sent me on this errand, but that was no good, for Ben would be sure to tell him.

I re-buckled the portmanteau. 'You have secrets yourself, don't you, Ben? Secrets about Mr Jenkinson's possessions, remember?' I felt at my neck, pulled out the topaz cross from where I now kept it, and held it out for the boy's inspection. Ben's eyes widened. Above our heads the capstan had begun to turn. We were anchoring, and Peter Williams would likely soon be here to collect the prize in his shoe and take it ashore.

'If you keep my secrets, I'll keep yours, child. Is it a bargain?' I stuck out my hand. After a moment Ben put his small fingers in mine, and I squeezed them. 'Good boy. Keep your mouth shut and I'll do the same for you.'

It was cruel to threaten him. I left the boy looking rather dejected and went back to my cabin, closing the door with a sigh of relief. But when I pulled the paper out of my pocket and unfolded it, it was not a page of the Treaty either. I swore under my breath, first in disappointment and then in surprise, for instead, it was part of a letter, neatly torn across the bottom. On one side, gibberish written in Your Lordship's hand. On the other, your signature. It was that missing portion of Jenkinson's instructions torn from the letter I had found the day of his death.

The cypher for that letter was now on my shelf, removed from Jenkinson's cabin when Bruin moved in. I seized the book and turned quickly to the same page as before, decoding as though my life depended on it. I could hear Peter Williams's voice calling out, harassed, from the mess. Surely to God he hadn't already discovered his loss?

We do not fight the French and go to all these lengths to appease the Americans, only to see our interests injured by other means. We have had too little information, I am afraid, to help you further, and you may very well question such draconian orders, but you must trust that the organs of intelligence at our disposal see this matter as vital to the Country's interests as the Treaty. The main thing is to

apprehend the perpetrator and his prize, so that others may
be discouraged from imitation.

The letter made little more sense in translation. And why the devil did Peter Williams have it? Where had he got it from? Had he stolen it from Jenkinson's cabin before I got there, on the day the War Office official died? I thought I remembered meeting him in the shadows outside Jenkinson's door that day.

But, if so, what on God's earth had possessed him to tear that particular paragraph from the rest of the note? Peter Williams would not have been capable of its translation, since he did not have the key to the cypher. What did he think it was? What had Jenkinson *told* him it was? Had Jenkinson, in fact, torn the sheet himself and given this piece to Peter Williams? Was it an act of self-defence? A desperate attempt to repel attack and save his own life? Had Peter Williams, *tall and vigorous*, as Philpott had once observed, also been responsible for Jenkinson's death?

But I was wasting time. Whatever the circumstances, if Peter Williams had had this from Jenkinson weeks ago, then it was not the paper that he had caught out of the air the previous night. That paper must still be in his pocket, and I had to find him before he had the chance to damn himself entirely.

By now we had anchored, and I could hear bumboats already arriving, cheerful rough voices raised in welcome. When I got on deck, I saw that we were moored hardly two hundred yards out from land, and Peter Williams was already ashore, walking away briskly into the ragged crowd.

In the excitement I had forgotten Max. What he and Lizzie might be up to, now we were moored, was a question I hadn't the time to answer until the cook stopped me on my hasty way through the mess.

'Your breakfast, sir? I don't believe you've had it.' His face was mottled and hectic, and I surmised he'd been at the rum.

'No need, Mr Hind, I'm going ashore.'

'Oh but sir, you must never go ashore on an empty stomach. 'Twouldn't be healthy.'

'I'm afraid I haven't time.'

'A little coffee, then?' The cup was already in his hand. 'It's the last of the water, but we'll be taking on more within the hour.'

Mr Hind's coffee, made with the dregs of the scuttlebutt, seemed the least possible inducement and I shook my head impatiently, but he was blocking my way and in the end I drank it off to please him. It was more than usually brackish and foul.

I thrust the empty cup back into his hands. 'Have you seen the Frenchman? Or Lizzie McKendrick?'

'Frenchie's in his cabin. Woman just went ashore.'

If there had been the slightest shred of doubt in my mind that Lizzie was involved in some nefarious plot, it evaporated in that moment. I ran up on deck where the rest of the passengers were in dialogue with a very convincing local. There was a tavern he could heartily recommend, and where under no circumstances would they be robbed or kidnapped. This seemed a faint endorsement, but I climbed down into his boat anyway, and bid him row me ashore across the choppy waters of the harbour. I could see Mr Gibbs watching forlornly from the entry port, and Philpott waving for me to return, but I ignored them both. The island's governor was the only man with the authority – or the dungeons – to imprison my suspects. I would go to him first and set up a search for Lizzie. Then I would look for Peter Williams. Even if he still had his snippet of Treaty, and handed it over, it would be of little consequence to the state of nations. It was the Treaty's accumulation of clauses – which taken together were so detrimental to the Americans and satisfactory to the British – that mattered in the wider scheme of things.

As I stepped ashore on to the filthy cobbles of the quayside, the solid earth smacked against the soles of my feet, and I staggered. The world tilted, and a wave of clammy nausea washed over me. The boatman laughed. 'Sea legs!' he shouted, apparently highly amused. There was no time for such weakness now – Peter Williams had shown none. But my stomach griped strangely as I raised my head and surveyed my surroundings.

Behind the landing place, the ground rose in a series of scrubby terraces to the town. Beyond that, in the far distance, mountains loomed. The earth was russet red, the sparse vegetation grey-green. It was hot and dry as I climbed the hill, up towards the centre of the town. After so many idle weeks aboard my legs were unused to the effort, and I began to pant and sweat under my collar as I passed low, whitewashed buildings that straggled haphazardly up the hill towards the mountainous interior. My stomach was definitely uneasy, and the place looked menacing. Somewhere in the back of my mind, I had known that Cape Verde was a slaving post, being so conveniently placed between Africa and the Caribbean, and on the universal shipping road of the trade winds. Looking back down at the harbour I could see a couple of large Guineamen, anchored further offshore than the *Tankerville*. They would not want their cargo escaping, and among the Europeans that swarmed the streets I saw hard-faced officers, likely from those dreadful hulks, bargaining for provisions with equally hard-faced merchants. I hadn't the faintest clue how to find Peter Williams, and now I also feared for his safety among these traders in human flesh.

I paused, meaning to ask directions to the governor's residence, but then a wave of sickness overtook me, and I bent double. More urgently than anything now, I needed somewhere to empty my churning guts. I stumbled on, coming out into a marketplace. There were crowds all around, stalls of spices and vegetables, and bolts of vivid cloth. I stopped abruptly, and a woman walking behind me with a basket of fruit on her head nearly came to grief. I muttered an apology, but Jesu, the urge to shit was coming on me like a wave, and I was running with sweat. I hobbled sideways through the crowd until I came to a narrow street that led off the marketplace and petered out into scrubby wasteland and trash. Humiliating as it was, it would have to do, and I fumbled at my breeches buttons feverishly. There was something terribly wrong, something worse than sea-legs. What had I eaten? Whatever it was seemed now urgently bent on seeing the light of day, and I had no choice but to squat there, like an infant just out of napkins. Or like Mr Jenkinson at the heads. An image of his haggard face rose before my eyes, and remembering how I had laughed at him, I groaned with pain and mortification.

There was no nausea any more – that was one blessing – but I was utterly incapable of finding the governor or pursuing Peter Williams. As my guts cramped and cramped again, I imagined the slave handing over his scrap of the Treaty and demanding cash, somewhere far away about the town. But which would be more valuable? His paper or himself? He was tall, handsome and educated. And, from where I squatted abjectly, I could see down to the docks where a slave auction seemed to be in progress. Just one or two figures in chains, and hard to see from this distance whether they were male or female. A small affair – one of no interest to any but those concerned – and yet an epoch in the lives of those sold, their whole future existence determined by the mere pass of a coin between two hardened palms.

I could see the *Tankerville*, too. She was taking on water at a feverish rate – Captain Morris had declared his determination to get in and out of lawless Praia without mishap, and that meant speed. He would damn me roundly if I was late back to the ship. And the longer they waited, the more time Lizzie would have to find her French contacts. Would the French now be in pursuit of Peter Williams too, and the one piece of paper that remained from the document they were so eager to find? Even a clause or two of the Treaty's contents would be information they did not now possess. Between the French and the slavers, Peter Williams might be lucky if the only news that came back to ship was of his desertion.

My body could scarcely contain anything more, but each time I rose to my feet another spasm came. In the end I was just passing water. What had the sailors said about Jenkinson? *Ins and outs all backsyfore.* The joke seemed nearly as grim in my case as in his own. And then, as I squatted there, for longer than you could conceive possible, My Lord, I remembered the cook's strange insistence that I drink his foul-tasting coffee and I was suddenly sure I had been poisoned. Had Lizzie felt my hesitation, my suspicion, last night, even as I held her in my arms? Had she used her charm to persuade Hind to pass me something fatal, and stop me acting upon those doubts? What in God's name had she given me? Kidd, the surgeon, might conceivably save my life, but only if I could get myself somehow back to the ship.

The procession of water barrels to the *Tankerville* seemed to be petering out, and even from here I could see figures at the rail, looking out towards the shore. The sun was past its height. I remembered something about leaving with the tide. I peered down again at the shore, the dusty sand of the beach. There was no dark line to be seen at the high-tide mark. Unless the stiff hot breeze had blown away the moisture, the tide must be at the full. I needed to get down there, or risk being left behind and stranded.

I got to my feet and nearly fell. I was as weak as a new-hatched chick. I redid my buttons with trembling fingers, and for my own self-respect kicked a cloud of dust and rubble over the mess I left behind. The cramps were still coming, but I was spent, dried out, and at least I could walk again, though bent double like an old man.

I began this wretched progress back along the street into the marketplace, where the stalls were now closing and the crowds thinning. No one spared me even a cursory glance. An ill foreigner was of no use to the stallholders. But beyond the marketplace a group of children began to gather behind me, slipping out of doorways and whispering. They reminded me of the street children of Lincoln's Inn Fields, who were fierce as they were motherless, and they could see I was weak. They would pounce, when their numbers were large enough to bring me down, and they would take whatever valuables I might possess. I wished for Mr Gibbs, back on board the ship, and then realised that if I missed the *Tankerville*'s departure, I would be left here penniless, alone and helpless, food for the rats that scuttled at the edges of my vision among the piles of rubbish.

My head was pounding from squatting so long in the blinding sun, and I was ragingly thirsty. My body ached as if a wave had picked it up and dashed it against the rocks. I thought of the dying captain entirely without pity. I wished Peter Williams luck in his chosen path and had no more desire to find him. Even Lizzie could take the Treaty and I would not complain. Not if I could only escape these predatory children, get to the peace of my bunk, and feel Gibbs's affectionate lick on my hand again.

I turned to snarl at my pursuers and came face to face with Peter Williams.

'God help me,' I said weakly. 'I am ill. Dying.'

He put his arm around my back and pulled my hand across his shoulder.

'I was looking for you,' I said. 'Did you sell it?'

'Sell what?'

'The page you saved. I saw you with Fletcher. Saw you—' I broke off. Accusing the only man here to help me of murder would be stupid. Might be the last stupid act I would ever be permitted to perform. But at any rate he didn't answer, only tightened his grasp on my waist and pulled me along more firmly.

'The tide,' I babbled on. 'They'll leave on the tide. Captain Morris said so.'

We were on the brow of the last terrace, looking down over the harbour. The stiff breeze carried the shouts of the crew across the water. 'They're leaving,' Peter Williams said, and went plunging down the sandy slope towards the quayside. I could hear the turning capstan and the faint shouts of the crew, but more vivid to my mind was Peter Williams's laboured breath, the clattering of scree under our feet, and the ever-present fear of falling. We were going too fast, and I was weaker than ever. Then, as in a dream, I saw there was a boat at the dock, waiting. Our boat, from the *Tankerville*, with the third mate standing in the prow, scanning the hillside, the rope in his hand. I could have wept for joy.

But he had seen us too, and for some inexplicable reason he was angry. He held up his palm as if to ward us off. Peter Williams kept going. I wondered if I was feverish, for I almost thought I could hear the third mate shouting 'no, no!' as we came hastening along the cobbles.

I turned up my eyes to squint at Peter Williams as he bellowed at the man in the boat. 'I'll not leave him behind. He'll die here. And you'll have another curse on your heads.'

'He won't *die*.'

'He'll be robbed and beaten, and worse.'

'None of our doin'.'

'Come, Mr Rogers, I've told you—'

'Told us quite enough. Damned if I don't leave you both.'

'I'm so thirsty,' I said. The idea of robbery, beating, rape or murder seemed just at this moment less alarming than the sudden terrible dryness of my throat. 'Please to God, give me a drink.'

Peter Williams tightened his hold on me. He was quivering with pent-up fury as he stared at Mr Rogers. 'Very well, then. I'll stay with him, at the risk of my own neck, too. Get back to the ship, and may God damn your soul to hell.'

The third mate had already untied the rope from its half-rotted post. As he let go, a cannon boomed across the bay behind him. Rogers turned to look. A ship was emerging from behind the headland to the right of the bay, tacking into a cross breeze that carried her neatly round the point. The cannon at her bow was still smoking.

'It's the French,' Peter Williams said with what seemed like unfounded certainty, and there was actually satisfaction in his voice. 'See, Rogers, your bad luck holds whatever you do.'

'God-damned bastards.' The third mate glanced up at the hill. 'And look, there ain't a single fucker at them guns.'

Peter Williams flung me on to the boards of the boat and jumped in after me as Rogers turned his eyes back to the approaching ship and dived for the oars. There was no further time to argue. The clank of the capstan came to us more urgently across the water, the *Tankerville* apparently intent on flight out of the bay as soon as the anchor cleared the water and before the new ship could block her escape. I looked up where the third mate had pointed. He was right. I could see the cannon on the hill, black against the blue sky, but there wasn't a soul from the Portuguese garrison manning them.

The salt spray on my lips and the breeze revived me a little. The tide had turned and was taking us with it swiftly, sped on by the oars worked feverishly by Rogers and Peter Williams. The anchorage was deep, thank God, and the capstan was still turning, to the captain's bad-tempered annoyance, for we could hear his voice rising in a flurry of shouted orders. Other figures were climbing down the ship's side to meet us, calling encouragement. I saw the dark shape of the anchor as it emerged dripping from the water behind the comtesse's windows. Then there were arms reaching, the boat's rope tossed deftly into the hands of the bosun, and a sharp tug, as the ship gathered way and took us with it. I don't remember much more. I was half-fainting as they lifted me up the side.

'God-dammit,' a voice said. I thought it might be the gunner. 'Not aboard again?'

'We'll not shift 'un so easy, seems like,' another answered. I was almost certain it was the cook, but the comtesse was now upon us, and directing operations in a way that brooked no argument. A glorious stream of water was poured liberally over my head and into my mouth. Such profligacy, I thought, as I was carried below, tenderly laid on my bunk, and Mr Gibbs, who had padded after us, with surprising devotion, jumped on to the bunk and settled in the crook of my knees. Kidd poured me a few drops from the little glass phial at my bedside, and despite the French ship and the hurry of activity above my head, I soon slept as soundly as I had feared to do among the Cape Verde rats.

30

CANNON FIRE WOKE ME, as it had all those weeks ago in the Channel. The illness that had struck me down had passed as suddenly as it had come. I was weak, but the cramps and pains were gone, and with recovery came a new desire to live. I climbed out of my bunk, my legs trembling, eager to find out what in God's name was happening on deck.

We were still in Praia harbour, and anchored once more, our sails furled. I glanced up at the hill. Still no sign of life around the Portuguese guns to help us against the French ship, which was squarely between us and the open sea. Another boom, and more smoke eddying around her decks. This time her cannon had been fired to draw attention to a white signal flag at her masthead. 'Truce,' a sailor said, as he passed behind me. And now I could see activity on the Frenchman's deck. Their boat was being lowered, and a figure in blue was standing stiffly to attention beside it.

'The captain's coming over.' Captain Morris closed his eyeglass with a snap. 'Prepare the mails for sinking, Mr Peters, but don't let it go just yet. If he fancies to talk, we may yet persuade him to leave us be.'

'What kind of a ship is it?' I asked, as the boat pushed off from the ship's side. It was much smaller than the warships of the Channel. Not so very much bigger than ourselves, in fact, but broader and more clumsily built.

'That, Mr Jago, is the *Lovely Lass* – or was. God knows what they call her now. She was captured by the French last year and fitted out as a privateer in America. I thought your old master, Grenville, had agreed with President Washington to keep her in port at Baltimore, but it seems she's free again.'

'Can we fight her?'

'Never in the world. She has twice our guns and a crew used to warfare.'

As the small boat approached, Theodore came up the ladder from the mess, followed by Peter Williams, and they took up a position either side of the captain. With uncharacteristic acumen, Theodore also turned his eyes up to the battery on the hill, whence, just at present, cameth no help at all.

'What's been going on? While I was asleep?' I asked Philpott, who was at my elbow.

'Just a deal of staring. We tried to slip past her, but she had the wind with her, and there was no escaping.'

'Where's the comtesse? Where's Max?'

'Down in her saloon, keeping out of sight. And Lizzie McKendrick's still missing.'

Was it Lizzie's doing that the French had found us? She had seemed somehow in league with Max, but she had fled the *Tankerville* alone and now we were trapped in Praia harbour at their mercy. 'Lizzie McKendrick is almost certainly on that ship,' I said. 'I'm sure she acts for the French and has been looking for the Treaty like everyone else.'

'Lizzie!' Philpott was frowning, but he caught my warning look and spoke low. 'What makes you think so?'

'Mr Jenkinson was expecting a French agent aboard the *Tankerville*. I read so, in his letters, the day he died.'

'And kept it from me?' He looked affronted. 'Good God, Laurence, that might have helped our investigation a great deal.' The cogs in his mind were turning. 'But why the devil were you rummaging through his papers at all?'

'You remember the letter and the money you brought me? At home in Cornwall? Lord Grenville bade me come with you to Philadelphia in return for that bag of coin. To guard the Treaty and keep it secret. But the game's up now, seemingly.'

'Keeping secrets?' Philpott's frown was evolving into a smile of uncertain paternal pride. 'My dear boy, you astound and amaze me.'

The French ship's boat was approaching swiftly, propelled by half a dozen oarsmen, and aided by the tide, which had turned again. I must have been asleep some hours.

'Affects to look like a navy officer,' Captain Morris was saying from the wheel, scathingly. 'I'll warrant he's not dressed so fine when he's cutting our merchantmen's throats.'

Philpott spoke low in my ear. 'He'll be after the Treaty, Laurence. For the love of God, do you know where it is?'

I shook my head. 'In the sea, so far as I know.'

'You think Jenkinson sank it?'

'No. Fletcher. I saw him toss it overboard last night, before he followed it into the sea.'

'Are there any more astonishing secrets you wish to share, my boy?'

I shook my head. But the cogs were whirring again in Philpott's brain. 'Are you sure it was the Treaty Fletcher was sinking?'

'What else?'

'But why the devil should he want to?'

That was a question I had hardly had time to ask myself, and I found I had no ready answer. I was quite sure the main body of the Treaty was gone. But there was still Peter Williams's sheet, as yet unaccounted for, of which I wouldn't speak until I knew what Peter Williams had been doing in Praia this morning. Did he still have the page he'd saved, or had he already sold it? And if he had, why was he back aboard, instead of making his escape? He had been returning to the ship when I met him in the marketplace, I was sure. I looked at his profile, and for the first time thought I saw suppressed excitement there.

The French boat was scraping up against the ship's side. There was no ceremonial welcome as its captain climbed aboard, but he saluted anyway, on his best dignity. Likely he was a former officer of the French King's navy and clung to the decorum of his old position.

Captain Morris stood forward and returned the salute sketchily. 'I'm the captain of this vessel,' he said. 'And your flag of truce don't mean much when you're forcibly detaining us in this harbour. Moreover, it's Portuguese waters, sir, and therefore you are on enemy ground.'

'Not for much longer.' The man spoke English with an accent as strong as the comtesse's own, but he seemed fluent. 'The French and Portuguese will soon be allies.' He pointed up to the silent guns on the hill. 'Does that not show you?'

'If you say so.'

They looked at each other for a moment, Captain Morris apparently unwilling to open negotiations. The French captain inclined his head. 'A quiet talk over a glass of Portuguese sherry would be agreeable, Captain.'

'Very well, sir. Come below.' Captain Morris glanced around at us and nodded for us to follow, perhaps thinking there was strength in numbers. Accordingly, we all trooped down the ladder and took our seats at the mess table. The captain and then the first mate, Mr Peters. Next to him, Theodore, Peter Williams, Philpott and me. On the other side of the table, the French captain sat alone, looking down his nose at the cramped conditions, while Peters called for Mr Hind, the cook, who forthwith appeared with a bottle of Madeira and glasses for all of us. The cook looked at me fiercely as he poured the amber liquid into my glass, and I remembered the strange exchange between him and the gunner that morning when I had been carried aboard. It seemed he had in fact poisoned me quite of his own accord, without any prompting from Lizzie, and was only sorry to see I'd survived. But any reflection on this revelation would have to wait for later.

The Frenchman watched his own glass fill. 'Captain …?'

'Morris, sir. And you are?'

'Captain Benoît. Of your pleasant ship the *Lovely Lass*.'

'Oh, I know the ship, sir. And what can I do for you, besides striking my colours and handing you the *Tankerville* to add to your pirate navy?'

'Yes, yes, we would be glad to have that pleasure some-day. But, in fact, I do not now have the time. Paris urgently requires my return, and if we can come to terms we will leave you to go on your way while we take ours.'

'Most kind.' Captain Morris already had a good idea of what the said terms would be. He looked admirably cool, considering that we were in no position to satisfy the Frenchman. I found I had already emptied my glass in my anxiety. The two captains had not yet touched theirs. Now the Frenchman put his fingers around the stem of his glass, and tilted it a little, so that the lantern illuminated the wine within to a deep brilliance.

'We have information that you are carrying Mr Jay's Treaty to America. The British have candidly refused to apprise Paris of the terms – no great surprise in an enemy – but we were disappointed to find Mr Jay equally unforthcoming. It is of great importance to France to know the terms agreed. Mr Jay's silence makes us fear your countries have reached an accord most detrimental to our interests.'

Theodore spoke up. 'I am the envoy's son. I can assure you that the terms of the Treaty are quite indifferent to you.'

The young captain stared at Theodore as if committing his face to memory, and I shivered. If the French ship did end up taking us, Theodore might find himself the subject of uncomfortable interrogation. I hoped he wouldn't reveal I knew the terms more intimately even than he did. But the French captain was now smiling pleasantly. 'I'm afraid we cannot take your assurances as fact, *Monsieur* Jay. I must beg to receive the Treaty at once, in order to pass it on to Paris, where it is eagerly awaited.'

His calm intensity, alone here among half a dozen enemies, seemed very brave until I remembered his ship across the bay with its cannon trained on us. We were in no position to bargain.

'I suppose Miss McKendrick led you to us,' I said. 'Did she not also tell you that the Treaty is unfortunately lost overboard?'

He turned his eyes to me with the same studied gaze. 'On the contrary, she knows exactly who has it, and that it is as safely sealed and entire as the day it left London.'

'Nonsense.' Captain Morris gulped at his Madeira. 'We have been searching for the damned document since the Channel. In fact, I am so well persuaded of its loss I give you permission to search the ship from stem to stern. If you can find it, you're a better man than I am.'

This was an easy promise in the circumstances, since he likely knew as well as I did that the Treaty had gone overboard with Fletcher. But the French captain only smiled again, and finally sipped his drink. 'A good bottle, Captain Morris. I congratulate you.' He set the glass down again. 'You are very kind to make such an offer, but of course I know you will give the order to sink the mails and the papers as soon as we leave this cabin. Better by far that we remain here, in this room, until we can agree. My ship's cannon have you in their sights, and if we set foot on deck, they are ordered to fire at my signal. I'd take it as a kindness if you produced Maximilien de Salles and his aunt the comtesse at once.'

Philpott swore ripely and Captain Morris frowned. 'Max de Salles?'

'I know they are aboard, Captain, so there is no purpose in denying it.'

Captain Morris hesitated for the merest moment before conceding. 'If they are, they have sanctuary on this ship, Captain Benoît. If you want them, you must win them along with everything else.'

'Which I am sure will be accomplished in very short order. Especially as I believe I hear *Monsieur* de Salles on his way.'

He was right. Max was coming along the corridor from his aunt's saloon into the mess. We all looked up as he came in, probably expecting to see alarm or his customary anger at such a disastrous turn of events. But he stopped just outside the orbit of the table lamp, so his expression was veiled.

'Good day to you, sir.' The French captain spoke to Max in English, apparently for the captain's benefit. 'I'm glad to find you still at liberty.'

'At liberty, and very happy to see you,' Max answered in the same tongue, equally amicable. Despite all my former suspicions, and the strange relationship I had lately discovered between him and Lizzie, it still seemed like a dream as he came to the table, nodded to the rest of us, and sat down.

'Miss McKendrick tells me you have the business all in hand,' the French captain went on, coolly indifferent to the fact that Philpott had turned quite puce and was swelling visibly.

'I do. Theodore Jay has been most obliging in sharing his secrets with her. It is all quite in order, and my aunt is packed and ready to depart.' Max turned to Theodore. '*Monsieur* Jay, I believe you have an item for me.'

Theodore bent his head so that his face was hidden. I peered at him through the lamplight but could only make out mild regret on his face. He avoided Max's eye and instead looked at the French captain. 'Will you let me send my manservant to my cabin? It's just in that corner, there.' Theodore turned to the rest of us, his young eyes earnest. 'I'm sorry, Captain Morris, but I think we must know when we are defeated.'

'You God-damned lily-livered scrub,' Philpott said with unusual deadly calm. For myself, I was now quite bewildered. They seemed certainly to be talking of the Treaty but how was such a thing possible? I glanced at Captain Morris and saw that he knew nothing of this either. He must have thought the copy of the Treaty he had given to Fletcher was the only one aboard. As for myself, I could only turn my eyes speechlessly between the parties like some dumb mannequin with wood for brains. Philpott was not labouring under the same difficulty. 'You lobcock,' he was going on, levelly. 'You despicable dunghill.'

After a moment's hesitation the French captain nodded his assent, and Peter Williams rose to his feet and padded away. Another moment while we all stared at Theodore. Did

Philpott's insults fit the bill? For myself, I thought the boy had merely been played as a fool by Lizzie, and the only wonder was that he had had something worth pilfering at all.

Peter Williams was coming back. When he came within the orbit of the lantern, I saw a rectangular package of creamy paper in his hand. Copperplate clerk's handwriting like my own on a sheaf of papers folded and folded again, like a letter for the post, so that Grenville's crabby signature, and John Jay's firm one could be seen above the stamped scarlet wax blot that sealed the package closed.

I jumped to my feet. 'Good God! Theodore!'

But the boy waved me back, only looking at Captain Benoît. 'I'll not see bloodshed on account of mere paper, sir. Besides, I don't doubt the knowledge of the contents will become known to your Government in time, so all's one in the end. Take it.' He offered the package across the table. 'Take it and leave us in peace.'

'Young fool. He'll sink us anyway.' Captain Morris was yellow; under the stress of these revelations he seemed to have aged ten years. 'He might not take us as a prize, but he'll never allow us to go on our way unmolested.'

'There is no need for such drama, Captain Morris,' Captain Benoît stood up. 'If you also bring me the mails our business will be at an end.' The rest of us rose to our feet automatically as he turned for the ladder. 'And fetch your aunt, *Monsieur* de Salles. We shall be delighted to receive her as soon as she is ready.'

Max stopped Philpott with a hand on his arm. 'You have been most kind to the old lady, *Monsieur* Philpott, despite all your vulgar curiosity. You asked me once why I chose America instead of London. In fact, I have chosen France. The family chateau. Immunity from a Jacobin tribunal.'

'A pleasant prospect.' Philpott was still dry, his small eyes unflinching.

There was a thumping overhead, as of large, weighted portmanteaus being brought to the side. 'The mails,' Captain Benoît said. 'I'd be grateful if you'd hurry and tell your men not to sink them, Captain Morris, or I will destroy your ship after all, and that would be a sad end to your career.'

'And Lizzie?' I asked, as Max turned away. 'What was she doing here? What was her purpose?'

'Oh …' He looked at me a degree more pityingly than I liked. 'If you ever see her again you can ask her yourself.'

Captain Morris was gesturing the Frenchman to precede him up the ladder into the light, and I reflected that it was highly unlikely I should ever see Lizzie again, touch her waving brown hair, or kiss the scattered freckles on her slender body.

Then, as the French captain's heels disappeared through the hatch on to the deck, there was an explosion of such crashing force that the ship lurched, and I fell back into Philpott's arms. Captain Morris swore, and flew up the ladder after the Frenchman, while the rest of us struggled for a moment at the foot. Max pushed us aside as another explosion came. The comtesse was now among us, white as paper, but she followed Max aloft without looking at us.

'*Madame*, I beg you …' Philpott was on her heels, but she didn't answer.

The bay was full of cannon smoke, and as a third volley came echoing off the hills I realised it was coming from the land, not the sea. The battery on the hill was now fully manned, I could see through the drifting whiteness, and it was training its fire on the *Lovely Lass*. God damn them, what had kept them so long? I was furious with them, and furious with Theodore, for another moment or two and the French captain would have been fleeing empty-handed. Instead, if he could only get out from under the cannon fire, he would have achieved his purpose.

But at least the mails were forgotten. The French captain had already jumped down into the boat, and Max was handing the comtesse down to him. She looked back at us as Max leapt down beside her, and her face was working. She had no idea what was happening, that much was clear. But the French were expecting them, and they were welcome. For the second time in twenty-four hours, everything I believed I knew had turned out to be false.

The battery was improving its aim a little. The clustered splashes in the water were creeping closer to the French ship. If only they could hole her! At least then the Treaty would go to the bottom rather than back to Paris. My fear had turned to bloodlust, and I was shouting encouragement at the battery guns, clutching my head as they missed again and again. The French boat was almost back with the *Lovely Lass* – rowing frantically through the maelstrom, the occupants soaking wet.

'Poor Emilie!' Philpott was saying in my ear. 'For God's sake, Laurence, leave off shouting. You'd not have her drown?'

The small boat tied up and they were climbing aboard as I continued to tear at my hair, if now in obedient silence. Max had chosen his side and he must take the consequences. But, of course, I feared for the comtesse. The cannon shot from the battery was faltering – perhaps they'd run out of ammunition for a moment – and it seemed enough for the boat to be hauled in. A moment later and the French ship's sails bosomed out into the wind.

'They're getting away.' Theodore was speaking to Peter Williams quietly behind me.

'I believe they are. One more volley and they'll be out of range.'

'I only hope—'

But I wasn't interested in Theodore's hopes. 'And thanks to you, they have the Treaty.' I was suddenly furious. 'After all these weeks – all this trouble – you bloody fool.'

'They're out of range,' Peter Williams said calmly. 'And not a scratch on 'em.'

'Damned poor shooting. She was a proverbial goldfish in a bowl.' Captain Morris sounded regretful. 'Ah well. Now we must wait to see if the Frenchman's true to his word. If they really are called back to Paris and will leave us be.'

'How will we know?' My breathing was slowing, but the blood was still fizzing in my veins.

'We shan't. Not until we set sail again, and find her either waiting for us or safely gone.'

Theodore was unruffled as a church parson. 'I believe Lizzie will make sure they turn straight for France. She had no thought for anything but the Treaty.'

'I thank you for your opinion, Mr Jay.' The captain was angry, too.

'Want something to eat?' Peter Williams asked me, as I turned for the ladder, with the dog at my heels, suddenly in need of my quiet bunk again. 'You must be hungry.' He had helped Theodore give away the Treaty with such alacrity that I was sure he was involved somehow. But why had he been chasing Fletcher about the deck, if Theodore had had the Treaty all along? And what had he been doing ashore in Praia?

Still, I was tired, and trembling, and I gratefully remembered his strong arms helping me back to the ship. 'Thank you,' I found myself saying humbly. 'I believe I am.'

'No FEVER, AND a healthy appetite.' Kidd shook his head the next morning. 'Just an unaccountable frenzy of the bowels, poor bastard.'

'Will it come back?'

'Likely not, but naught's sure except for death and taxes, as they say.' He took his hand from my forehead with this comforting judgement, opened my cabin door and retreated to his brandy.

I sat up and swung my legs over the side of the bunk before cautiously jumping down. I was still weak, but that would doubtless pass if Kidd was right and I wasn't mortally ill. The ship had set sail again, and the boards were humming against the scudding waves beneath my feet.

Up on deck, my hair whipped about my face in the stiff trade wind. We were bound for Barbados once more, and, with no sign of her on the horizon, the *Lovely Lass* seemed to have turned back for Europe as Theodore had predicted. The only sails we saw were of the slave ships – one had left Cape Verde the day before we sailed, but we quickly overhauled her, and she was now a dwindling speck in the distance. Peter Williams watched her impassively – perhaps as I might have watched a ship full of English convicts bound for Botany Bay on trifling charges. Kin, and yet not kin, lives moving on different paths.

'When I was ill in Praia,' I said to him, 'you had an argument with the third mate.'

'Irritable feller.'

'He threatened to leave us behind. What the devil had we done to upset him?' He didn't answer, though I could see he could tell me if he wanted to. 'Do you know, sometimes I think the crew dislikes me.'

He raised his eyebrows a fraction, and his lips twitched.

'I wish I knew what I'd ever done to offend them,' I added, 'beyond taking that infernal cross from Jenkinson's body the day he died.' Peter Williams stirred but stayed silent. 'And you?' I said. 'What were you doing ashore in Praia?'

'Stretching my legs.'

'And that's all?'

He wasn't going to give me a satisfactory answer, I could see.

31

A ND SO, MY LORD, I come to the end of my report again.
The Portuguese battery opened fire in time to save the
mails but too late to save the Treaty, and my duty is all at an
end. Max de Salles, Lizzie McKendrick and the Treaty are all
gone, and I will arrive in Philadelphia with nothing to give
the Ambassador, and no prisoners in tow. Nothing to deserve
Your Lordship's thanks. And no sweetheart, however false, to
start my American life withal.

I have written this new report over the quiet days at sea
since we left Cape Verde. As the captain promised, the sea
has been kind and the winds steady. I think I have arrived
at an understanding of most of it now. Max de Salles knew
his family were in danger in France, regarded as enemies of
the state due to the gallant actions of the comtesse's son in
saving aristocrats from arrest, even before the true horror of
the Terror and the guillotine were known. *My son was a hero*,
the comtesse told us. *For many, many others, he helped to flee
the blade.*

As all rationality evaporated in Jacobin bloodlust, the only
fate that confronted the de Salles family was death or escape

from France. But Max was too proud and too fierce to accept either choice. Instead, he resigned – or fled – his commission in the Royalist army and resolved to court the Jacobin leaders and make himself indispensable to them. It was a degradation in its own way, and part of me is surprised he would deign to bargain with such men, but the instinct to live – and thrive – is very strong. He agreed to bring his aunt aboard the *Tankerville* to make a show of flight, but in reality he intended from the first to steal the Treaty, which he already knew was aboard, and hand it to Lizzie, whom I now think he had arranged to meet in Madeira.

But the Treaty was hidden before he could snatch it, and he arrived in Madeira empty handed. He must have feared abduction back to France and an appointment with the guillotine after all. I remember his relief when the captain forbade all visitors from the shore, and his alarm when Lizzie forced herself aboard with her improbable bear. But when he saw she meant to help, not kill him, Max made his peace with the woman, and together they examined us all and found out Theodore's secret. The rest was inevitable. Theodore was far too feeble a character to defy them and die in defence of the papers he so surprisingly possessed. They had scuttled the water butts to force a prearranged meeting with the *Lovely Lass* in Praia, where he had spinelessly handed them over.

Barbados is only a day or two distant and will be a matter of little consequence to me now, just a staging post on the way to our destination and a new life with Philpott in Philadelphia. Theodore spends hours at the rail, gazing into blue nothingness. I hope he is racked with remorse. Peter Williams seems on some new bad terms with the crew, and the atmosphere in steerage is snappish. Philpott worries for the comtesse and Bruin pines, lying moping in his hammock all day and padding sadly about the deck at nightfall. The captain has taken back his saloon, and Bruin now scratches at its door in vain.

The ship feels very quiet. My bunk is cold, my arms empty, and my mind filled with tormenting self-reproaches for being such a fool, and – in truth – as easily gulled as Theodore. When Lizzie was not with me, was she lying in *his* arms, inveigling the whereabouts of the Treaty from him with her body and fairy charm? I will not ask him. I will not seek to know if I was cuckolded as well as deceived.

With no women aboard, the ship also feels rougher. The crew shout coarse jokes loud enough to be heard down in the mess. But despite my complaints to Peter Williams, I believe they are softening towards me a little, even if they only show it by good-humoured lewd remarks.

I think a good deal about our reduced numbers, lying awake in the dark. First, of poor Mr Jenkinson, whose cabin Bruin now occupies, and who scarcely survived the journey beyond Ushant. Whether the spar that killed him was wielded in anger I am still not sure, but it had been well hidden afterwards, and there can scarcely be another explanation for that. The paper I found in Peter Williams's luggage, torn from Jenkinson's letter, links the slave inexplicably to the man from the War Office, and it still surprises me that he assented to the loss of the Treaty they had guarded so long, with such little demur.

Some other things still bother me. There were clearly two copies of the Treaty aboard, after all, since Captain Morris sold his to Fletcher, before Theodore handed the other to Benoît. Were either of these the copy Jenkinson had hidden, or is a third still at large? Perhaps Theodore could tell me, but we still aren't on speaking terms.

But most of all, my mind keeps returning to Peter Williams.

He was there when Fletcher fell to his death; he followed Lizzie ashore in Praia. His actions have certainly been the most mysterious of all. Did Lizzie seduce him, too, just as she persuaded Theodore and deceived me? Did she promise him freedom in return for his help? And, if so, does he now repent? I suspect I will never know, for Peter Williams is nothing if not tight-lipped.

Yes, we are a much reduced company, now that Lizzie's sparkling presence is gone, and Max and the comtesse are bound back for Paris. I sincerely hope they will be rewarded with immunity and the return of their lands as Max hoped. If anything good is to come out of this business, My Lord, it will be a life of unexpected peace for the old woman. No doubt you will think me sentimental, for you have shown your ruthlessness time and time again.

How I will comport myself in Philadelphia remains a question. Whether I will make myself known to the authorities, as Jenkinson instructed, or slip quietly into a life as Philpott's apprentice I have not yet decided. It is, therefore, perhaps for the last time I may style myself

Your obedient servant, etc. etc.
LAURENCE JAGO
25 January 1795

PART THREE

A dungeon horrible on all sides round
As one great furnace flam'd; yet from those flames
No light, but rather darkness visible

John Milton, *Paradise Lost*, Book I

It is a sober thing to watch a Man fall, John. Not from a Tree or a Horse, I mean, but from Virtue into Evil. Yes, I am uncommonly solemn for once in my Life – as solemn, indeed, as I felt at the sight of the poor Shoemaker at the bar of the Old Bailey last November. I feared for that man's Life. Now I fear for another man's Soul.

Max de Salles had been a good Soldier in the Bourbon cause. He did not choose to be born into Wealth and Privilege, but he embraced the Duty to his King such a birthright demanded of him, and he fought in the Fields of Flanders, without fear, for many months.

But, like the rest of us, he was fallible. His Cousin, and by association the whole Family, had become particularly odious in the eyes of the new Regime, and Max de Salles thought his cousin an Idiot for putting Ideals above Self-preservation. As foolish as a Jacobin Dreamer, perhaps!

Satan whispered in his Ear, just as he whispered to poor Eve. Instead of Knowledge, this time he promised Redemption in the eyes of the French, and the quiet Enjoyment of the family's old Possessions. And, at once, Max fell, as fiery and flaming as Lucifer into his Pit! Well, he is gone, and let him enjoy his Triumph for a little While. If he is indeed another Satan, I predict with Confidence that he will find his Bed d—d uneasy.

32

M Y LORD,

Two weeks have passed since I finished my last report, but I must take up my pen again, for the *Lovely Lass* is back. For a full day we didn't recognise her, flying along in our wake, a mere dot on the horizon. But we were in no particular hurry, and she grew in size inexorably over the course of the following day. By the time the lookouts realised that she was in tearing haste, they had also made out that she was a brig, and a tolerably clumsy one at that.

'The *Lovely Lass*,' Captain Morris said grimly. 'Her captain has changed his mind and means to take us as a prize, I dare say. The *Tankerville* would make a formidable privateer, with her turn of speed and a few more guns. Fortunately, we can use that speed to keep us ahead of the damned *Lass*, now that we know she's chasing. We're scarcely twelve hours from Barbados and safety.' The first mate was supervising the trimming of the sails as he spoke, and the ship was surging faster under our feet. 'But why she's here, now, and so far from home, is a mystery. I could have understood it if she'd been lurking off Cape Verde, but after a fortnight's absence! And further from Paris every day she chases us.'

It was mid-afternoon, and Philpott was dozing in his cabin, snoring loudly, but the rest of us were in the captain's saloon, which smelt worse than it had under the comtesse's occupation but was otherwise unchanged. Even the wig was still on the skull. Now Theodore looked up at Peter Williams from his seat under the window, as if asking for permission, and after a moment Peter Williams nodded imperceptibly. The sea was grey outside the window, the sky cloudy and dull, though it was still very warm.

'I'm afraid it's our fault, sir,' Theodore said. 'Peet's and mine, that is. I've been fearing this for days. Kept looking out at the horizon and hoping to see nothing there. It had been so long, I thought we'd got away with it.'

Captain Morris looked displeased and shifted in his chair at the table. 'I'd be exceedingly obliged if you'd explain what exactly you were hoping to "get away with", and how it might affect my very valuable ship.'

I was looking at Peter Williams, and so was Theodore. 'Will you tell them, Peet? After all, it was your idea.'

Would there ever be a time that Theodore would take responsibility for his own actions? I thought I probably wouldn't live to see it, as Peter Williams came to the table and sat down in the chair across from the captain.

'The presence of the Treaty was a mighty trouble to our journey,' he said. 'So much scheming and snooping, and every French ship apparently aware we'd got it, so that fetching it to Philadelphia seemed a terrible hazardous business.'

Captain Morris grunted, picked up his pipe and reached for his tobacco pouch.

'Mr Theodore and I reckoned it might be convenient for the Treaty to be found, sir, and captured. That way we might be left alone to get on quietly with our voyage.'

Captain Morris looked quizzical. 'Without the Treaty there'd be little point to your journey, however.'

'Without the *real* Treaty, yes,' Peter Williams answered, but Theodore was breaking in eagerly.

'In fact, it was Mr Jenkinson that first put us up to it. He had a supply of Ministry paper and a War Office seal that looked official enough to an ignorant eye. We mocked up the front and end papers. I could forge my father's signature, and Mr Jenkinson gave us a scrap of his instructions with Lord Grenville's on it. Peet practised all those three days we spent trapped in the winds off Ushant before he could get it right. Then we sealed the package up and stamped it with Mr Jenkinson's seal. I kept it under my shirt until the day we sailed into Praia. It was the one place I knew no one would look – except for Lizzie McKendrick.'

'And it was this you gave to Captain Benoît?'

'It was.'

'And what did you write inside?'

'Nothing.' Theodore bit his lip. 'And now I'm afraid they've opened it and found us out. We thought of inventing a set of clauses, you know, but it seemed too risky. Anything we wrote might affect the state of nations quite as much as the real provisions.' He looked out at the growing black shape of the *Lovely Lass* behind us. 'You know, I have pondered it, and I believe that's what poor Jenkinson meant by his *nakedness*. You remember – when he lay dying. He was reminding me of the plan. Nakedness within, you see, concealed by a false cover.'

This seemed the most egregious straining after gnats of meaning and I was nettled. It was a humiliation to find I'd been left in the dark by them all – that Jenkinson hadn't told me what they were up to, even though you had named me his *colleague* in his instructions. I'd assumed it was my own copperplate handwriting I'd glimpsed on the false Treaty, but I realised now that it was a style all too easy to mimic, being the ubiquitous hand of every clerk in Whitehall. More proof of my own insignificance. More than anything, though, my teeth were set on edge by the new knowledge that Lizzie's hand had slipped inside Theodore's shirt as I had feared, and that she was once again so near us, with all her lies, and deception, and charm.

Theodore sighed. 'I did hope they'd carry it home without meddling, but I'm afraid we've failed. I'm sorry, sir.'

Captain Morris came over to where Theodore was sitting on the window seat and put a hand on his shoulder, apparently mollified. 'Well, well. If your ruse had succeeded, it would have been a splendid feather in your cap. And as it is, we're scarcely any worse off. If it hadn't been for the battery at Praia finally coming to our aid, we should be sunk in the harbour there already.'

'Oh, that was Peet's doing, too.' Theodore looked pleased by his imaginary feather. 'He went to the governor as soon as we landed, and hatched a plot, you know. We believed Miss McKendrick had gone to fetch the *Lovely Lass*, for once I realised she had designs on me, I made sure to let her see that I had the lost Treaty after all. Peet agreed with the governor that the battery would stay out of it until they saw us reappear on deck and Captain Benoît get ready to leave. He would have the Treaty by then, you see, and could be safely scared off by the guns. They never meant to hit the French ship, for that would have ruined the plan entirely. We wanted them to escape and return to France post-haste with the false document and leave us be.'

Captain Morris nodded. 'Well, it certainly raised no suspicion, for the Portuguese are notoriously bad shots.'

'They have been gone so long, I suppose they must have turned for France, as we hoped, but then something roused the captain's suspicions. I wonder if Max de Salles persuaded him to open the package?'

'Good God,' I said, leaping to my feet as though a bee had stung me. This aspect of the business had not hit me until now. Max and his aunt would no longer be favoured allies. 'The poor comtesse!'

The captain frowned at his unlit pipe. 'I have no sympathy with the young man at all, but it's a pity about his aunt, I admit, for all her oddities. But we'll likely never know what befalls them, for if this wind holds we'll reach Barbados and the safety of British waters by dawn, long before the *Lass* can catch us.'

Back on deck, I sought out Peter Williams. 'I've wronged you,' I said. 'I began to think you in league with the French. I even found that scrap of paper Jenkinson gave you, and suspected it was you had bashed his brains in.'

He raised his eyebrows, politely refraining from offence at such a dreadful suspicion, and forbearing to ask exactly when I had rummaged through his belongings and found the paper. But as he walked away, I remembered why I had been doing so. The matter of Fletcher's death, which I had seen with my own eyes, and the paper Peter Williams had snatched from the air, was still quite unexplained. My apology for suspecting him of all ill doing might, in fact, be premature.

THOUGH THEODORE'S RUSE would, in normal circumstances, have delighted him extremely, Philpott took the news very badly. We were leaning over the stern rail. The sun, hidden behind banks of cloud, was halfway to the western horizon. Mr Gibbs had satisfied himself as to the state of my health and had abandoned me again in favour of the cabin boy.

'Poor Emilie.' You might almost have called Philpott wan, in the grey afternoon light.

He pressed his lips together in an uncharacteristic frown. 'Max, and Emilie, and Lizzie McKendrick, too! They'll be in the brig in chains, I don't doubt.'

'But, you know, sir, none of it makes any sense. If the real Treaty is still missing, Theodore's elaborate ruse was mere vanity. The French might have left us in peace, but we'd still have arrived in Philadelphia empty handed.'

'Do you know, my boy, I'm not so sure of that after all.'

I looked at him. 'What? What is it? What do you know?'

'It was the comtesse who heard it. From her window again, you see.'

'Who did she hear this time?'

'The night after Fletcher's death, while we were hurrying back to Praia, the captain and Peter Williams were at the rail. The captain was congratulating him for something.'

'He didn't say what it was?'

'No, not a syllable. Not as far as she heard. But the dear creature heard the captain say something about Peter Williams's deplorable situation as a slave, and she heard him answer, "Not for much longer, Captain Morris. Perhaps I'll return with my family and sail with you to Falmouth a free man." It struck me as peculiar. Did he not say to us, Laurence, back before Madeira, that his promised freedom was revoked? And yet now he admits to new hope! He was cheerful, the comtesse said, very cheerful. Far more than if he'd merely saved one page out of a score to carry to the President in Philadelphia. Laurence, I am having something of a thought.'

Philpott looked at me solemnly, and I conceded to myself that so far he had been right oftener than he'd been wrong. But I thought I already knew what he was going to say, for unbidden, the captain's voice had come back to me. *Without the Treaty there'd be little point to your journey, however,* he had said, and Peter Williams had answered, *Without the* real *Treaty, yes.*

'I begin to believe the whole Treaty is still aboard, untouched,' Philpott said. 'That Peter Williams has known where it is, all along; and is promised freedom if he gets it home.'

All this while we had been gazing at the ship's tidy wake as she skimmed along in the steady wind, her sails trimmed for utmost speed, and the quickest possible escape from the *Lovely Lass*, which was falling behind with every passing mile of deep Atlantic water. I had grown used to the empty void of sea and sky. We had not seen a gull in days, and the porpoises that had gambolled in our wake on the African coast were long gone. I was opening my mouth to ask Philpott who exactly he imagined had promised Peter Williams forgiveness on such terms when a crashing thump exploded under our feet, quite as if one of the Frenchman's cannon had holed us below the waterline.

Of course, they were far too distant for such an eventuality. In fact, the shattering blow had come from the very depths of the sea below our feet. We hadn't seen the huge creature come up, nor did we see it go again. The only sign of its existence was a single ribbon of blood that trailed momentarily behind us through the water. Then there was a dreadful sound of tearing timber, the metal plate that held the rudder to the stern exploded, and the two heavy chains that connected it to the ship's wheel snaked out violently. All this was explained to me afterwards. At the time, all I saw was a violent spasm of flying wood and metal, and then the sails whipped out of control, the mizzenmast boom swung with tremendous force above our heads, and the ship span about into the wind so fast we lost our footing and hurtled together across the deck, coming to rest in each other's arms against the unyielding hull.

If it had been any kind of sea, Captain Morris said later, we would have broached to and sunk, but as it was, when the madness settled we found ourselves only bruised, helpless and drifting at the whim of the winds. *In irons*, they call it and, in our case, it seemed quite apt, for the *Lovely Lass* was still coming on unencumbered, and the captain's certainty that we could outrun her had proved entirely unfounded.

PHILPOTT'S NAVAL SUPERSTITIONS

To be inserted after Jonah, and before Mermaid

K

The Kraken is no Fancy, I know that now, for I have seen it. The sailors say it acts on the orders of a resentful Spirit, and will return for its helpless Prey, but Captain Morris is not to be defeated by a damned Cuttlefish, however cantankerous a Party it may be.

33

A SERIOUS CONCLAVE OF men with worried faces gathered around the stern as the ship wallowed helplessly, prow to the wind. The first mate glanced repeatedly at the sun, sinking into the west, and the black dot of the *Lovely Lass* coming closer with every passing minute. The captain and Spiers, the carpenter, pored over a miscellaneous heap of parts they had assembled from every corner of the ship, from which they apparently meant to fashion a new rudder.

'There's no way we'll out-run her now,' the captain was saying. 'How long till nightfall, Mr Peters?'

'An hour, I reckon, Cap'n, till dusk. And p'raps another half-hour till full dark.'

'Then I'm afraid we must play cat and mouse again, as we did off Ushant. Let us work as quick as we can until night falls. Fashion any kind of rudder we can manage – a drogue will do it, if the rudder can't be fixed in place so quick – and creep off as soon as darkness hides us.'

'She'll expect us to do it.'

'Then we must creep more nimbly than she can follow. At least this cloud's a godsend – maybe the Almighty's on our side.' But he didn't sound terribly hopeful. 'Oh, and Mr Jago, be so good as to shut your dog in your cabin. He has a damned propensity to yap.'

I obeyed him, and then came back to the deck to watch events unfold. Whether the *Lovely Lass* knew the exact nature of our predicament wasn't clear, the first mate told me in passing, but if she got within range of an eyeglass before dark, she would soon learn of it and guess our strategy. Never have I longed for darkness so sincerely. The lookout was in the crow's nest with the captain's glass, ready to tell us when the French ship came clearly into his sights, and therefore us into theirs. Every time he raised his voice to shout a comment down to the crew on deck, we passengers startled like sheep. Theodore was on deck, but the violent heaving of the ship had made him sick again, as was only to be expected.

At length dusk fell, and the distant lights aboard the *Lovely Lass* became visible over the water as a pinprick of brightness. We had lit our own lanterns, feigning normality, the captain said, but the third mate stood ready to extinguish them on command.

'I reckon she can see us now, Cap'n,' the lookout called down. 'But it's mazy, like, in the cloud and gloom. *What* she'll see I don't know.'

'Well, we've no choice but to follow our plan,' the captain said to the first mate. 'On my command, out with those lights, Mr Rogers.'

The third mate's voice came out of the gloom. 'Aye, aye, sir.'

The sky was darkening. Where a minute before I could see the gunner lounging against the mainmast, he was now only a black shape silhouetted against the lamplight. The wind seemed to drop, and the sea to hold its breath.

'Lights.'

One by one they snuffed out, and we were in blackness.

There was no gleam from the grey sea around us, for the sky was cloudy and the moon veiled.

'I'll thank you passengers to stay on deck and have no lamps below. We are in far worse straits than last time, sirs, and the merest glimmer will be fatal.'

They had thrown out the drogue already, a trailing contraption of chains and ironwork which was a makeshift replacement for the lost rudder, and now they trimmed the sails in utter silence. The trailing chain clanged as the helmsman turned us into the wind, and the captain growled a rebuke.

'Surely to God they can't hear us from so far away?' I said to Philpott's outline in the darkness. The French had the weather gage, the wind blowing from them to us.

'The captain believes we'll be taken,' Philpott answered quietly. 'That's what makes him testy. And if he thinks so, then I'm afraid we had best be prepared. At least we'll be in irons in company with poor Emilie and can comfort her.'

At first glance, this didn't seem to me to be the main concern, but on reflection, what else was there to be glad about? And now my earlier conversation with Philpott came back to me. Was it possible that Peter Williams really did know where the Treaty was hidden? And, if so, would he now finally reveal its hiding place?

'I'm going to the heads,' I said, and slipped away from Philpott's side into the deeper gloom. It was unlikely I could find him in this impenetrable darkness, but I wanted to know where Peter Williams was, and what he was doing. If necessary, I'd dog him about the ship until the very moment we were taken.

I set off with tolerable confidence towards the rail, where I'd last seen him standing, watching affairs quietly from Theodore's side on the quarterdeck. But now the space expanded before me far too vast. I held out my hands and rough linen brushed against me, the sleeve of some passing crewman. They seemed to be like cats, able to see in the dark, for I could hear them going about their duty as if it were broad day. Then, for the merest moment, the clouds thinned, and a glow of moonlight illuminated the deck. I had taken hardly a step away from Philpott, though it had felt like yards. Peter Williams was now squatting on a pile of rope for a makeshift seat, further forward towards the hold hatch and the foredeck. As the clouds closed again, and the faint light died, there was a murmur of relief all around me, like a hiss on the wind. Like them, I should have been glad of the covering gloom which hid us from the pursuing ship, but I stretched out my hands again, and had to force my feet forward into the void.

When my fingers collided with the mainmast I knew I was near him. I listened for any sign he was still in his place among the ropes – a sigh, a cough, a word to a passing crewman. But everyone aboard appeared to be holding their breath. Reluctantly letting go of the mainmast, I inched forward into the void once more. The coil of ropes where I'd seen him sitting was on the far side of the hatch to the hold. My foot came up against the raised edge of the hatchway, and I felt carefully over it with my bare toes. Nothing. Good God, the hold was open, and another step would have seen me plummeting ten feet into blackness. I pulled my foot back, my heart thumping. Then a hand grasped my arm, and another came across my mouth. I gave a stifled cry, before a rough weight pushed me forward, and I tumbled head-first into the hole.

34

MY FALL WAS BROKEN by a crowd of waiting bodies. One gave out a recognisably ursine grunt. There were whispering voices all around me. Among them I recognised Smith, the gunner, and Rogers, the third mate. Mr Hind, the cook, was also there, and the sailmaker, whose name I still didn't know. My feet were wet, and I'd taken a tremendous blow to the elbow.

'What in Christ's name are you doing?' Fear made me belligerent. 'Why aren't you on deck?'

'Off watch, ain't we?' The sailmaker spat audibly into the three inches of water we were paddling in. The ship was labouring into the winds, and her joints were working. 'They'll call us if they need us.'

Bruin gave a low moan from somewhere to my left. 'You're not hurting the bear?'

'Just tied up, that's all. Don't you worry about him.'

Just then another body came suddenly through the hatch, with no warning in the blackness, and knocked me off my feet. The water was cold, and when I stood up again I could feel it trickling down my calf like blood.

'Goddamn you all,' the new figure said. It was Peter Williams. 'You're all crazy. Touched in the head.'

'Not crazy in the circumstances, Mr Williams, not crazy at all. This business has gone on long enough.'

If the third mate meant the *Tankerville*'s voyage, he was right, and it certainly would soon be over if the *Lovely Lass* sank us, but I didn't think that was what he meant. I remembered the sailmaker's hiss on New Year's Eve, aimed at the comtesse, and my sudden realisation that we were alone with men cut loose from all social bonds, save those of the sea.

'It's none of Jago's doing,' Peter Williams announced, in a remonstrating tone that went some way to answering my questions and was not at all comforting. 'We tried everything, remember? You even stranded him ashore or tried to. And the *Lass* turned up at that very moment.'

''Cause you was bringing him back aboard.'

And now I finally understood why the cook had drugged my coffee. It hadn't been for Lizzie at all; instead, they seemed to believe me some kind of Jonah. 'God damn you, Hind, *you* poisoned me?'

'Only a prodigious dose of Epsom Salts.' He sniggered. 'No mortal danger.'

'More's the pity,' another voice I didn't recognise put in. 'If he'd kept shittin' another hour we'd have been shot of him.'

'There's only so much shit in the human frame,' I said feelingly, remembering the unpleasant watery aftermath of the attack. 'But what in God's name made you do it? What the devil have I ever done to deserve it?'

'Devil!' I could almost hear the third mate ticking off the list on his fingers. 'Summoned that accursed bird off Ushant, and put Satan in his very form, God damn you. Frayed them ropes in the rigging. Stole Jenkinson's holy cross. Helped that Frenchie raise the dead gennleman's ghost, and then that bloody bear came aboard the very next day and sleeps in the dead 'un's cabin, and damn near killed poor Ben. Cursed the cap'n with a mortal illness. Broke the water. Killed that other man, gone overboard. Brought on this fucking French ship agin us. And now broke the rudder so we're certain to be had.'

Even I had to admit this was an impressive list of misfortunes. 'But that's absurd. Why hold *me* accountable for all that?' My mind rather whirled under this onslaught of accusations and I clutched at the ones I could remember. 'It was the comtesse held the *séance* and I have had nothing whatsoever to do with any ropes. And how in the world do you make out that I raised that poor bird?'

'It was your own fault,' Peter Williams said from the direction of my elbow. 'Harping on about Satan sitting like a cormorant in the tree when they were all in a panic about the French ship that day. When the creature cacked in your eye, they took it as a certain sign it favoured you. I found the Milton on the mess table, tore the page out with the verses you quoted at them, and burned it at New Year to please 'em, but still they weren't satisfied.'

'Because it didn't help a particle,' the third mate growled from out of the darkness. 'Look at us! No, it's this damned ghost that's behind the trouble now.'

'For which I am hardly responsible,' I said; but remembering poor Bruin, hastily added, 'and nor is the bear, for God's sake. He's no more Jenkinson than you are.'

There was another hiss. 'Slit its throat,' Rogers said. 'Toss it overboard. Say a prayer. Settle its spirit.'

There was a general growl, and another unrecognised voice said, 'I ain't hurting a dumb animal.'

'Cut them both, mix their blood, then. Put the ghost into Jago and put *him* overboard.'

'Another murder won't settle it,' Peter Williams said reasonably.

'No one never got cursed for dumping a Jonah.'

'*Another* murder?' I said. 'God damn me, what do you men know about it? Do you know who killed Jenkinson?'

A general shuffling, and I remembered the spar hidden in the hold. 'You do know, God damn you, *you* hid the evidence. Then why not bring the murderer to justice? That will settle your ghost for you, once and for all.'

'What the devil do 'ee know about it?' Rogers was angry.

'If you kill Jago, you'll be cursed again, whatever Rogers says.' It was Peter Williams again, as reasonable as if he were haggling over the price of a herring. 'Two wrongs don't make a right. If you won't give up Jenkinson's killer to the captain, then for God's sake, let us merely exorcise his ghost from the bear. That way, no one else need go overboard.'

A general intake of breath.

'Exorcise 'un!' It was the sailmaker. He was doubtful, but there was prurient excitement in his voice that made me a shade more hopeful. 'Without a rev'rend aboard?'

'I could try.'

Another general growl.

'Beggin' your pardon, Mr Williams, you ain't done no good at all.' It was the gunner. 'Damn me if I don't wish we had that French woman here again. But being as she's gone, I reckon we need that Philpott down 'ere. Always quizzin' the men about signs and portents, and full o' how he raised that storm in Ushant by whistlin'. Happen he has the gift.'

Assent, in mumbling whispers. '*And* the Frenchie asked him to talk to the dead 'un the night of the see-ance.'

'Go get him, Smithy. We'll bide here a while.'

'This is absurd,' I began to say, but Peter Williams poked me sharply in the ribs and I fell silent. He was right. Better a ludicrous charade than a lonely death overboard for me or Bruin, or a less lonely one together. As in Praia, I regretted the absence of Mr Gibbs, still shut in my cabin. Smith climbed up the ladder quietly, and I half-wondered if we could take the rest with a sudden rush. But there was no way of communicating this idea to Peter Williams even if I wanted to. Then my mind went back to Rogers' hostility. They knew who the murderer was – had connived at hiding the evidence – and I wondered who they could possibly be protecting.

WHEN THE SITUATION was explained to him, Philpott was silenced for the first time in living memory. He had come climbing down the ladder after Smith, breathing heavily.

'I know it's nonsense, sir, but for God's sake do what they want,' I said. And then, for the benefit of the onlookers, 'The comtesse did call you a sensitive soul, remember?'

'She did.' The words were drawn reluctantly from him, and then, behind him in the deeper shadows, Bruin unexpectedly sneezed. 'Christ in heaven! What the devil's that?'

'The bear, sir. Who is also relying on your help, for they say they'll drown him otherwise.'

'Over my dead body.' The prospect of Bruin's danger seemed to stiffen Philpott's sinews more than my own had done. 'Oh, very well, very well. God damn me, if someone had told me that, while locked in mortal combat with the French, I'd be down in a hole summoning ghosts, I would have told him to put a cork in his brandy bottle.'

'We should sit in a circle,' Peter Williams said, from somewhere in the darkness.

'Bugger that. We're paddling already. I'll not meet the French looking like I've pissed my breeches. We can stand, can't we? Talk to Mr Jenkinson's spirit, man to man.'

There was another shuffling in the dark that resolved itself into a circle of heavily breathing bodies beneath the open hatch to the deck. Bruin was poked and prodded into the centre, and I felt a moment's superstitious fear that the business would degenerate into some druidical ritual. But, of course, that was reckoning without Philpott.

'In any other circumstances, gentlemen, this damned witches' coven would be called a seditious meeting, and you'd all be dangling at the rope's end. However, we ain't in London and for the first time I think it's a damned pity. Now Bruin, my dear fellow, just stand here and look at me.' An aside to the rest of us, 'God damn me, it's so pitchy I don't know where he's looking, but 'tis all one, I suppose. Come, gentlemen, let's be quick about it. Close your eyes and think of the world beyond the veil. Spirits! Attend!' Philpott tried an approximation of the comtesse's sepulchral tone, marred somewhat by his Hampshire burr. 'Come out, come out, wherever 'ee are, and speak to us, Mr Jenkinson. I'd be most especially obliged if you'd be promp—'

A shaft of light came straight down through the hatch, pinning Bruin in its glow. There was a cry of fear, and the seamen around me fell back, away from the light and into the shadows. Bruin, for his part, was fast asleep despite the rope around his neck.

'Sail ho! Sail ho!' A shrill voice came down to us from the deck. 'Cap'n Morris, sir, she's right here upon us, to starboard!'

A thudding of feet across the boards above our heads, and

the first mate's strident yell for men at the sails. After a fraction of hesitation more, the crewmen around us swarmed to the ladder and were up into the bright moonlight that now flooded the scene.

Peter Williams and Philpott went thundering up after the rest, while I paused to untie the rope from Bruin's collar. He was sleepy and not inclined to be budged, but when he finally noticed the racket above us, he consented to be prodded to the hatchway. With an excess of affection, he tried to climb the ladder in my arms, but I pushed his round backside up ahead of me and came out into the moonlight to see what new terrors awaited us both.

THE EMERGING MOON revealed the *Lovely Lass* lying less than a hundred yards away, across the choppy water. There was a stir of activity on board the *Tankerville*. The mails were finally being thrown over the side in their large portmanteaus, the seamen struggling and sweating under the weight of the pig iron. As they hit the water with a dull splash, the *Tankerville's* occupation was gone, and so was her captain's. He was bellowing orders to strike the colours as I hastened over to Theodore, who was standing alone on the quarterdeck, vulnerable in the glare of the cannon mouths across the water.

'Best get your things, gennlemen,' the first mate said, passing by. 'They may take us off any moment. Confine us, in any case. Anything you want to keep, you'd best get it now.'

Theodore made no move.

'Listen to me, Theodore,' I said quietly, 'if you've got the Treaty hidden away, I think you'd better fetch it.' He turned his face to me, soulful in the moonlight, and shook his head.

Philpott had apparently received the same instruction from the mate for I could see him plainly in the moonlight, hastening back below. It was then I remembered Peter Williams and my previous plan to follow him, which had ended so unexpectedly in the hold. Where was he now? Not on deck, that was soon clear. I ran for the companion ladder in my turn, almost colliding with the gunner, who gave me an old-fashioned, unfathomable look, before hastening on. Bruin appeared out of the shadows as I came to the hatch and thundered down the ladder behind me, wide awake now, and excited by all the commotion.

Down in the mess, the lanterns had been lit again, there being no use in secrecy now. Philpott's cabin door was open, and I could see him rummaging through his papers. He was hurrying as though the devil was on his heels, stuffing the closely written sheets in every pocket. He even took off his hat, and shoved more inside, before ramming it back on his head.

Bruin had wandered off into steerage, but it was deserted when I followed to find him calmly gnawing on a mouldy old crust he'd turned up somewhere. The crew had had no leisure to fetch their own dunnage, poor souls. I hunted among their sea chests as Bruin finished his meal and began to hop nonchalantly from hammock to hammock, but Peter William's bag was missing. It seemed he had already been and gone.

Out in the mess again, Philpott was banging out of his cabin and running up the ladder to deck. Bruin followed him, but I hesitated, wondering what I should save from among my own possessions. I had brought nothing of value. No letters from home. I was a mere shadow with no substance at all. I snatched up the bag of guineas you had sent me, and, on a whim, my copy of *Paradise Lost*, which seemed a commentary on our whole voyage. And there was one other thing the searching Frenchmen should not find – this report to you, My Lord – and, as should be clear from the fact I am still writing, I took it up and slipped it inside my pocket, and then bade Mr Gibbs follow me back into the mess.

I heard a noise aft, and went quickly past the other passenger cabins and the water closet until I could see the door to the captain's saloon. It was open, and Peter Williams himself was inside.

'What are you doing?'

He looked up. 'Nothing.' He held out his hands to show me they were empty. 'You were lucky, Laurence, for once.'

'Lucky?'

'If the moon hadn't come out – showed 'em the French – you might be overboard by now.'

'I believe I should have been over weeks ago – or stranded in Praia – if it wasn't for you.'

'They're superstitious fools.' He was looking about him absently. 'What goes on in their minds is beyond fathoming, Laurence. Anyhow, they have thought themselves cursed.'

'And made me their scapegoat!' I was foolishly nettled, but just at that moment there was a dreadful grinding from above which made me break off. The *Lovely Lass* had driven herself alongside us. There was a hammering of footsteps, and then voices – French voices – shouting to each other on our deck. Peter Williams cast his eyes up in the direction of the commotion, then returned to the business I had interrupted, lifting Jenkinson's wig from the skull on the captain's table.

All in the brief moment it took for him to hesitate, look at the thing with apparent loathing, and settle it, swiftly and incongruously, on to his own head, I remembered a number of things at once. Jenkinson coming up from his cabin, the day of the first French ship, clutching the same wig to his head. It was always troublesome, always slipping as a well-made wig should never do. I remembered Jenkinson's bald head as he proffered the comtesse his wig. I remembered how insistently he handed it over to complete her disguise. And now I recalled a flash of satin fabric as their hands met, satin fabric that had no business inside any wig I had ever seen – no wonder it had such a shocking propensity to slip. I remembered the darning needle I had knelt on the following day, on the floor of Jenkinson's cabin. I remembered Philpott stuffing his papers into his hat. I knew all at once, and with absolute certainty, that Jenkinson had spent those brief moments alone in his cabin, unpicking the wig's unusual lining, and sewing it up again with the needle from his huswif, a needle he had dropped in his haste. And how roomy a hiding place after all. Big enough to contain a whole volume of *Paradise Lost*, if Milton himself had been contraband.

Shouts and clamour from the deck. I swallowed the hundred questions on my lips and followed as Peter Williams ran back through the mess where Kidd had just appeared from his cabin, staggering under surgical instruments. I murmured an apology as I pushed past him to the ladder, where Peter Williams's heels were disappearing up into the moonlight, with the dog close behind him.

35

THE FRENCH HAD taken over the ship while we were
below. Captain Morris was in conversation with Captain
Benoît, his hands spread in a gesture of denial, while other
French seamen were herding our crew off the ship on to the
Lovely Lass to be confined. Our sails were furled, and the
makeshift rudder in the water rattled and clanged with every
passing wave, like the last tolling of doom. Another handful
of French seamen were fanning out across the deck, searching.
Bruin materialised at my shoulder as I went over to where
Theodore was in the custody of a burly French officer.

'*Pardonnez-moi, monsieur,*' I said. '*Qu'est-ce que c'est qui passe?*'

'Orders to search the ship,' the officer answered in French.
'And for you gentlemen to come aboard the *Lass* for your own
safety.'

'*Il faut absolument que ces créatures viennent avec moi.*'

The man looked at Bruin, grinning at my shoulder, and Mr
Gibbs at my heel. He shrugged. 'As you wish.'

Peter Williams, preposterous in Jenkinson's wig, had now
come up with Philpott, and the officer shepherded us all –
man and beast – over the rudimentary gangplank thrown

up between the two ships. I looked back as I stepped on to the French deck. The *Tankerville*'s officers were surrounding Captain Benoît, still arguing, their faces dancing in and out of shadow with the rocking of the ship's lanterns.

'If you'll follow me, *messieurs*.' The French officer poked us a good deal less politely than he spoke, herding us across the boards towards a companionway ladder that led to the deck below. Ripped away from the comfortable familiarity of the *Tankerville*, I finally remembered to be afraid. Here everything was the same but different – on a slightly bigger scale, perhaps – and with unfamiliar smells and sounds. There was a dim light in the square of the companionway, and I remembered my sally to you, My Lord, about Max looking down into hell and backing out again, only scorched. Now he was confined down there, somewhere in that dull orange glow, like Satan on his lake of fire.

But there was no one in sight, as we were herded through the officers' mess into the captain's cabin, a larger version of the saloon I had grown to know so well aboard the *Tankerville*. 'Ask him about the comtesse, Laurence,' Philpott muttered in my ear, but before I could open my mouth to ask, the French officer bowed and went out, locking the door behind him.

Captain Benoît might be a privateer, but everything in his cabin gleamed with naval order. I sat down on the window seat with Bruin and the dog and watched as the others settled themselves about the room. 'Something's afoot,' Philpott said. 'Did you see their faces as we came across? Captain Morris looked like he'd lost a child, not a command.'

'You can't blame him. The voyage has been a total failure from start to finish.'

'No, no, there was more to it than that.'

'He's dying, and this was his last command.'

Philpott stared at me. 'God damn me, Laurence, I am grown quite tired of these incessant thunderbolts.' But his eyes had already turned to Peter Williams. 'And wonder upon more wonders, my dear sir, what possesses you to wear that shocking monstrosity on your head?'

Peter Williams put his hand up to straighten Jenkinson's wig. 'Thought to disguise the comtesse again, when we find her, and get her safely away.'

Philpott smiled at him, some of his rosiness restored, despite the circumstances. 'God damn me, sir. God bless you.'

I supposed it was a passable excuse, and Peter Williams was canny, for we still had the Treaty, and all might not be lost after all. Out of nowhere a curious peace descended upon me. We had played chase with the French all across the Atlantic, and Lizzie had turned out to be a part of it, but they had won fair and square, and now the worst had finally happened, it was curiously restful. The ship rocked gently. The noise from above was muffled and, thus at peace, I even dozed a little on Bruin's furry shoulder. Philpott alternately sighed, paced and whistled inauspiciously. I hadn't the energy or the inclination to stop him, and, in any case, I could hardly imagine worse bad luck than we'd already suffered.

After about an hour the door opened, and Captain Morris and his three officers came trooping in, along with Mr Kidd the surgeon and the cabin boy. The door closed again behind them. The captain saw our questioning faces and stroked a tired hand across his hair.

'They're taking the *Tankerville* apart, looking for the Treaty. I told them it went overboard with the mails – taking a leaf from your book, Mr Jay, and hoping to gull 'em into letting us go on our way – but they didn't listen. At any rate, I can't believe they'll find anything.'

I thought he was right about that, since I was sure the Treaty was, in fact, scarcely an arm's length from where I was sitting. 'And what will happen to us, sir?'

'I don't know, Mr Jago, but fortunately the captain's a gentleman. Perhaps, after they've satisfied themselves the Treaty's gone, they'll let us go. But more likely they'll take the *Tankerville* as a prize, for she's a pretty ship, and we'll be put off at some foreign port to find our way home.' His hand had strayed to his belly, and his tone was wistful. He was probably wondering if he'd live to see Falmouth and his family again. 'In the meantime, the crew's confined below in damned uncomfortable conditions, and I only rescued Ben, here, by objecting to the lad being buggered by the whole French crew. The captain took some offence, but as they're raping the poor old *Tankerville*, I don't care much for his pious protestations.'

DAWN WAS GREYING in the east when we were taken up on deck again without explanation. The *Tankerville* was lying away at some distance once more, perhaps a couple of hundred yards from us across the water. Captain Benoît came over from his place on the quarterdeck and saluted.

'Well, we have searched every cranny, Captain Morris. We have checked every sack of grain, every sack of sugar. We are grateful for your stores of salt beef and your trifling powder and shot – most wise in you to strike your colours before you need expend it.'

'Not having the means to sink you, sir, my duty was to protect my ship.'

'Quite so. I am sorry, then, to find they will come in handy after all.' Captain Benoît nodded over to the distant *Tankerville*, where a handful of seamen were still dawdling about, up and down the ladders. 'We cannot let you back aboard the ship with the Treaty still unfound. I would face *Monsieur* Guillotine if I were made a fool of, and the paper reached President Washington despite all my pains.'

Captain Morris turned his head to glare at him. 'She's a fine ship. Fast and handy.'

'So she is. A pretty one, too. But we have no time for prizes, I'm afraid.'

'And us?'

'I will send you home as soon as I am able. Your crew are too hungry, and your bear *trop puissant.*' He smiled briefly. 'But before you return below to your temporary quarters, I am afraid you must submit to an examination of your possessions, and a search of your persons. I shall send my first officer to attend to it, once this sad matter of your lovely ship is concluded.'

He wandered away. Captain Morris leaned on the rail and rubbed his face with his hands. The Frenchmen aboard the *Tankerville* were now climbing down into the ship's boat. She had drifted even further away with the wind, while the captain had been speaking. Taking the oars, the knot of seamen began striking manfully back towards the *Lovely Lass*, leaving the *Tankerville* empty and abandoned.

But the small boat had scarcely reached us when I saw a dark shape at the top of the companion ladder, a glint of orange light. I thought for a moment it was someone coming up with a lantern. Jenkinson's ghost aboard a ghost ship. But then the dark shape resolved itself into a coil of smoke, dissipating instantly in the breeze, and the glint transformed into a tongue of flame. Unmoored, the *Tankerville* was scudding away from us in the stiff wind, and there was perhaps half a mile between us when there was a loud thump which sent a wave hurtling towards us across the water, and the *Tankerville*'s timbers lifted into the air and showered down on the water. The fire had reached the gunner's stores.

All heav'n resounded; and had earth been then, all earth had to her centre shook.

The ship split in two, and within a quarter of an hour she was sunk.

From the captain's log

10 February 1795
The Tankerville Packet taken at Latitude 24 °, Longitude 60 °
Burnt and sunk

We are confined aboard the Frenchman, but with a promise from
Captain Benoît to land us as soon as is practicable. He has the
French aristocrats in custody and, despite the responsibility I still
feel for their welfare, he will not listen to my representations on
their behalf.

36

'FOR GOD'S SAKE, take this and put it among your papers,' I said to Philpott, still numb, still shocked from the wilful murder of the ship I had inhabited these many weeks. I was thrusting this report at him, My Lord, while the French officer elaborately and thoroughly searched Theodore's pockets. Philpott cast his eyes over the first page.

REPORT OF LAURENCE JAGO

For the attention of Foreign Secretary Lord Grenville, Downing Street, London

Philpott shaped his mouth in a soundless whistle and shuffled the thick wad of closely written pages in among his own just as the French officer reached him.

As soon as the officer had established there was no wax-sealed Treaty among Philpott's copious writings he was polite enough, and only skimmed his eye across the bundle that contained my own. Yes, indeed, the officer replied to Philpott's enquiry, he had certainly heard of the *Weekly Cannon*, and knew *Monsieur* Philpott was often admirably hard on the British Ministry. *Monsieur* Philpott should write up these events and send them home at once, so that the English should know that they could be defeated at sea, whatever they liked to pretend.

I was, in the end, far more anxious when the officer came to Peter Williams. He ran a hand over his breast, under his jacket, felt through his pockets, and, with a quiet murmur of apology, even around his balls. 'Your costume is most bizarre, *monsieur*,' he said, standing back and looking at the wig, which had slipped sideways at a rakish angle. 'And this bear is your companion?' Bruin was watching with interest as the officer felt inside Peter Williams's sleeves. 'I think you perform with him, *hein*?' The officer twisted his fingers in a little pirouette. 'A pretty dance?'

A look of withering scorn was Peter Williams's only reply. The officer took Jenkinson's wig from off his head with a pitying smile, but after the merest glance the fellow seemed content. A moment more and the officer was passing it back and I allowed myself to breathe again. Jenkinson had certainly known his business. Peter Williams settled the wig back on his head as firmly as he could, then took off his shoes as he was bid. One cursory look inside, and the officer had passed on to the rest of us.

Having nothing else to hide, the search was soon over, we were led back down below. This time we turned right, instead of left, at the bottom of the ladder. There was no common mess. Instead, the space was divided into two smaller areas separated by a partition. Morning sun was filtering down through a skylight as we passed through the first. The officer ahead unlocked the second door and bid us enter. This room had no natural light, and no other way out. There was only a single lantern, a few hammocks stowed away around the walls, and a small table, at which the comtesse and her nephew were sitting.

'My dear lady!' Philpott, surprised into sudden motion, smacked his head off one of the low beams and fell at the comtesse's feet with rather more drama than he might have intended. 'What a delightful consolation to find you! Are you well? Do they treat you kindly?'

'I am well.' The comtesse returned the pressure of his offered hand and smiled. She looked tired, grey and much older. 'And they treat us *ainsi que l'on pourrait espèrer.*'

'Laurence?' Philpott turned to me eagerly.

'*As well as might be hoped*, sir.' In the heat of the moment no one seemed to notice that he sought my aid, or my unexpected knowledge of her tongue. I slid into the seat on her other side and bowed. 'I'm glad to see you, *madame.*'

The *Tankerville* officers remained huddled and speaking in quiet voices by the door, as the comtesse took my fingers and squeezed them too, then looked up at Peter Williams, who seemed bent on melting into the shadows. '*Mon Dieu*, I think for a moment you are *Monsieur* Jenkinson, when you come in wearing that thing.'

''Tis for you, ma'am,' Philpott said eagerly. 'A disguise again, don't you know. We'll get you away, never you fear, when the captain puts us ashore as he promised.'

'I've my suit of clothes,' Peter Williams added. 'If you're minded to try.'

Max had half-risen as we came in, and though he had subsided at my nod, he was wary. More than that, he was ashamed, for he'd left us so full of his own success, and now found Theodore had outsmarted him after all. 'Escape?' was all he said. 'How the devil do you propose to do that? And which noble soul among you will volunteer to remain behind in her stead, dressed in her clothes, so that the escape of the only woman aboard goes unnoticed?'

Such practicalities were beyond Philpott at present. 'Captain Benoît is a decent man,' he said. 'Open to reason, surely to God. The comtesse has done naught to deserve his ire. He'll let her go, I'm certain.'

"E is a gentleman, *certainement.*' The comtesse glanced at Max meaningfully, but her venom seemed half-hearted, as though she had finally reached the bottom of her well of ill humour and could summon no more. 'But 'e says 'e is obliged to do 'is duty, *Monsieur* Philpott, and take us back to Paris for judgement.'

'Nonsense! You are a woman and can have done no injury to their infernal revolution.'

'They 'ave no particular tenderness for ladies in the *Place de la Revolution*, and never for those who bore an enemy of the state in their womb.'

'Your son?' Philpott was dismissive. 'Whatever he did, you're not responsible, ma'am.'

'But in fact, I am,' she contradicted him. 'If only a very little. There was a *conspiration*, as I told you before. A plan to 'elp men escape the guillotine. It was the wish of every nobleman, so it is no surprise my son was a part of it. And, *Monsieur* Philpott, sometimes I 'elped him.

'They 'ad a leader,' she went on. 'One who made the plans, organised the escapes, arranged the safe passage, and so on. Even 'id the men in the cellars of 'is chateau. No one knew 'is name. It would kill 'im to be exposed. They called 'im ...' She paused. 'I do not know the English word. A small creature. With fur.'

'A cat? A dog?'

'*Non, non.*' She was impatient. 'A small, furry creature that lives *souterrain* – under the earth.'

'A rabbit?' Philpott looked perplexed.

'She means a mole,' I said. The drum had started up again in my temple. '*Une taupe.*'

'Yes, yes, *une taupe, exactement.* Everyone in France knew of 'im, but none knew 'is real name.'

'And …?'

'He was taken,' I said for her. 'He was betrayed.' I had not known it for certain until that moment. So many pieces of information had flown around Whitehall that we seldom heard the upshot.

'Just so.' The comtesse dabbed at her eye. 'And before 'E died, 'e gave up many other names. No one blamed 'im. Who would not weaken, *monsieur*? But no one forgives 'im, either. Among others, 'e gave up the name François de Salles, *mon fils*, who 'ad 'elped 'im.'

'And after your son was taken? Did they pursue you, too?'

'François was closer-lipped than *Monsieur Taupe.* 'E would never betray me. But then Max came to the chateau. We were no longer safe, 'e said. They knew I 'ad 'idden men for François. Max brought me 'ere. But it was all a ruse. In fact, 'e 'ad made a bargain with Paris, to find this Treaty. 'E only needed me to make 'is story seem true, the pretence that 'e was fleeing.'

Max had been staring into the shadows, his arms folded defiantly. 'Our lands were forfeit. You admit you helped François. You would have been fodder for the guillotine in the end, if I hadn't come to save you.'

'François would never 'ave done what you 'ave done.'

'Then he was a fool. As if *Taupe*'s secret plans wouldn't leak, and themselves be caught.'

I had grown accustomed to guilt, hovering like a black line at the edge of my vision. Now it spread inwards, so that I could barely see.

*I*N MY TIME *I have been a traitor and a spy.* But, of course, you know it. Even Philpott knows it, and though both words are ugly enough, I do not think you will recoil from me as much as I do from myself. After all, treachery and espionage are your bread and butter. To me, they were a sacred cause, at least for a time, a hope of a better life for my cousins in France and a dream of revolution in England that died with the coming of the Terror in Paris.

I knew very few useful secrets, and passed on even fewer to the Frenchwoman I had known in London as Aglantine, but what I did reveal came from the messages I spent my days decoding in the Foreign Office garret. As the persecution of the French aristocrats grew through the early years of the revolution, very many fled to England, and the details of their journeys were sent to us, to aid and abet them in their escape. I can barely bring myself to write down the following words but will press the ink into the paper until it cannot be erased.

I passed on one or two names. One or two places where those named might be captured.

I told myself it was nothing of any possible consequence. That the flight of the aristocrats was always a hasty business, as likely to go awry from ill management as from betrayal. And that I would never know the outcome of my actions. But in the dark of sleepless nights, when all past sins come back to haunt us, I remembered those names. Remembered, especially, the heroic *Monsieur Taupe,* and only strong black medicine had the power to lay his accusing ghost. War broke out in early '93, and with it came the end of my informing. Since then, I have thrown myself into loathing and defiance of those in power above me. If someone else was guilty, then perhaps I was not.

But, in the end, I was no match for you, My Lord. My efforts against you were only a feeble failure. Then, in your munificent kindness, you offered me protection – a way back into favour – by acting as your secret, degraded, agent aboard this ship. How could I know that by accepting, I would find myself face to face with the reality of my own vilest wrongdoing?

And now I saw myself for what I was. Every man dreams himself a hero, supposes himself a moral creature until his moral resolve is tested and found wanting. But what I have lost in innocence, I might still gain in wisdom. It is a sweet irony that at the moment I saw this truth and might have become a far better spy in your service, I was no longer your obedient servant. And that being the case, I highly doubt this report will ever reach you.

'**B**UT IF YOU PRODUCED the Treaty after all?' I said, after a moment's silence. 'Do you think Benoît is enough of a gentleman to forgive you? Keep his word?'

Max's eyes widened at my tone, but he kept his voice low. 'I hope so.'

'What are you saying?' Philpott had run out of commiserations and could sense something was afoot. The comtesse had also turned her head to me.

'Do you have a pin or some such about you, *madame*?'

The comtesse hesitated only for the merest moment, then reached down to her stomacher and pulled out a pin from its quilted folds. I took it carefully from her fingers, and pointed the pin at Peter Williams, like a preposterously small sword. 'If I may, sir. The wig.'

He gazed at me quizzically, then shrugged and pulled it off his head.

The *Tankerville* officers had turned to us now, and the captain's voice was harsh. 'What are you doing, Mr Jago?'

'Making some recompense.'

'You think the Treaty's in that damned wig?' Philpott's piggy eyes were popping.

'I know it is. It can't be anywhere else.'

'I charge you to think what you're about.' The captain was coming over to the table, his officers with him. 'If it is there, it's the property of the Crown.'

'Or the property of whoever offers you the best price?'

He looked astonished. 'God damn me, sir, what's got into you? You'll find yourself at my sword's end if you insult me again.'

I was too eager to argue. 'Remember how it was always slipping?' I said to Philpott. 'I believe it has a smooth lining sewn in. A perfect secret pocket. And begging your pardon, Captain Morris, I'd as soon see it give the comtesse and Max their freedom, as hand it to some trifling official in America.'

The captain grunted, but now, like everyone else, he was leaning forward. Only Peter Williams was still aloof, while Theodore looked bemused. Philpott, apparently too excited to argue the question, pulled the lantern closer, so that the wig was bathed in a pool of light as I grasped the pin ready to tear at the stitches. I turned the wig inside out. Stared, hesitating my pin over it, unwilling at first to admit what I saw.

It was only a common-or-garden hairpiece, such as I had worn every day of my London life. Hair on fine threads woven through a cap of netting and tied off neatly. A narrow ribbon covering the bound edge at the front. This was the satin I had glimpsed when Jenkinson passed the wig to the comtesse that day, and which I had subsequently built in my own mind into a lining to the hairpiece and therefore a possible hiding place for the Treaty. The wig had slipped on the billiard-ball smoothness of Jenkinson's head only from bad manufacture, nothing more. But still I began to rummage my hands through the curls, feeling for the concealed pouch I was sure—

'There's no secret pocket,' Peter Williams said, without satisfaction, from the shadows.

'Leave it, Laurence.' Max sounded suddenly tired and slumped back. 'It was a clever guess but a wrong one. God forgive me, for a moment I almost had hope.'

I stared at the loathsome thing, now entirely without redeeming feature, and with a rancour worthy of Comtesse de Salles herself, I hurled it as hard as I could against the opposite wall, where it fell to the floor as limp as a dead cat.

37

I N THE SILENCE THAT followed, Peter Williams retrieved
the wig from Mr Gibbs's cheerful jaws, and handed it to
the comtesse without a word. Philpott sighed heavily, and
produced his wad of papers, from which he began extracting
the pages that were not his own, which turned out to be a
good deal more than just my report. He passed the pages back
to their rightful owners. The first mate nodded his thanks and
slipped his into his pocket. The surgeon carried what seemed
to be a half-finished letter to the table and began to scribble.
Peter Williams took a single folded sheet out of Philpott's
hand without a word and returned it to his portmanteau. I
glanced over these pages, and then settled at the mess table
beside Mr Kidd, under the swinging lantern. It was a kind of
dogged determination born of despair that gripped me, and
made me resolve to finish my account of all that has happened
on this journey. It was no longer for Your Lordship's benefit. I
knew I had committed an act of malfeasance in even thinking of
trading your valuable document for the de Salles' freedom, and
that therefore this report could never be sent. In fact, I should
likely throw it overboard, as Fletcher had his mysterious papers.

And, in any event, it was useless. I had failed to find the lost Treaty, failed to find Jenkinson's murderer; was none the wiser about why Fletcher was throwing his papers away, or why Peter Williams had helped him to his death that night at the bowsprit. Even my traitorous attempt to save Max and his aunt had come to exactly naught, all my clever guesses, as Max had said so flatly, *wrong*. Glancing back over these pages, all I found I was qualified to do was write a decent account of failure. If nothing else, I might be fitted for a journalist.

They brought us food and wine towards evening. The flat, freshly baked bread and salt cod soup was so delicious I might have congratulated the comtesse on her imprisonment if things hadn't been so serious. The packet officers grumbled, and the third mate fed his bowl to the dog. Under the hum of conversation, I found Max again.

'Is Lizzie McKendrick still aboard?'

'We've not touched land since we left you. I dare say she's still here.'

'She is not locked up with you.'

'No.' His fierce face grimaced a smile. 'She is no aristocrat, nor an enemy of the Jacobins in Paris.'

'Then who is she?' I asked. 'Did she ever tell you?'

He looked at me somewhat pityingly. 'She never told me anything about herself, except that she acted for the United Irishmen, and was here in their interests.'

'I've heard of them but know very little.'

'They are not unlike your Radical societies in London, the one your shoemaker belonged to, I believe.'

'Mr Philpott would say they have fouler aims.'

'Freedom from British rule, Catholic or Protestant alike, if you call that foul. Perhaps a republic like the French. She told me they long for the Jacobins to aid them, and offer what help

Paris requires, to win favour and perhaps one day be rewarded with an invasion fleet to cast you out.'

'I wish them joy of that. An invading French force would scarcely leave again.' What had Philpott told the comtesse? *Politics makes fools of us all.* Perhaps I hadn't been uniquely naïve.

'She hoped you might know something about the Treaty if the papers didn't appear. *Once a Government man, always a Government man*, she said to me. *And always watching.* She didn't believe that story of your disgrace for a moment.' He grinned, unkindly, perhaps in revenge for the false hope I'd raised over the wig. 'She said, *He knows as much about women as I do about bears.*'

THE SHIP LABOURED on through the night, against the waves, and the other prisoners fell asleep one by one, snoring and scratching their day-old beards, while Mr Gibbs twitched and dreamed in Ben's arms. Confined as we were in near-darkness, I lost track of time. I took the lantern down from its hook and trimmed it to the merest glow, to be sure it would last. The first mate snorted from his place at the other end of the table, and soft breathing came from all around me as I leaned my cheek on my palm and bent my head over the first page of my report. Here, in my hand, at least, was a full account of everything that had happened since we left Falmouth – if nothing else, my clerk's training had made me thorough, and I would try one last time to understand what truths underlay its cluttered surface.

But I was disturbed by the captain, watching me from where he lay in his hammock. 'What did you mean, Mr Jago?'

'Sir?' I peered at him in the faint orange gloom. He spoke

softly, and there was only weariness in his face, now, instead of anger. 'You accused me, before all these people. A serious allegation. I'd have you tell me what you think I've done.' He looked very ill, but perhaps it was just the yellow lantern and dark shadows. 'You said I'd sold secrets to those who would pay. I'd like to know who exactly you think I sold them to.'

'Oh.' I tapped my fingernail against the pile of papers, finding myself unqualified for the role of inquisitor. 'Mr Fletcher told me he'd bribed you with a promise of money for your family after your death if you gave him the Treaty. And the night he died his hands were full of papers. And then, when Theodore produced the false Treaty and gave it to the French captain, you looked puzzled. I thought it was because you knew the thing was already gone overboard.'

'You thought Fletcher's papers were the Treaty?' The captain grinned, painfully. He looked now like nothing so much as the skull he had kept in his cabin – the cabin and skull which were now, unimaginably, at eternal rest on the seabed.

'What else could they have been, sir? It wasn't hard to add two and two, for it was all he wanted.'

'Not quite all.' Another voice came from the shadows. It was Peter Williams, who now came venturing into the light, and sat across from me at the table. 'You've seen the paper I saved from him that night, Laurence. Don't you remember?'

He had the folded paper Philpott had given back to him, and now spread it out on the table. I bent over it. Letters, numbers, 'Arkwright'. A diagram in pencil and ink.

'This?' I looked up at him. 'Yes, I saw it in your dunnage. But what is it?'

'Plans.' Peter Williams's long finger tapped the drawing. 'Or, at least, one remnant of many more. He was taking them to America.'

'Plans of what?'

The captain had climbed down from his hammock stiffly, and now joined us, leaning over the paper under the lantern. 'A new-fangled kind of spinning machine. When I searched the ship before Madeira, he tried to hide the plans from me, but, of course, I soon found them.'

'He practically told us what he was doing, the first night he came aboard,' Peter Williams put in. 'Do you remember? We were running from the French. He showed us his cotton gin. And he said—'

'That the Americans couldn't make a cotton industry of their own, for want of the machines.' I scrabbled through my own pile of closely written pages. 'I've just been reading it. *Your Government locks up any man who smuggles his know-how with him to America.*'

The captain sat down, passed his hand across his hair with his characteristic gesture. 'It was my duty to confiscate the papers, of course, but at first I said nothing, for I had other more pressing business on my mind, and I didn't like to condemn a man for so abstract a crime. But then he tried to bribe me for the Treaty.'

'And you resisted?' I was looking from his face to the sheet of diagrams.

'I didn't have it – we none of us did, surely you know that, by now?' The captain hesitated. 'But then I guess the devil got into me, Mr Jago. I met him again, and I tried to turn the tables on him. Said I wouldn't sell him the Treaty for his windfall of cash, but in return for the same financial favour, I'd turn a blind eye to the papers I'd seen he was carrying.'

'And if he didn't pay you?'

'Then I'd see him turned over to the authorities in Praia. Well, a more sensible man would have struck the bargain to keep the papers. For a man willing to put the plans to use and build a cotton mill, it would prove a far more profitable enterprise than the mere sale of ginned cotton – or a quick speculation on the market with inside knowledge of the Treaty.'

'But he didn't agree?'

'He preferred the bird he had in his hand to the one singing for him in the bush,' Peter Williams said. 'He couldn't bring himself to part with all his cash for the sake of so intangible a prize. So, he chose to dump the incriminating papers overboard, to thwart the captain of his money and the authorities of a prisoner. What a fool. He saved a few hundred dollars at the cost of thousands.'

'But you?' I asked. 'What were you doing there?'

'Mr Williams also had business of his own,' the captain said, smiling slightly. 'God damn me, there was nobody aboard the *Tankerville* without secrets, I do believe.'

'It was Lord Grenville,' Peter Williams said. 'He couldn't help but hear about my troubles with Theodore in London. Learned how Mr Jay had withdrawn his bargain with me. I guess he felt sorry for me. Made me another offer.'

'To find the *agent* with the plans,' I said, with a sudden rush of bitterness that almost floored me. I didn't have to look up these words, for they were words I had thought referred to myself. Of course, they hadn't, I saw that now, for no one had ever said them to my face, nor paid me the scantest attention, least of all Jenkinson. Nevertheless, the words were etched on my heart. In return for *full immunity from all former slights, and the fulfilment of all promises personally given by—*

'Grenville promised to step in with Mr Jay,' Peter Williams was saying, 'and I was very happy to oblige.'

I began to see a glimmer of light. 'So you followed Fletcher and tried to take the plans from him, as proof of his crime.'

'Yes. The whole thing was an abject failure, especially when he slipped through my fingers and I lost him as well as his papers. I was instructed to catch both the perpetrator and his prize, you see, so that—'

'*Others may be discouraged from imitation.*' I remembered these words, too. Peter Williams, not I, had been Jenkinson's *colleague*. Had they not also concocted the story of the fake Treaty together?

'For God's sake, Peter,' I said, using his given name for the first time in all our acquaintance. I had always feared to sound like Theodore, patronising him with familiarity, but there was no longer any need. 'Did Jenkinson tell you where he hid the Treaty?'

'No.' He was looking at me with a strange kind of sympathy. 'But if I'm not mistaken, he tried to tell you the truth of it, before he died.'

I didn't know what he meant, and I didn't believe it. I had been so far out of all their confidences that Jenkinson would have scarcely given me a second thought. Lord Grenville had called me a pious fool. And hadn't I deserved their neglect in any case? I had just proved myself willing enough to betray them.

Max and his aunt were huddled together in the furthest corner, hammocks slung in some attempt at privacy, and again I remembered all my past sins; again I remembered the poor *taupe* dead at my hands. I spoke slowly, but I was thinking fast. 'I have done great wrong in my time. Such wrong, that in fact I can't blame Grenville for dismissing me, nor for keeping me in the dark. Why he even asked me to come on this journey I've no idea. But, as I've done worse in my time than anything he invented, he won't be so very disappointed if I fall further.'

'Laurence.' Peter Williams was frowning at me.

'I can't let them kill Max and the comtesse. I shall go to the captain and tell him I know the contents of Jay's Treaty by heart, even if the copy itself is lost. I wrote out the clauses so many times I can cite them verbatim. I'll tell him the contents, in return for their freedom.'

'There's no need for such drama. No need to sacrifice yourself.' Peter was shaking his head. 'You'll be finished in England.'

But there was such a need, if not for their sakes then for my own.

Weary from illness and the loss of his ship, Captain Morris made no attempt to stop me as I rose to call the guard and ask him to take me to Benoît. Instead, it was Peter's hand that tugged at my sleeve, and I turned back to find him thrusting a paper into my fingers. 'Take this instead. In the end it will be of as much value to France as America. Offer this for their release.'

It was the plan of the spinning machine. I looked up at him. 'But this is your passport to freedom.'

He shook his head. 'As far as Downing Street's concerned, it may as well have gone overboard with the rest.'

I was so bitter that his kindness baffled me. 'Why help me? Are you still so set on saving the Treaty from the French you'd risk your own happiness?'

He smiled at that. 'Believe me, Laurence, I care for Mr Jay and his Treaty considerably less even than you do. But don't fret, I had other duties, too, ones which have met with far more success. Whatever happens, I'll fare better than Max and his aunt.'

'But still—'

'For God's sake, Laurence.' Philpott, I now realised, had been listening from the shadows and understood it all. 'What the dear fellow is trying to tell you in his own stiff way is that he is mighty fond o' you, as I am, and we neither of us desire to lose you to your own pig-headed tomfoolery.'

Bruin stirred in his sleep, disturbed by our voices. He had tucked himself under the comtesse's hammock, nose resting on his paws quite contented. There was no accounting for the heart's sympathies, and though I didn't deserve either man's good opinion, my vision blurred with sudden, grateful tears.

38

PHILPOTT HAS A FAR more florid account of what followed, in his *Cannon*, very detrimental to the French and very flattering to himself, but I shall be brief and to the point. The *Lovely Lass*, proceeding on her path of piracy, shortly after took a Spanish merchantman bound for Cuba with a cargo of wine. The cargo was welcome, but the clumsy ship no use to them, so the captain kept his promise of release, bundling our hungry crew aboard her with some relief. He left us adequate provisions for the journey to Barbados, now again a few days distant since our frantic chase had taken us back halfway to Bermuda. He shook Morris's hand cordially. 'Let it not be said a Frenchman is without honour,' he said. 'I release you, as I promised. But I am as sure as I can be that you will arrive in Philadelphia empty handed, and therefore my task is done. Adieu, *messieurs*.'

I climbed down into the ship's boat last with the two animals, my heart a little too large for my chest. Max was watching us from the rail. Captain Benoît had agreed to overlook the comtesse's 'escape' in return for Fletcher's fragment of manufacturing secrets, but he would be sent to the guillotine himself, he said, if Paris got wind that he had released Maximilien de Salles after he had failed in the task they had set him. The crew turned an elaborate blind eye to the comtesse where she sat in the waist of the boat, her face pinched and drawn under Jenkinson's wig, Peter Williams's clothes still a little too tight for her. She never took her eyes from her nephew, who now raised his hand. The farewell between them had been dreadful.

'Good God,' I said. 'How am I to bear it?'

Philpott's large, beefy hand closed over my own. 'His sins ain't yours, Laurence. He knew what he risked.'

'I tried to save him.'

'The captain could never let him go. You know he couldn't.'

'How will I live with it?' By that, I meant much more than he could possibly know, but he nodded wisely, understanding me by his own lights, which were, as usual, of more depth and brilliancy than I had expected.

'You'll have to, my boy. Ain't you learned yet that one sin can't be atoned for by another? God damn me, guilt never goes, whatever we do. You could be the angel Gabriel himself, and still tremble on your death bed for some trifling sin.'

The ropes were cast off, and the small boat pushed away from the side, the crew shipping their oars on one side to turn for the lumpish unarmed Spanish merchantman waiting for us fifty yards away across the water. As we pulled away from the *Lovely Lass*, I finally saw Lizzie, also watching us from further along the rail. Her hair was blowing in her face, and she pushed it out of her eyes with a familiar gesture. Her gown clung to her slender body, and I remembered the smell and taste of her in the dark when I had been happy. I wished I knew who she really was; how such a creature could have found herself caught up with the state of nations. How small a thing I was, by comparison. She had likely been as indifferent to my happiness as she was to Bruin's. I had been no more to her, in fact, than a performing animal to be used at need, and then carelessly discarded.

In this, if emphatically in no other way, My Lord, she made me think of you.

THE SPANISH CREW greeted us with broken English and some fellow feeling from their own capture, but they were glum from the loss of their cargo and there was no celebration as the anchor rose and the ship gathered way westwards. Captain Morris closeted himself with the Spanish officers, while the rest of us went below to our cramped quarters. The comtesse was granted the master's cabin, while the rest of us would spend the next three days camping in the mess, sleeping on the floor as we had done aboard the *Lovely Lass*. But the adventure was nearly over. In Barbados we would find a ship bound for Philadelphia, and in little more than another week Peter Williams and I would present ourselves to the British Ambassador. Peter had had other duties, he had said that night under the swinging lantern, ones he had fulfilled, and which would atone for the loss of Fletcher's plans. I still didn't know what he'd meant, and there were many more questions than answers. What did he mean by saying Jenkinson had been 'telling me the truth' when he lay dying? And, above all, who the devil had killed the poor man, and hidden the evidence – the spar, which was now turning to coral at the bottom of the sea?

I DID NOTHING BUT READ, aboard the Spanish ship. I reread my three attempts at reports to you, My Lord, and, finally, no longer afraid to face my own personal fall, I finished *Paradise Lost*. I went back to that fateful page, now missing, where Satan arrived in Eden in the shape of a bird, and pressed on through all the serpent's blandishments to Eve, his promises of knowledge and Godlike wisdom did she but eat the forbidden fruit. She ate, she fell, and for love of her, Adam shared in her sin. Eyes opened to the dismal realities of the fallen world, like me they hid from God's vengeance. It was then, with a shock, that my eyes met the following words.

> *That thou art naked, who hath told thee? Hast thou eaten of*
> *the tree*
> *Whereof I gave thee charge thou shouldst not eat?*

There were the words Jenkinson had babbled as he lay dying on the forepeak. *Thou art naked.* His brains had been oozing out of his skull, and his consciousness with them, drifting towards the blest place where he would finally meet this puzzling deity, who planted the Tree of Knowledge in the midst of Eden, with the full foreknowledge that poor Eve would eat and fall. But Jenkinson's mind had been so taken up by these words that he had repeated them over and over in his death throes. *Thou art naked.* Words from the book, I saw now, that I had been reading on the day of his death, and which he might easily have seen lying on the table in the mess.

The words drummed in my mind all the next afternoon, as I laid aside the last sheet of my report, closed *Paradise Lost*, and sat back to consider everything that had happened. I watched Ben, as he went about his small duties among the crew, and I began to wonder. Jenkinson had whispered those curious words to Ben, and Ben – eight years old and as pale as a corpse himself that day – had remembered them faithfully. When exactly had Jenkinson spoken? Had anyone else heard him? And what had the boy been doing there at all, to witness such horrors?

WE WERE EIGHT hours out from Barbados, and night was falling, when I rounded up the comtesse and Philpott, Theodore and Peter Williams, and the ringleaders of the superstitious crew, who seemed to have taken the events of the past days as certain confirmation that they were cursed and groaned in corners when relieved from their light duties assisting the Spanish seamen. 'We must meet in the passengers' mess at once,' I said. 'And bring candles.'

'Another *séance*?' The comtesse looked weary, and almost afraid. 'My dear *Monsieur* Jago, 'ave we not 'ad enough of ghosts?'

'We have indeed,' I answered. 'And it's time to lay them.'

The crew were no more willing. When they realised my purpose they would have bolted, if I hadn't got Ben by the sleeve and dragged him down to sit beside me at the table in the mess. 'Look,' I said. 'Even the child is braver than you. For God's sake, be men.'

Peter Williams watched all this with a raised eyebrow, but he joined the circle without demur. Bruin had hardly left the comtesse's side since they were reunited, and could not have been kept out of it, which was fortunate as he was to be the main player in my performance.

'For God's sake, Laurence,' Philpott said, settling his coat-tails to either side as he sat down reluctantly. 'You don't mean me to talk to Jenkinson's damned ghost again?'

'No,' I said. 'No, it's all right. This time I'll do the talking.'

The comtesse smoothed her loosened hair and closed her eyes. The shadows gathered around us, blacker with every moment as we gazed into the candle flame at the centre of the table. Kidd had not joined the circle, but instead watched from a shadowy corner, as cynical as Fletcher might have been. I closed my eyes.

'Spirits, attend.' The comtesse was no longer imposing, but it didn't matter. The crew were impressed enough. I could hear their ragged breathing in the dark.

'I am here,' I answered.

Even with my eyes shut, I could imagine their astonished eyes turning to me. The raised eyebrow of Mr Kidd. Peter Williams's ghost of a smile.

'*Monsieur* Jago?'

'Jago no more.'

'Mr Jenkinson?'

Smith the gunner gave an involuntary moan.

'Nor him neither. I am no man. I am small, light, dark-feathered.' I paused. 'I am the cormorant at the masthead.'

'God preserve us,' the third mate said hoarsely. I had Ben's hand under the table, and I squeezed it with what reassurance I could muster.

'I saw it all,' I added. 'I was watching.'

Ben's small hand stirred in mine.

'Someone tried to shoot me, but I escaped the gun. Is the man who fired it here?'

A moment's guilty silence, then an assenting groan from the third mate. 'That bloody Frenchie lent me his pistol, didn't he?' I was afraid he might bolt, but opening my eyes a fraction, I could see the gunner had him by the wrist.

'And I also saw a child. Is *he* here?'

'Yes, sir.' Ben's voice, small and impressed.

I squinted at him disapprovingly. 'Don't sir me, Ben. I'm no man just now, but a bird, remember?'

'Begging your pardon, sir.' No more than a whisper.

'This child in the rigging,' I resumed. 'What was he doing?'

'Chasing you.' Ben again. 'Scarin' you off, see?' He had finally submitted to the fantasy, and I was no longer *sir*. ''Twas early mornin' and you was still there in the rigging.'

'But I was not to be scared off so easily. And there was a man below us at the heads. A bald man. Egg shaped.'

'*Jenkisson*.' A breath among the crew.

'A snapping sound. A crack. I fluttered into the air, surprised into flight. What happened?'

'The rope did part under my feet,' Ben said in his small voice. 'Where a bullet had chipped it, see? And the spar did fall.'

'The spar did fall,' I echoed. 'And Jenkinson did die.'

'Not right away.' Ben's voice was a whisper. 'I did go to him.'

'I saw you. From the sky. You comforted him.'

'Yessir.'

'You were kind. And then others came. *You* others,' I added, opening my eyes at last to look severely at the rest of them.

'We seen what happened,' the gunner ventured. 'Hid the spar, didn't we, while that fucking navy ship was there and no one looking.'

'But why?' I asked, forgetting for a moment to be the bird in the rigging. 'Why hide the evidence when it was only an accident?'

A general shuffling. No answer. No reason at all, it seemed, except the collective panic that had gripped them in the grey morning, pursued by enemies, and the instinct to save the child from blame.

I sighed and resumed my cormorant form. 'Mr Jenkinson, are you still with us?'

Peter Williams obligingly poked Bruin, who woke up and yawned widely.

'Spirit, your work is finished. The story is told. The men repent. The boy is innocent. You may return beyond the veil.'

The sailmaker spoke waveringly. 'He'll never rest without his damned—'

'Cross?' I already had it in my hand. 'Mr Jenkinson, what would you have them do with it?'

Another poke from Peter Williams, another yawn.

'You are so very weary, sir, I can see it, and all you desire is rest. If the boy returns the cross to you, at the bottom of the ocean where you lie, will he be absolved? Will all these men be forgiven? Will you go to your sleep and leave them be, for ever more?'

Silence. And then the candle ducked horizontal with a passing breath of air.

'So be it.' I turned Ben's hand palm upwards and folded the cross into his fingers. 'Go,' I said. 'Go and be forgiven.' And then, leaning down close to his ear I whispered, 'You were always forgiven, Ben. You did nothing wrong. But all this flummery will please your friends. Will you lead them away?'

His wise child's eyes met mine, and then he nodded. I let go of his hand and he made for the ladder. Mr Gibbs followed him at once, while the rest of the crew rose to their feet sheepishly, stumbling and shuffling in the boy's wake.

We others remained at the table. The comtesse and Philpott. Peter Williams and Theodore and I. Peter Williams stood up to light the lantern and the shadows receded into the corners of the room once more.

'Well,' Philpott said, 'a fine, dramatic way to wrap up the mystery, my boy.'

'Nothing less would have satisfied them.' I smiled at Peter Williams, and then frowned. 'At least, now, Bruin and I may hope to live to see Barbados.'

Theodore began to rise from his seat, and the comtesse to

bundle her hair at her neck, but I stopped them with a raised hand. 'Begging your pardon, but I think the most mysterious of all the puzzles is still unsolved.'

'Puzzles? Nonsense.' But Theodore looked wary.

'Don't fear, Theodore. We'll keep your secret, for the race is run, and your task very well accomplished. But I think we owe Max de Salles' aunt the courtesy of the truth, don't you?'

She turned to me now. So did the others, and I closed my eyes again.

'I think, in my cormorant shape I see another ship. Likely some distance to starboard now. Likely even coming into an American port as we sit here. Do you see it, Peter Williams?'

'The *Thomas*, sir?' He sounded faintly amused and, I flatter myself, for the first time a little impressed.

'Is that her name? And what kind of a ship is she, pray? I can't quite see from this height.'

'A merchantman, bound for Virginia.'

'With a passenger?'

'Several. But I suppose you mean Mr Blaney.'

'An acquaintance of Mr Jay's, I imagine?'

'Quite so.'

'What drivelling nonsense is this, Laurence?' Philpott asked. 'What are the pair of you talking about?'

I opened my eyes again. 'The true whereabouts of the Treaty, sir.'

Theodore had slumped back on the bench, but it seemed that, if Peter Williams was willing to disclose the truth, he no longer objected.

I looked back at Philpott. 'Does it not strike you as odd, what a collection of well-known personages were aboard our little ship? Yourself, a famous journalist. The son of Mr Jay the envoy. And the very solid figure of Mr Jenkinson of the

War Office. If that wasn't an announcement of the presence of some item of importance aboard, what would be? Not to mention the fact we delayed in port in Falmouth, while Theodore and Peter Williams thundered down by coach from London, probably announcing their destination at every stop. If the Treaty was to go swiftly and secretly to Philadelphia, I think it might have been done more quietly.'

'And therefore?' Philpott hadn't yet caught my drift.

'Peter told me that Jenkinson meant me to know the truth. *Thou art naked*, he said, and lately I found that they were words from a book he'd seen me reading. Well, I still doubt he meant very much by anything, in those last minutes, poor devil, but it did set me thinking. Adam and Eve did not know they were naked until the serpent opened their eyes. And that made me think in turn of an old tale my mother used to tell me when I was a boy. Three rascally weavers impose upon a foolish king that they have woven him a suit of clothes only men born in wedlock can see. Of course, the King is mighty troubled to find *he* cannot see it, but equally he can't say so, or his birth – and therefore his crown – would be in doubt. "Oh, yes," he says. "What a marvellous suit. I shall wear it at once."'

'I entirely fail to see where this is going, my boy.'

'Why, sir, that *we* have all been as naked as the new-born babe these two months, for the Treaty never was aboard this ship at all. We were merely a decoy, while Mr Blaney of the unnoticed *Thomas* now presents the actual document to the Ambassador in Philadelphia with the compliments of Mr Jay.'

Philpott turned to Theodore with a face suffusing a deeper red than I had ever before witnessed. When he opened his lips, he was hoarse with emotion.

'Is this true?'

Theodore hesitated, then nodded. 'Yes, sir.'

'You never had the Treaty at all?'

'No, sir.' Theodore's face was flushing as pink as Philpott's.

'Nor Mr Jenkinson?'

'No, sir. But everyone believed we did, and my father will be ever so pleased.' Theodore's blush resolved itself into a radiant smile. He might infuriate his father, but all the boy had ever really wanted was his approval.

I reached out my hand to the comtesse. 'Poor Max came aboard the wrong ship, gulled like all the rest. I am so sorry, *madame*.'

Emilie de Salles pulled herself slowly to her feet and took the Indian shawl from her shoulders. 'Mr Jay and Mr Jenkinson were not alone in deceit. My nephew took a gamble and lost, *messieurs*. 'E meant to mend our fortunes, but 'ow could I ever 'ave returned to that chateau, knowing my peace would be at the cost of betraying my own son's principles? François was willing to die, *messieurs*, and therefore I must be willing to be born again, in a new life, if I am to honour 'im.'

I almost spoke then. Almost confessed that it was I had betrayed her son, by betraying the man who then informed on him. If I'd thought it would help her, I hope I would have done it, but in the end I stayed my mouth. What good would it do? It would only bring her pain and set her at variance with the few friends she now had in this wide world.

'You look pained, Mr Jago,' Kidd said from his corner.

'It's nothing, sir. Only a headache.'

'Will you take a drop of laudanum? I saved a bottle from the ship, if it would ease you.'

I hesitated. The warm glow that would spread from my belly like golden candlelight. The peace, if only for a happy hour.

'No, thank you, sir. I dare say it will pass.'

The happy hour would end, and the pain that really troubled

me would return. I remembered Philpott's words in the boat. Nothing would ever ease my guilt, no matter how much I wished for it.

And you, My Lord? Do you have sleepless nights, reflecting on the things you have done to prevent a revolution in Britain? Do you repent of those you hanged, and are you secretly relieved that the jury freed the shoemaker you tried so hard to convict of treason as a warning to others? We have all done dreadful things, intending to do good by our own lights, and though I once thought you only attacked the radicals to preserve your own life and property, I dare say you yourself believe you did it to prevent a dreadful Terror like that in France.

Philpott was smiling at me, pleased with my answer to Mr Kidd. It seemed he had known of my return to the laudanum, and beneath his tomfoolery remained as canny as ever. He would say that there are no devils among us, only men obliged to live with the good and bad outcomes of their actions, just as I am. And it was in that moment, My Lord, that I finally forgave you.

REPORT OF LAURENCE JAGO

Bridgetown, Barbados

For the attention of Foreign Secretary Lord Grenville,
Downing Street, London

The *Tankerville* Packet, from Falmouth to Halifax, in Latt 24, Long 60, was taken by a French Brig of 14 guns, and burnt at Sea. The Crew sent to the West Indies.

39

THE NEW THEATRE on Chestnut Street was only middling full on a Wednesday evening in February. The tiers of boxes rising to the ceiling were sparsely populated, while even in the pit we were able to stand unharassed, except by the pretzel sellers who plied their trade, entirely indifferent to the activities on stage. A minute ago, a Frenchman had been reciting from the *Droits de l'Homme* to much applause. Now a jobbing actor from England was strutting and fretting his hour upon the stage, in front of the curtain, while scenery changes were being made behind it. Philpott was examining the ceiling and the rich ornamentations of the new theatre, his head flung back and hands on hips. 'Extraordinary,' he was muttering. 'What a story. An allegory for all life, you know. And especially our voyage. Truth and illusion.'

Peter Williams took a pretzel from a passing vendor and drowned it in a thick white sauce of doubtful composition. I followed suit, willing to be guided in the ways of the city. Since setting foot on shore at the squalid docks, I had eaten Pepper Pot and Snapper Soup for the first time, with mixed results but, thank God, no repetition of the horrors of that day in Praia.

Philadelphia is an English town set down in a swampy wilderness between two rivers. Half its streets are still only ideas, while the actual life of the city thrums along the waterfront and up Chestnut Street, where the nation's Government makes its temporary headquarters, while some hundred miles away, the new capital, Washington, grows slowly out of the mud of the Potomac.

We had visited the British Ambassador earlier in the afternoon, Peter Williams and Theodore to report their ruse successful – even if the *Tankerville* had sunk as a result of their chicanery – and I to hand my own report to the Ambassador for transmission back to London. 'Hm.' The Ambassador had regarded the single sheet I handed him with some disapproval. 'Succinct, I'll grant you that. But surely there must have been more to tell than this, if you'd had the energy to do it?'

'Much more, sir. And I did consider sending a fuller report. But, in the end, none of it seemed of any official interest.'

He had nodded, the whole business already filed away and forgotten. I reflected then, as he dismissed Peter Williams with cool courtesy, that my role in all this was not uniquely slight. As a mere decoy to the real Treaty's progress across the Atlantic, we were all of us only pawns in the Ministry's larger game.

The Englishman on stage was now coming to his climax, all sound and fury signifying nothing, which I rather thought an apt description of the thick wad of papers I had chosen to keep in my own possession instead of handing over to the Ambassador. I shall keep them, and perhaps, in some long day of futurity, they will be of passing interest to persons as yet unknown.

'What next?' Peter Williams asked me now. 'What did the Ambassador say?'

'That I'm to meet President Washington tomorrow.

Apparently, Mr Blaney and the *Thomas* are still stuck off Virginia in bad winds, and they don't expect his arrival for another fortnight. In the interim, I'm to tell the President all I know of the Treaty.'

'You're honoured.'

'Am I?' I chewed on my pretzel, which was as stale and hard as an old boot. 'They do seem to hold their president in remarkably high esteem.'

'Half do. Half would drag him up Market Street at the cart's tail.'

'And you?' I swallowed down the last mouthful and looked at him with a good deal of affection. 'What are your plans?'

'Back to Mr Jay's establishment in New York until he arrives home, and we hear from Grenville. At the very least, I hope the original terms between us will be restored.'

'How old will your children be when you get home?'

'Six and three.' He shook his head. 'Doubt they'll even remember me.'

He will leave a good deal more to posterity than I will, for I am thirty, with nothing to show for it, not even a child. But then, I reflected, I was to attend on President Washington the next morning, while Peter resumed his old, invisible life in the Jay household. I had bitterly envied him his collaboration with Jenkinson and Theodore, yet it was I, with my knowledge of the Treaty's contents, that still had some part to play in the story. Perhaps I wasn't such a failure as I had thought. And then it struck me that the *Tankerville* had, after all, carried a copy of the vital papers in the shape of my own person. I was a living embodiment of the Treaty. A second, uncaptured, copy.

There was a smattering of applause as the Englishman on stage bowed and departed. A moment more, and the curtains behind him opened. Philpott grasped my arm and began dragging me towards the front. I went, not at all unwillingly, with Peter Williams at my shoulder.

A darkened stage. A table covered over with a cloth, and a single lamp. A woman wrapped in an Indian shawl, with her hair loose down her back. From this distance she looked much younger. And in the chair across from her, a bear, similarly attired.

A collective sigh went up from the audience. A murmur of laughter, as Bruin yawned widely and folded his hands on his belly. The comtesse shuffled her tarot deck and spread the cards out with a swift hand into a crescent on the table before her. Bruin solemnly roused his portly figure and picked up a card with careful claws, a feat which raised a sigh of admiration from the onlookers. Then, on cue, a large curtain fell down behind them from the unseen flies, painted with a careful facsimile of another card I remembered well from her pack. The capering figure of the Fool. The comtesse turned her head to look, shook it with elaborate disapproval. Sighed. Shrugged. And then rose to her feet, her hand held out to Bruin's enquiring gaze.

A knowing look at the audience. 'Now, my dear creature? *Attendez-moi. Un, deux, trois . . .*'

The music struck up, her skirts flew, and Bruin's fur bounced, as they revolved about the large stage to a French tune. The bear showed more enthusiasm than execution, being disinclined to let her go for the second measure, and more eager to twirl than was proper in a male partner, but the leaps and turns of the gavotte came naturally to him. Her breathless smile and dewy forehead – the bear's warm paw in hers, and his gratified snuffling – I hoped these brought her joy and eased her fears of the future. As they came at last to a giddy halt, and Bruin bowed with the utmost aplomb in answer to her deep curtsey, that future was assured. The crowd cheered and stamped their feet. In fact, the Marvellous Comtesse and her Astonishing Bear would pack out the Chestnut Street Theatre for a fortnight and would later transfer to New York with a good deal of fanfare.

L ATER, PHILPOTT AND I wandered home to his old rooms on the corner of a snowy Market and Ninth, where Mr Gibbs welcomed us affably at the door. The rooms had been as cold as the tomb when we first arrived, and the printing press in the front room had been dusty, but we had stoked up the fire and drawn the curtains before we went to the theatre, and now it was cosy enough. A man was coming in the morning to set the press in action again, and another to act as general dogsbody to our new enterprise.

In the absence of a maid, we sent out for bread and cheese and a jug of beer, and nestled by the hearth. Philpott looked up at me wolfishly by the firelight as he gnawed on a crust, with Mr Gibbs's eyes intently fastened upon him.

'Well, my boy, this has all worked out quite splendidly after all. I feel no sympathy at all for poor Mr Blaney, puking up his guts off the Virginia shore. Long may he vomit. President Washington will be all eagerness to hear what you remember of the Treaty, and you will be the second most celebrated man in town.'

'The second?'

'I shall dedicate the first edition of the *Philadelphia Cannon* to the whole story and shall, of course, be the first.'

'I'm glad you're happy,' I answered, somewhat tartly, as I cut myself a slice of dry cheese and stale bread worthy of the *Tankerville*, and felt suddenly homesick for Cornwall and my mother's cheerful, well-laden table. But I think Philpott is probably right and that for me – unlike so many others aboard that ill-fated ship – there are still adventures ahead; still some service I can render to my country, my friends and myself. I shall await the issue.

HISTORICAL NOTE

The details of what happened to the Jay Treaty, after it left London in December 1794, are sketchy. According to Lord Grenville, the British Foreign Secretary, two copies were dispatched, both accidentally put on the *Tankerville*, which was taken and sunk by the French privateer the *Lovely Lass*. This account is contradicted by John Jay's observation that one copy went on the *Tankerville*, the other with Mr Blaney on the *Thomas* (*The Avalon Project, Yale Law School*). From leaving Falmouth to meeting its demise, nothing else is known of the *Tankerville's* voyage. Whatever documents were aboard the ship when she sank, it is certainly the case that the Treaty finally reached Philadelphia in March 1795, from Mr Blaney's hand.

With so little information available (even the *Tankerville* herself is a shadowy presence, despite the help of the National Maritime Museum) I have felt free to invent and embellish these bare historical facts with what Philpott would doubtless call *damned impudence*.

I have borrowed some flavour and the depiction of Madeira from *Edward Lawrence's Packet Journal*, published by the National Maritime Museum, an account of Lawrence's last voyage as captain in 1776. Mr Smith's jokes at Philpott's expense are mostly taken from the *Packet Surgeon's Journals*, by James Williamson, also published by the Museum. Lizzie and Theodore are reading an extract from Thomas Gisborne's *An Enquiry into the Duties of the Female Sex*, which would not be published until 1797 but I am confident that Theodore and the curate conducted a regular correspondence. I am also indebted to *The Ancient Language and the Dialect of Cornwall* by Fred. W. P. Jago, published in 1882, while Laurence's final report to Lord Grenville is taken from the *Lloyd's List*'s laconic announcement of the ship's loss.

I have used the names of other real ships and their captains throughout, but for the purposes of my story, purists may find them far from their actual stations in December 1794. The only real historical personage aboard the *Tankerville* is Peter Williams, though even he was actually in France with John Jay during this period, soothing ruffled feathers in a Paris dismayed by the agreement of the Treaty between the United States and Britain. John Jay and Peter Williams, along with Jay's real son, Peter, returned to America in early summer, to discover the Treaty already an object of detestation and Jay himself being burned in effigy.

John Jay went on to be Governor of New York, while Peter Williams worked out his remaining period of enslavement until 1805, when Jay decreed he had made sufficient recompense for the cost of his purchase; the sacrificed bank interest on that substantial sum; the risk of total loss (presumably if the purchased individual died), and the entire cost of the board, lodgings and other expenses he would have paid over the years as a free man (*Selected Letters of John Jay and Sarah Livingston Jay*, 2005).

ACKNOWLEDGEMENTS

The National Maritime Museum in Falmouth was a great help in the writing of this novel, and even has a mock-up of a passenger cabin on a packet ship of the period, a circumstance of utter delight to a novelist. Tony Pawlyn's book, *The Falmouth Packets 1689–1851* (Truran Books 2003), told me everything else I needed to know about life aboard the Post Office ships, and any mistakes are my own.

Drew Davies very kindly examined a number of treaties for me at the British Library, with a view to seeing if they would fit inside a wig. Eloise Logan read several drafts, while Emily Rainsford advised on Irish dialect and drew Philpott's delightful map.

Captain Morris is a portrait of my late father, who enjoyed terrorising my childhood imagination with dreadful tales of death and injury from his maritime career. This inspired a love of naval literature, from Nicholas Monsarrat to C. S. Forester, and finally to the greatest of them all, Patrick O'Brian, whose benign influence devotees will recognise behind everything good in *Blue Water*.

My thanks to everyone at Viper Books: especially Drew Jerrison, Rosie Parnham, Flora Willis, Alia McKellar, Graeme Hall and my exceptional editors Miranda Jewess, Therese Keating and Alison Tulett.

ABOUT THE AUTHOR

Leonora Nattrass studied eighteenth-century literature and politics and spent ten years lecturing in English and publishing works on William Cobbett. She lives in Cornwall, in a seventeenth-century house with seventeenth-century draughts, and spins the fleeces of her Ryeland sheep into yarn. Her first novel, *Black Drop*, was published in 2021.